FIELDS OF FIG AND OLIVE

The cover drawing, "The Mount of Olives"
is from a water-color by Nabila Hilmi

FIELDS OF FIG AND OLIVE

Ameera and Other Stories of the Middle East

Kathryn K. Abdul-Baki

An Original by Three Continents Press

First Edition by
Three Continents Press
1901 Pennsylvania Ave. N.W.,
Washington, D.C. 20006

Library of Congress Cataloging-in-Publication Data

Abdul-Baki, Kathryn K.
    Fields of fig and olive: Ameera and other stories of the
Middle East / Kathryn K. Abdul-Baki. – 1st ed.
          p. cm.
    Summary: A collection of fourteen stories portraying Arab
life in the 1930 to 1990 period in the Middle East.
    ISBN 0-89410-725-9 : $18.00. – ISBN 0-89410-726-7 (pbk.) :
$10.00
    1. Middle East–Fiction.   [1. Middle East–Fiction. 2. Short
stories.] I. Title.
PS3551.B56F54 1991
813'.54–dc20
[Fic]   91-27966
                                            CIP
                                            AC

ACKNOWLEDGEMENTS

Some of these stories appeared originally and in somewhat different form in the following publications: "Nariman" in *Shenandoah*, "Ameera" in *Confrontation*, "Hashish" in *Phoebe*, "Skiathos" and "Hala" in *Union Street Review*, "The Wedding" in *Erotic Fiction Quarterly*, and "Solomon and Bilqis" and "The Marriage of Sima" in *Middle Eastern Dancer*.

"Nariman" and "Skiathos" won the 1984 Mary Roberts Rinehart award.

THANKS

To my parents, Jean and Khalil, for telling me stories; to my husband, Ahmad, and my children Shereen, Omar, and Yasmeen for keeping faith; to Jim and Sandy, Nora and John, Nabila, Soha, Shafiq, Aisha, and to each and every member of my family for their love and support.

DEDICATION

The fig and the olive, the sweet and bitter fruits, eternal Eastern symbols of man's destiny, of good and evil, of peace.

To *peace* for all peoples of the Middle East.

INTRODUCTION

Tales set in the Middle East by Western writers have always been available, but literature created by a native Arabic speaker, written in English, is a rarity, and only one of the unique aspects of this collection of stories by Kathryn K. Abdul-Baki.

Because of the recent Gulf war, and the massive coverage of it by television news, the complex and vital Arab civilizations which once seemed vaguely dismissible as Third World have entered our consciousness, and many of us who wanted to know more went to encyclopedias and history books. As we searched, we found we could locate facts, but the true human history eluded us. Now, with this collection, readers interested in finding out more may take up these stories, as desert travelers might reach for a cup of cool water at a green oasis. The variety of viewpoints presented here, whether set five or five thousand years ago, opens a door to understanding the human complexity of the world of the Arabs, and of the broader spiritual nation of Islam. It is almost as though the ancient gates of some great and exotic city were finally thrown open, and strangers invited to walk in and explore a previously secret and puzzling world.

This author's vivid imagistic scenes of Arab life, both ancient and modern, could well accompany an historic text of events in the Persian-Arab Gulf, illuminating that history. As in the best not only of the Arabs and Persians, but of Christians and Jews as well. In this wonderful retelling, King Solomon acts as the crafty monarch he probably was, and scheming Sheba is his worthy match. This version, while faithful to the one we know from the Old Testament, also incorporates Arab legends that have grown around the original account and the scene of this famous meeting becomes even more vivid when retold with freshness, wit and irony. For a moment, there is a provocative sense of "if only," an idea muted or missing from the biblical account, but altogether appropriate, given what we know of past and present history.

The writer does not venture into Islamic teaching any more than Tolstoy or Chekov mentioned the Czar or Russian Orthodoxy. There are no priests or streltsy in the stories of either Russian writer, yet how influential both church and state were to daily life. We do not miss this element in the Russians, and we do not miss the ingredient in this collection of stories, because it is the private, human moment that counts for everything, and this is what these stories give us in rich and generous portions. The detailed scenes of family life and portraits of Arab women reveal more about the customs of Islam than any historical text could ever supply. "Ameera," a female rite of passage story, while it reflects Arab and Islamic culture, speaks first of all for the eternal female experience, the emotions of a girl about to enter womanhood.

Two of the most accomplished stories in this collection, "The Lady" and "The Mouse" take place in Jerusalem during the British mandate. In "The Lady" the writer creates not only two women from different cultural and economic backgrounds, but in a few brilliant scenes gives us the emotional texture of the life of these women, their place in society, as well as relationships between men and women, all in the context of lives conducted by unwritten rules, within the divided Arab/Jewish city. The subtlety of the women's conversation reveals tolerance and suggests what might be, if people were left to conduct their lives without politics. In this story, we see the tremendous civility and tact required for people to live in harmony, and when civility is observed, how stunning and moving it is. As in the story of Solomon and Sheba, the reader is reminded that individuals of separate cultures have lived peaceably, side-by-side, in Jerusalem for thousands of years, despite politics, despite wars, and that there must be hope that they will again.

In "The Mouse," also set during the time of the British mandate, an Arab man tells of the anguish of arriving at a personal decision made more difficult because of politics. Like the characters in "The Lady," he must walk a fine line both to avoid giving offense or receiving it. His willingness to do so becomes a moral decision, above politics or cultural concerns.

In two contemporary stories, "Flight" and "Nariman," both set in war-torn Lebanon, the writer reveals the effects of war, not by direct statement, but through individual lives. "Nariman" surpasses even that theme in that this story of a young girl violated becomes the story of all victims of assault, and we are able to see the results of violence on personality, a major concern everywhere, America not excluded.

These stories then are not only tales of the Arab world, but universal. Kathryn Abdul-Baki's persistent theme is the human being faced with a choice, often an ethical one. Her other accomplishment is her variety of approaches. So often collections of stories, while accomplished, leave one impression, each story much like all the others in tone and voice. In this collection, each of the tales has something memorable to distinguish it from the one before, important for the reader hoping to learn more about the area we call the Near East, or the Middle East. Certainly the culture of this area is not strictly homogeneous, as many non-Arabs continue to believe.

While some of the stories are set in Jerusalem, "Skiathos" and "Jellyfish" are set in modern Greece. "Petra" and "Jellyfish" involve Americans traveling in the Near East—specifically Jordan and Greece. In both tales, couples discover truths about themselves as well as each other, but only when forced to view themselves through foreign eyes.

The characters in this collection are an eclectic mix: young and old; sophisticates as well as housewives; single women; merchants and scholars—a human world as varied as the geographic quilt of marketplace, schools, inns, and Arab dwellings. The writing, rich in metaphor and description, creates a great mural of Arab life, and readers from both East and West are fortunate to have this pleasure available to them in one volume.

Ellen Stone

Contents

AMEERA

Some years ago, in a village on the Mount of Olives overlooking Jerusalem, there lived a young woman, Ameera (Princess in Arabic). With a few goats, chickens and a cow in her backyard, she earned a living supplying several families in the village with milk and eggs and she brought us fresh goat's milk each morning.

She would knock just at dawn, as the first prayers were being called from the mosque across the street, and pour the warm milk from her tall, tin pail into my mother's saucepan. Her fair hair would be escaping in wisps from her white headdress and her gray eyes would be moist as, despite the early hour, she paused to chat; usually to recount her latest battle with her mother-in-law.

"We could live like milk, like honey, if it weren't for her," I would hear her lament as I lay in my bed enjoying those last minutes before my mother would call me to go down the stone steps to the garden where I would straddle the well, rope in hand, to draw up the day's water.

Sometimes, Ameera's pinched face would grow white as she rolled up the sleeves of her blouse beneath her long, embroidered *thob* to reveal purple welts on her arms where her husband had beaten her the night before. Once there were even several small knife wounds. My mother, wincing, could only nod and say, "Come now, be patient. Allah is merciful." And Ameera would replace the pail on top of her head, saying, "Oh Allah, oh, Great One," and

a ride into town. He was dark-skinned like his mo[ther]
his father was a blue-eyed Turk, and I remember[ ]
liar attraction to him, watching the way his chest e[ ]
he laughed and the way his trousers hugged his th[ighs]
the other men's did. Once, I saw him nearly come[ ]
man at whom he shouted, "Your mother!" so loud[ ]
mother dragged me by the arm to the other side o[f]
of ear's reach of whatever else he might say.

Some other woman would have sought refuge fr[om]
band at her father's house where her male kin wou[ld]
her and where a husband would have to humiliate[ ]
ging his wife to return to him along with an entour[age]
plead his case. But Ameera's father had been ser[ ]
years and she had no other male relatives to speak[ ]
dured her husband's behavior and blamed it on he[r]
to give him a child in their ten years of marriage.[ ]
likely, singled out my mother as confidant because[ ]
we were still considered city people from Jerusalem[ ]
siders. Although we had been renting our house on[ ]
Olives for seven years, we were still not privy to far[ ]
drawn into the village's feuds. Thus Ameera saw in[ ]
deep well in which to bury all that was in her heart.

One night when I was fifteen and preparing for[ ]
tions to enter the girl's high school in Jerusalem, An[ ]
our house. I had been studying at the dining room[ ]
determined to qualify, for only two of my friends an[ ]
ning to go on to the three years of high school. Th[ ]
had already quit in order to get married or to help[ ]
While my parents were not enthusiastic about my c[ ]
studies—besides the daily bus ride into town, alone[ ]
that high school would only reinforce my independ[ ]
they tolerated it because my father was, himself, a s[ ]
and valued an education. Also, in lieu of a suitable m[ ]
school seemed best...

stride on down the street to continue her r
rose over the Old City.

The old mother-in-law lived alone down a
a sloping field of fig and olive trees. Her hov
stone arches and domed roof, was unkempt an
ugly weeds. My cousins and I roamed the fiel
mother and aunts picked figs for breakfast o
and sage for tea. There was a Russian monas
hill where some nuns, 'brides of Christ' the
lived in complete seclusion. Sometimes we cli
walls and peered into the gardens, just as
lowering the basket with the nuns' daily groc
ing to glimpse them. But we never did.

We knew enough, however, to stay clear of
law, for, if ever she saw us near her house she
doorway to shake her broom at us, to empty a
to spit in the dust and hiss, "May your mother
the devils in *jehenam* take you!" There was a wo
left foot should have been, and we would hol
went back inside, imitating her stooped limp.
life hell, too. On the rare day when there had
between husband and wife, the old woman wou
go mad again and Ameera wouldn't hear the e

Everyone in the village knew that Ameera
good, that he preferred loose women and
games of late-night backgammon to his wife's cc
a concrete roof over a hard, dirt floor with
tables and stools for playing backgammon or
empty during the day except for Ameera's hust
sitting on a cane stool, smoking a waterpipe. Sc
be leaning against the door of the barbershop
eyes lowered like a cat's, watching passersby in
ing his throat to spit in the dust.

I saw him whenever my mother and I walked

Ameera's shrill and hurried voice in the next room that night
meant that something new was the matter and I got up from the
table to see what it was. She had never before come on a purely
social call and certainly never at night. I had gotten used to her
voice blending in with the pale dawn and the heady smell of fresh
milk, but in this new context, her cries were very disturbing.

There she was, standing in our foyer, rubbing her hands over
the brazier. Outside, the mountain wind whimpered; Inside,
Ameera's long scarf had softly slid off her head to loop about her
neck. Her village dress, more than usually frayed and dusty, looked
as though she had caught it on a bush or a rock. Despite her youth,
she looked wan and haggard beside my dark and ample mother.
Yet her eyes were ablaze as I had never seen them before when she
said, quite unexpectedly, "The old bitch is dying."

This was shocking news but my mother told Ameera to sit down
and calmly asked her some questions. It appeared that the doctor
had been summoned that morning when the old woman could
not get out of bed, but he had left soon afterward saying that there
was nothing to be done and that she probably would not last much
past evening. Her heart, he told Ameera, was no stronger than a
chicken's. Since then, Ameera had been sitting alone at the bedside watching and waiting for the end.

Nobody else had shown up, she told my mother. Even the daughter-in-law in the next village had sent word that her son had the
measles and could not be left. Ameera's husband had, of course,
left for the cafe as soon as the doctor had gone.

"They can't be bothered, that's all," Ameera said. "They all hate
her but since I've got no children they think I should be the one to
put up with her."

"Is she conscious?" Mother asked.

"God knows," Ameera said, shrugging. "But it'll take more than
a bad heart to stop her, believe me."

She hesitated for a moment, then began, "Om-Hatim—" for my
mother was known as the mother of 'Hatim', my older brother, but
my mother stopped Ameera before she could finish.

"I'll come and sit with you," she said.

"I hate to ask..."

"That's all right," my mother said, glancing into the sitting room where my father was smoking a waterpipe and talking to a friend.

"I think I'll lose my mind if she stops breathing suddenly," Ameera said.

Or gets better, I thought, feeling wicked but wondering if it were not that which was really bothering her. Ameera could only gain, after all, from the old woman's death.

But it would have taken a heart a thousand times harder than my mother's to turn Ameera away. Mother often sat by relatives and friends in death, comforting the grieving family, sending food or cooking meals right in their homes, serving the required bitter coffee, and helping the distraught family fulfill its obligations to society. She knew the women who would come to wail or to recite the *Koran* or poetry at the homes of the dead and could be counted on to locate them quickly. Ameera had no one else to turn to so, of course, mother would go back with her.

"I'll come too," I said, suddenly.

I had not gone near the old house in years and I was curious. The scornful face and rasping voice came to mind, now, as though I had been there only yesterday and since Ameera's stories had brought the old woman so vividly and hideously into our midst lately, I felt obliged to witness her end if it were to be. I brought my mother her black, chiffon scarf and helped her on with her coat. Then I put on my own coat.

My mother turned to me. "This is no work for a girl. What about your studies?" she said, sharply, raising her eyebrows. But she let me push past her to heave open the heavy, iron door against the wind. It clanged shut behind us. I knew that my coming along unsettled her, but it was too late for her to argue. We three descended the long flight of steps from our landing to the street in silence, my mother clapping her hand over her head to keep her scarf on, Ameera's long dress whipping at her ankles.

I could not help regretting the end of Ameera's plight. Surely with the mother-in-law out of the way she would lead a more reasonable married life. But to me this meant the end of her need to unburden herself in the morning, stories to which I had become accustomed. Through Ameera's frank, unabashed conversation I gleaned more of what went on between a man and a woman than I ever could have from my proper mother. The more amusing tidbits I shared with my girlfriends at school since our appetite for this forbiden topic had grown insatiable. But most of the information I kept to myself, turning it over and over in my head, mystified.

It took us only minutes to walk down the dirt road to the high wall enclosing the field. We went through the iron gate. From then on the ground was steep and rocky and covered with a thick brush. The olive trees shimmered in the moonlight, their leaves rustling like fingers tapping the wind. Above us loomed the Russian monastery, a giant shadow, as we descended the field to get to the small house with its dimly-lit window.

When Ameera opened the front door for us we were met by such a damp, acrid smell that it was all I could do to walk inside. My mother's compulsive habits, which she had by now instilled in me, included daily scrubbing of floors—even the outside steps and veranda—and never eating out for fear of the uncleanliness of others. Still, I followed my mother and Ameera through the tiny hall and into the bedroom as though drawn like a magnet to the place where the old woman would be.

The blue-green walls were mildewed and the paint was peeling. The old woman lay stretched out on an iron bed in one corner of the room, her head turned away from us and an old gray quilt covering her up to her chin. The flickering light from the lantern burning on the nightstand seemed to lick the tufts of white hair on the pillow.

I must have expected to see her thrashing about, screaming some obscenity at us for I was surprised and disappointed to find her so passive, so clearly oblivious to our presence.

8

Ameera pulled out a mattress from under the bed and hauled it over to the doorway for my mother and me to sit on. As mother loosened her scarf and removed her veil she shot me an angry look, suddenly re-aware of my presence. She was forever warning me of the evil-eye to which the young were particularly susceptible. As a precaution, now, her lips moved in prayer to clear the room of any sinister spirits.

Then, through the silence, came Ameera's voice: "I wasn't as old as *you* when I first saw her."

"What?" I said, surprised that she was looking at me. Usually it was through my mother that she addressed me, if at all, and sometimes I would answer her myself to prove that I had a tongue. But there was no mistaking who she was talking to now.

"I said I wasn't as old as you when she came asking for me. I wasn't as tall as you, of course, but I had thick, blond braids to my waist and a round face," she said, illustrating with her hands. "I was well-fed in my father's house and never did any work. That's why she fancied me for that no-good son of hers."

I did not doubt this. With a few extra pounds and her fair hair and complexion, Ameera might have been considered pretty. My own brown hair which I wore in a severe braid down my back and my olive skin were not the sort to draw attention although I felt my brown eyes did have a certain almond shape.

"My father was a generous man, too, and important enough in those days," she went on. "When she came asking for me, she set me on her lap and pretended to like me. She touched my hair and looked at my teeth. She even felt my breasts—they all do that. She agreed to the sum my father asked for and you should have seen the gold bracelets and new outfits of clothes they sent me. You'd have thought I was a queen the way they threw their money about. My wedding was the talk of the entire village and the trays of lamb and sweets were sent to my father's doorstep for an entire week."

We had heard this before, even the part about her crimson-

9

stained wedding sheets being hung for display from the upstairs balcony. Ameera always took pleasure in telling this.

"But that was the end of the honeymoon," she went on, brushing her hands together at what might have been. "We moved in with his family—his two brothers and their wives and dirty children lived with his parents—and who do you think was made to wait on them all? To scurry after those brats, to bake the bread, sweep, wash, *and* cook for them?

"Three years went by and I still had nothing to show for it—my stomach hadn't once swollen with child and I'd grown pale and thin as you see me now. Once she took me walking the whole day to get to Hebron where she threw herself on the tomb of our Lord *Ibrahim* beseeching that I be granted a son as Sara had. I kneeled and did as she did. What did I know? I was only a child.

"Then she began to give me potions. Don't ask me what they were—they tasted awful! But I drank them. I even took her advice and refused to let her son touch me for a whole month so that when he did force himself on me he was so fierce I was sure he'd left his child in me. I immediately rolled over onto my right side, the way she'd said, so that a son would grow. I rolled onto my left side, too. By then, I no longer cared whether it was a boy or a girl." As Ameera spoke, I tried to imagine what it must have been like for her. She would have been my age then.

"Nothing happened," Ameera said, her stare suddenly turning sharp as a scythe. "At first I was afraid he would divorce me. How could I return to my father's house in shame? I was no better than a servant with him but at least I was a married woman.

"But he didn't divorce me. Instead, he found a whore in the city and hardly touched me any more. Still they blamed me. 'What kind of woman,' they now asked, 'lets her husband run off at night like that?' But I pretended not to care. 'What kind of man would he be if one woman were enough for him?' I retorted.

"The brothers and their families finally moved out. I thought that things would be easier now that I had only the two old ones to deal with at home but the old man always sided with *her* whenever she started anything. He was afraid of her, you know. He was younger than she was."

"Really?" I asked, suddenly alert. This was a new twist.

"You didn't know?" Ameera said, looking at my mother.

"He died years ago. He must have been older," my mother said abruptly, obviously uncomfortable by Ameera's chatter in the presence of the dying woman.

But Ameera had taken her cue from the look of surprise on our faces and there was no stopping her now.

"Ha! Who wouldn't grow old living with her? But he was younger—much younger. And good-looking in his day. That's what they say. That's why she got him to marry her.

"Why, she was nearly thirty by then and never been asked for. Who would have wanted anything so ugly, anyway? And her reputation! Never thought twice about talking to a strange man, always passing time with soldiers at the well. That's where she met him. He was a soldier, you know, an Ottoman. Stationed right where that new hotel is. She'd even tell us the story herself," Ameera said, leaning toward us.

"She'd wait until it was time for the soldiers to water their horses, then she'd follow them and not come home for two or three hours. Why I could have filled two dozen pails of water *and* carried them home in that time!"

I tried hard not to laugh or to let on that I found this hint of scandal delicious. Yet I could hardly believe that Ameera was speaking of her mother-in-law, this old hag, older than my own grandmother. I sat and waited, impatient with her pauses.

"Then, one morning," she continued, "his regiment was moved to Jericho. They had, simply, disappeared. So what do you think she did?"

My mother and I were both silent.

"She put on her brother's uniform, saddled his horse and rode after them dressed as a man."

"You can't be serious?" my mother said.

11

"How would she have known the way? Would she have dared to follow him?" I asked.

"Who was to stop her?" Ameera said. "Of course her father vowed to kill her. How could he marry her off after such a disgrace?"

"Did she find him?" I asked.

"Shut up, girl!" my mother said, angrily.

Just then, there was a noise and I froze. We turned toward the old woman. As a child I had believed that she had the power to summon up evil spirits to punish those she did not like. Perhaps she had done so now, I suddenly thought, cursing myself for not having stepped over the incense burner with the rest of my family last month. My mother observed this ritual each Autumn by lighting incense in a small, brass dish over which each of us would pass, almost in jest, to safeguard ourselves against potential hazards. Even the pet cats were included. Because I no longer believed in such superstitions I had refused to join in. I now regretted my arrogance.

Ameera sprang up and tiptoed over to the bed. She stared down into the withered face and finally signalled to us that the old woman was still breathing.

"Of course she found him," she said, coming back to sit on the mattress and going on as though nothing had happened. "A pan finds its lid doesn't it? But her father had gone after her and when he found her he beat her and then he stabbed her in the foot. That's why she had to have her foot cut off. It rotted. But the slut came back to the village even without a foot—and with a baby in her belly. That's how she got him to marry her."

"Sss!" my mother hissed at us, horrified. "Have some shame, the woman is dying!" She was, clearly, distressed that I had heard such talk and I was too embarrassed to look at her. A child out of wedlock was unimaginable. I wondered if Ameera had not made it all up from the satisfied grin on her face.

"It's time you left," my mother said, nudging me roughly and thrusting my coat at me. "Your father's alone and he'll be wanting his supper."

"But who'll stay with you?" I said, not wanting to go out alone.

"You just go and see to your father. We can manage here."

I glanced at the old woman, hating to leave my mother and not wanting her to have to help wash a corpse if the woman died. But I knew she would not leave with me so I put on my coat and walked down the hall.

Outside, the lighted windows of the other houses were comforting, reminding me of the world I knew. Walking into the fresh night air was like walking through a pleasing dream and it felt good to stride along free in the wind. Passing by the house of a friend I almost stopped but, then, remembering that my father might be waiting, forced myself to hurry on.

I climbed up through the field and thought of the distraught woman riding to Jericho, risking everything in the fury of passion. My parents intended for me to live the life that they were patiently designing for me, a life such as my mother's. But my friends and I often talked of escape, of a life far away from our families, a life in another country, perhaps. What would my parents say if I told them that I, like the old woman, might bring disgrace on them some day rather than bend to the restrictions set on me?

Breathless, I reached the gate, haunted by the image of a young woman losing her foot because she was in love. I could not wait to tell this extraordinary tale to my friends!

I was about to go through the gate when I suddenly collided with a figure approaching from outside. I screamed, my heart racing for the second time that night. Then, stepping back, I recognized at once the smooth cheek and slanting eyes, the thick, black hair. It was Ameera's husband.

I had seen him only a few days before when I had gone to the village store for some vegetables. Neither my mother nor I ever did this since the errand boy always delivered our groceries to us. I knew that the street was no place for a girl and except for the walk to and from school, I rarely went out without my mother. But that

13

day the boy had not shown up with our order and since it was getting close to lunchtime, my mother had given me some money and told me to run and buy the items myself.

I had been nervous in the store, sensing the glances of the men in the cafe next door, and when I had selected an eggplant and some tomatoes, I paid and hurried to leave. But there was a small step at the doorway that I had not noticed and I stumbled out onto the street, just managing to hold onto my groceries.

"Praise Allah for protecting the glass limbs of young girls," came the man's voice from behind me, smooth as silk.

I had spun round, my cheeks stinging, to find Ameera's husband drawing a deep breath from the gurgling waterpipe he was smoking. I hated him as I watched his dark, handsome face break into a knowing smile.

But now he seemed as confused to find me at the gate this late at night as I was to find him. I had never been this close to a strange man before, close enough to smell the drink and smoke of the cafe on his breath, to feel the heat on my skin where his body had touched mine. I don't know how long I stood there feeling sure that my legs would give way if he came closer—I knew that he could be brutal. But I knew, too, that I could reach out and touch him if I wanted to and nobody would know. I wondered what he would do if I gave him some sign of encouragement. I wondered if he knew that I wanted him to take me in his arms.

But as though reading my thoughts he quickly grunted, "Good evening," and started on past me, down the hill.

I ran the rest of the way from the gate up the road to our house, stopping only when I had climbed the steps to our landing. My lungs felt as though they would burst. I turned to look back, but he had already disappeared. I knocked loudly on the door, the iron echoing mercilessly into the field. I thought of my mother and prayed that Ameera's husband would not tell her that he had seen me or that I had lingered so willingly beside him. I thought of

Ameera—strong, sad Ameera—and I thought of the old woman who had dared to delve into the abyss of love, a woman whose bitterness and real story Ameera could not even begin to tell.

It seemed that I stood there forever, waiting for my father to open the door, scanning the dark field for a man and wondering, frantically, if I would ever find the answers to my questions or whether I would always be in search of them, and of myself, in the heart of some man or another.

THE MARRIAGE OF SIMA

🐛 🐛

In those days a woman's world was all powerful.

Sima Darwishi, my grandfather's youngest daughter, was married off at thirteen. Though she had two older, more eligible sisters still at home, her marriage was the result of a simmering feud between my grandfather and the groom's father, Haj Farouk Mahdi.

The Darwishis and the Mahdis were two of the oldest and largest Arab families in Jerusalem, branching into several other equally large ones so that together they formed a sizable element of the population of that city. Due, however, to a dispute between the two men some seven years earlier, neither family spoke with the other.

One morning, a young Darwishi man was found stabbed to death at the foot of the Mount of Olives near where the Mahdis herded goats. His family called for revenge. But the Mahdis, swearing that they had had nothing to do with the killing, threatened to retaliate. Since no evidence had been found to link them to the murder, the crisis passed. But several weeks later, as though making amends, Haj Farouk and the elders of the Mahdi clan came to my grandfather and asked him for his youngest daughter's hand in marriage to his youngest son, Jamil.

My grandfather agreed to give the Mahdis his daughter to show his good will, people said. Perhaps he did it to put a stop to any further animosity between the families. Nobody dared ask my grandfather his motive at the time. He simply gave the Mahdis his daughter and showed the outside world no regret.

The Mahdis, on the other hand, had good reason to choose Sima. While both of her older sisters were homely, Sima was pretty, with skin white as yogurt and thick, blond hair. As a child, she had even refused to believe that she was full sister to her older and darker-complexioned sisters and brothers, insisting that she had been born by her step-mother Shakira, a blond, Cherkess woman my grandfather had married after the death of his first wife. Shakira had raised Sima from infancy and was sorriest of all at Sima's sudden marriage since Sima was the only one of her step-children to call her 'mother'.

To Sima, the marriage meant obeying her father. As simple as that. If anything troubled her about it it was the fact that she would have to move in with a strange family under the scrutiny of an old mother-in-law. Though she had been taught by her step-mother to pluck a chicken, cook rice that was never lumpy, and bring out the sweetness in the most recalcitrant child, as the youngest she was often exempt from the housework and the thought of having to serve the Mahdis made her nervous.

"You'll have to leave the Mount of Olives and move into the Mahdi quarter of the Old City," a sister said.

"You'll be shut away," another said.

Sima had heard all sorts of stories about the Mahdis: that their women were made to work all day and never leave their quarter, that they ate sitting on the floor instead of at a table, that they had no electricity, that they never bathed their children and dressed them in rags for fear of the evil eye. Worst of all, she would now have a husband she had never met, to whom she would be required to perform duties as yet unclear.

Most of the city's families had lived within the city walls at one time. Sima and her brothers and sisters had been born there in a large house with an enclosed courtyard where fresh fruit floated in a blue fountain. It had been called the 'Darwishi quarter.' Her grandfather had held a *majlis* there each Friday where men would gather to visit, ask advice, or air a grievance before partaking of the trays of roast lamb and *konafa* that were served.

Her grandfather had surrounded himself with sons who also raised their families in the Darwishi quarter. But these sons, like other young men with growing responsibilities, began to look for work outside the confines of Jerusalem. Some bought farms in Hebron and Jaffa, others went as far away as the Lebanon until only Sima's father, Mohamad, remained to sit alongside his father at the weekly *majlis*. When her grandfather died, mourning the scattering of his sons like so many grains of wheat, Sima's father moved his Cherkess wife and seven children out of the Darwishi quarter and the bleak passages of the Old City to the dry Mount of Olives.

From here, Mohamad Darwishi could still gaze down at the city's mosques, the fortress walls, the cemetery. But he could also smell the pines and hear the quivering leaves of the olive and fig trees. He continued to receive the guests who had crowded into his father's *majlis* and it was in this cool refuge that he received Farouk Mahdi the day of the marriage offer.

Farouk Mahdi, the son of a goat merchant, was a tall, ruddy-faced man with piercing blue eyes. He had eight children by his wife and was said to have sired even more by several roving gypsy women occasionally seen in the market.

His wife was a dark-eyed Syrian from Aleppo. Om-Jihad was her name and she had raised her children in the crowded Mahdi quarter among the other prolific wives of her husband's brothers, never once complaining at being treated as a foreigner or at having to do more than her share of work as the youngest wife. She tended the other Mahdi children as well as her own and could be counted on to aid any woman in labor or illness as well as feed anyone who stopped in, unexpectedly, for lunch. Even her

19

husband's escapades she accepted, simply, as just one other aspect of his manhood.

Her youngest son, for whom Sima was sought, was her favorite. Jamil had his mother's dark eyes and black hair and worked alongside his father as a dairy vendor in the cramped, domed shop in the old city selling yogurt, goat cheese, cream and olives. Nobody knew, then, that it had been Om Jihad who had fancied Sima for her son, or that until the day she had glimpsed the youngest Darishi girl in the market with her step-mother, saw the strong gaze of her blue eyes and the spirited lift of her chin, finding a worthy bride for Jamil had seemed as unlikely as finding a diamond in a sack of lentils.

The city talked about the Darwishi/Mahdi wedding for months. The Darwishi women did not want to hand Sima over to the rival clan.

"The groom's mother works magic. Perhaps it's a ploy to work some secret revenge on us," one Darwishi quipped. The Mahdi women were equally disconcerted that one of their strapping young men was being wasted on an outsider. "She's only a flat-chested child," they complained. "Her hips are so narrow he'll get caught between her legs like wood in a vise!"

For Sima, the wedding seemed little more than a fitful dream as she sat on the pedestal, eyes sultry with kohl, cheeks and lips rouged pink, her nails painted with henna. Her hair had been brushed until it shown like golden thistles and soft cloth had been stuffed into the bodice of her gown to indicate a bosom. As she watched the women sing and dance and pass out lemonade and candied almonds, as she changed into the different gowns of her trousseau for her guests to admire, she though of the other times when, similarly bored, she could run out into the street of the Mount of Olives for an ice cream or a falafel sandwich. Now, she knew, all that was in the past.

When the wedding party was over, she rode beside her father and brothers in the car to the city gates where she walked in a candlelight procession beside her stoic father to the Mahdi quarter to join her awaiting groom and his family.

The morning after the wedding, Om-Jihad Mahdi rose at dawn. She washed the droplets of blood from the bride's nightdress which had been left outside the bridal chamber and proudly hung it in the courtyard for everyone to see. Then, she performed her morning prayers. As she made the morning orange-blossom flavored coffee, she heated a cup of fresh milk for the bride, leaving the thick cream at the top. Once, again, she thought with pleasure and some trepidation, it had befallen her not only to marry off a son, but to raise a young girl to womanhood, to prepare the girl for the day when she would grasp the reins of power that she, herself, had held all these years. The challenge before her was in drawing the girl into the Mahdi fold, without alienating her as some mothers-in-law were known to do, so that in time this bride would build up her son's house.

Over the next few weeks, Om Jihad's home was overrun with guests coming to congratulate the bride and groom and be shown into the newlyweds' bedroom for a look at Sima's trousseau—the dresses, nightgowns and linens that had been brought especially from Damascus—and to stare at Sima who sat silently among them in one of her new outfits.

The Darwishis and Mahdis were slowly bridging the schism of the past seven years. Sima's sisters and step-mother were feeling a new kinship with the Mahdi women. Even Sima's father and brothers began to visit Haj Farouk Mahdi in the evenings to smoke *nargilas* and play backgammon, as though they had forgotten their past differences.

In fact, Sima's life in the Mahdi house did not seem much different from her old life at home. Although she had balked at the idea of waiting on the Mahdis before her wedding, in the mornings she now helped her mother-in-law dust, sweep, and rinse the floors, and even knelt on the tile beside Om-Jihad, surrounded

21

by several whirring gas burners and bubbling pots, to prepare lunch for the men coming home from the market.

Om Jihad taught Sima how to rip off the coverlets of the cotton quilts and then sew them back on again after they were washed, impressed at how the needle danced in the girl's hand as her small fingers sailed across the heavy quilts. She taught her how to core squash, carrots, and cucumbers without puncturing them in order to stuff them with rice and meat for lunch. Occasionally, Om Jihad asked Sima if her husband pleased her. Not only was she anxious that her son treat his bride with the delicacy that her young age demanded, but she was concerned for the safety of the young couple. She worried that the girl might not be invoking the name of God when Jamil entered her, inadvertently causing a *jinn* or devil to possess her first. To these subtle hints, Sima merely averted her eyes and nodded, which the matron could only assume was acknowledgement that all was well between them in the marriage bed.

In actuality, Sima saw little of her husband and father-in-law, for, when the men were not working in the market, they were usually at a friend's *majlis* or at the cafe. Jamil was quite formal with Sima in the presence of his parents and even when they were alone together in their room he treated her with the aloof fondness he might treat a kitten lest she become spoiled or worse, brag to the women that he was besotted by her. But Sima did not mind this. For she could more easily deal with his detachment than with his fierce embraces and wet kisses.

Om-Jihad worried during the month's festivities. Though eager to fulfill her family's duties towards the bride's family and the community at large, she was wary of all the attention being lavished on her new daughter-in-law. Though the girl seemed unaware of it, Om Jihad had sensed imminent danger several times in the eyes of certain women as they regarded the new bride. She decided to warn the girl. One afternoon when there were no guests to be received, she took Sima for a walk in the fresh air out of the Mahdi quarter.

Even now the old woman felt that others were admiring Sima's pretty, pink dress and scarf. When they reached a deserted side street Om-Jihad turned to the girl:

"My child," she said, "as you may know, I am considered a *wali* in the Mahdi quarter. People ask me to bless their newborn and to pray for their dead. You, too, someday will be like me. It will be your duty to guide and govern within the family—for that is the source of real power which passes like a thread from me to you. While I am with you, you are safe. But I must warn you against those who might harm you..."

Sima listened, understanding the urgency in Om-Jihad's voice more than her words. She was, of course, aware of the forces of which Om-Jihad now spoke—the evil eye—and knew she must beware of both envious looks and unbridled praise. In her father's house, her step-mother, Shakira, had frequently made the children leap over a smoking dish of incense, murmuring the Koranic verses to ward off evil. She understood about *walis*, too. They were good forces. Though she was not quite sure exactly what her mother-in-law's powers were, powers that she was told would be passed on to herself, Sima inferred that they were supernatural and was so stunned by this revelation that she barely spoke for a week.

Not two weeks later, the thing that Om-Jihad had dreaded happened. It was an autumn morning and she was waiting for the girl under the peach tree in the garden so as to have coffee together. The sun was so pleasant that Om-Jihad barely noticed that an hour had passed without the girl appearing.

Suddenly, the old woman was seized with panic. She could hardly breath. She ran back into the house calling Sima's name and flung open the door to her son's bedroom.

"What's the matter?" she cried, taking Sima's cool hand which lay limp on the bed.

The girl—white as the bed sheet—opened her eyes and mumbled something the old woman could not understand.

Om Jihad hurried to the kitchen. Trembling, she began to boil camomile and sage, cursing herself for her own vanity, for showing off the girl too much, for permitting Sima to go into the street barefaced. She was clearly a target. But no, it couldn't be, she prayed. Not this, her last bride.

"Didn't I warn you," she said, cradling the girl's head in her arm to get her to drink. "You are different from the rest, from all the Mahdis. Even when I'm with you I can feel their shameless eyes on you."

Sima did not answer. The steaming vapor from the cup caused something to ignite in her stomach and rush right to her head. She felt faint. She lay back on the pillow and wondered if this was what it felt like to be invaded by a spirit. That someone would wish her harm terrified her. She always involked God's name whenever she poured water, whenever she bathed, whenever her husband crossed from his side of the bed and caressed her breast. She tried to picture the face from which the evil might have emanated but even this was too much effort now.

Om Jihad placed her palm on Sima's forehead and began to recite verses. Then, as she expected, she began to feel a warmth creep into her own body, to cook her very bones as though she were standing before the cavernous rock ovens in the market, or the gate to hell. Her eyelids grew heavy as she battled the yawns that threatened to keep her from repeating the verses.

"My girl," Om Jihad said at last, "you are certainly infected with a spirit. Look, I have now drawn it into myself!"

By afternoon Sima was no better and word began to spread throughout the city that the Mahdi bride was dying. The quarter itself buzzed with the news that a spirit had been unleashed at their new kin and that she would surely be taken from them as swiftly as she had arrived.

Jamil rushed home from the shop when he was told, bringing

24

the doctor with him. When he saw the Mahdi women crowding into the foyer of his father's house, some of them weeping as if they were already in mourning, he flew into a rage.

"Is she already dead that you carry on like this?" he cried, as they all ran outside screaming. But, when the doctor came out of the bedroom looking puzzled, admitting that he did not know what was wrong, the bridegroom, too, hid his face in his hands.

When my grandfather learned of his daughter's illness, he suddenly let loose what he had kept bottled up within him all these months: that he had known all along that he would live to regret handing Sima over to a band of goatherders. He was certain that they had poisoned her to get back at him.

"My daughter is no cutoff woman without men to back her. If she dies, I'll avenge myself first with Farouk Mahdi's life!"

With his weeping wife and daughters, he arrived at the Mahdi quarter and pushed his way through the alley seething with relatives all the way into Farouk Mahdi's house. Shakira burst into the bedroom where Om Jihad and the other women hovered over Sima and placed her hand on the girl's forehead as she began to recite.

Once more the city was divided. The Darwishis and their kin boycotted the Mahdi shops and the Mahdis turned away their faces when they saw a Darwishi on the bus or in the market. My grandfather made no secret of his fury, while Farouk Mahdi cursed the day that he had sought a stranger for a daughter-in-law when there were dozens of Mahdi girls who would have caused him no trouble at all. Meanwhile, the threat of blood-letting hovered like a scorpion's tail, poised to strike.

The next day, after holding vigil all night while the girl neither spoke, ate, nor drank but an occasional sip of herbs, my grandfather decided that he had had enough.

He strode into the bedroom. "I'm taking my daughter home," he said.

"You can't move her in this condition," his wife cried.

"She'll die in her own home," he said, severely.

He walked past the women and bent down to take Sima into his arms to carry her out of the Mahdi house. But as he began to lift her shoulders and legs off of the bed, Sima let out a shriek that would have frightened the *jinns*. Each time he sought to pick her up, she fought him with her voice which burst from her limp body like thunder.

Seeing the girl resisting her own father's attempts to take her away, Om Jihad was roused from her own misery. She racked her memory for an antidote, hesitating, even now, to attempt the only alternative left to her. She knew that to rid oneself of evil one had to go to its source. It had been years since she had divined this way since it could produce adverse effects—even death—but as a last resort...

She called to one of the Mahdi children to fetch a chunk of lead from a certain gypsy woman in the market.

When the boy returned with the lead, Om Jihad sent him for a bucket of well water while she set to work melting the lead in a dish over a burner. Then, as Shakira and one of Sima's sisters held the bucket over Sima's head, Om Jihad poured the molten lead all at once into the cold water.

The old woman watched the lead harden, scrutinizing it to find what spirit had been provoked.

"Is it a bird—there is something resembling a beak—or is it a goat with a single horn?" she mumbled to herself. Both were unfamiliar signs to her.

She removed the lump and started to melt it over the fire, again. Somewhere inside the lead must lay the secret to Sima's affliction. She invoked the name of Allah, and was about to pour the lead into the cold water again when she heard Sima call out. The girl was asking for a drink!

Someone pressed a glass of water to the girl's lips.

"Fetch a bowl of soup from the kitchen," Om Jihad called to one of the Mahdi girls. She watched the girl, skeptically, not daring to rejoice lest the spirit be merely teasing her.

But when Jamil looked in a few minutes later, his bride was

sipping the soup heartily and talking with her sisters. Soon the room was bustling with well-wishers and word was out that Om-Jihad had saved the girl.

Days passed, then weeks. Sima grew stronger and her face rounder until she was the picture of health again. But, she was not the same. Her eyes had gained a new depth, like twin blue ravines that seemed to absorb everything she saw, and every word that was said to her sank in the same way that it did with Om Jihad. In addition, her clothes no longer fit properly and her belly began to swell. Her breasts, once unripe apricots, began to grow full and soft.

Soon illness and fear were forgotten as Sima and her mother-in-law realized that she was carrying a child. It must have been the child, Om Jihad conceded, not a spirit, that had infested the girl.

They began to knit and embroider in anticipation of the event.

Just before her fifteenth birthday Sima delivered a boy with the black hair and eyes of his father.

"His name is 'fahed'," Om Jihad said, as she rubbed salt and olive oil into the baby's skin to ward away the evil spirits and to ensure that he would grow strong as the leopard he was named for. She did the same with each of Sima's six children that followed—some blond like their mother, others as dark as their father.

One night, some years later, Farouk Mahdi died suddenly after a game of backgammon at the cafe. My grandfather had been with him. People said that as my grandfather helped lower his erstwhile rival's white-shrouded body into the earth outside the city walls, he wept like a woman.

Om-Jihad lived to see the youngest of Sima's seven children lose her baby teeth and the older boys begin to work alongside their father after school, ladling out cheese, yogurt, and olives to customers.

When Om-Jihad finally died, six grandsons raised her coffin to their shoulders to take her from the house to the cemetery, far from the wails of the women. When they reached the garden gate, however, they found themselves pulled backward several steps. Each time they tried to go through the gate, they were stopped. This happened three times. Finally, at Sima's insistence, Om Jihad's grave was dug within the garden walls, under the peach tree.

As a child, I was both fascinated and horrified whenever I visited my aunt Sima in the Mahdi quarter and witnessed her utter alignment with her husband's kin. Neither could I equate the formidable matron she had become with the dainty bride of whom I had heard so much.

I often wondered, during those visits in her crowded courtyard teeming with her children and in-laws, whether I would one day be made to break with my own parents as she had and, if I did, whether I would find it in me to flourish so vibrantly among strangers.

HASHISH

❦ ❦

My mother and I sit in the back seat of a taxi, waiting for it to fill up with passengers so that we can start on our way back home to Jerusalem from Hebron. We have just spent two weeks here on my aunt's farm and my father, returning from one of his trips to Turkey, was to have come to fetch us back to Jerusalem, himself. Though we have waited all week he has neither come nor sent word that he is back in Jerusalem. So my mother has decided that we will go home, alone, and we have been up since dawn this morning, packing.

I am eleven and I understand that my mother is upset at my father for not coming for us as he promised. She is morose and sullen, probably remembering the other things that he has promised and failed to do, like saving money to buy a house instead of renting the top floor of a souvenir shop. For two years now, my parents have been quarreling and mother sometimes runs off to my grandfather's, exclaiming that it is too much for her, that she is finished with my father.

Is she missing an arm or a leg, she asks my grandmother, that she has to suffer such a husband? She is still young enough to attract another man, she says. Although I love my father, he does absent himself for days at a time and I am beginning to wonder whether what they say about him is true: that he has another wife and child stashed away in Ankara. Once he got sick and had to spend three months there in a sanitarium. My mother never lets him forget this, especially when they fight. As if he should have stayed there.

In the taxi I am squeezed between my mother and a woman with a nasty smell who is clasping an infant to her breast. I can't wait to get moving. When the last passenger—a man—finally sits in the front seat, the driver lights a cigarette, shifts gears with two fingers, and starts along the road to Jerusalem.

The sky is a liquid blue and there is the promise of summer in the new grass covering the valleys which are dotted with grazing sheep and red and orange gypsy tents. The almond trees are thick with white blossoms. A black-robed village woman stands at the roadside with a water urn on her head, and as we pass her our driver breaks into a tune about a *Khaliliya*, a Hebron woman, who has bewitched him with her "pearly teeth, apple cheeks, and pomegranate breasts."

I press my face to my mother's arm in disgust, thinking him vulgar. But my mother does not seem to hear, suddenly beginning to knit. She does this whenever she starts to worry about my father, as though the clacking needles reassure her. At the moment she is making me a white cardigan which will probably be too small by next winter.

The woman next to me, equally oblivious, stares out the window as her swaddled baby lies in a rumpled mound across her vast belly. She looks too old to have a baby, her face slack and grooved with a certain tightness about her mouth. Darker than most Hebron women, she has an ugly mole the size of a grape on one cheek. She is wearing a long, russet villager's dress and a man's black cape is drawn about her shoulders.

The driver begins to harangue the man beside him who looks like some principal of a boy's school with his stiff, checkered suit and double chin. With spring vacation just over, I am eager to start school again. The two weeks on the farm in Hebron were boring since I didn't get along with my two cousins and, to make things worse, my aunt had recently read of a rash of kidnappings in the area and had forbidden us children to venture beyond the last row of grapevines at the back of the house. Being confined to the yard made me fidgety and now I can't wait to get home.

"When will we get there?" I ask.

"Try and sleep," my mother says.

"I don't want to sleep," I say, refusing her extended arm. "When will we get there?"

"In an hour."

"Will father be waiting?"

"It's hot," she says, changing the subject, starting to roll down her window. She stops to see whether the breeze might be disturbing the sleeping child beside me but the child is well hidden beneath its mother's cape and the mother seems unaware of the breeze or anyone else in the car. Balanced across her knees this carelessly, I think the child might tumble onto the floor any minute. My aunt calls her own baby her 'bundle of dreams' and would never carry my squealing, runny-nosed cousin this way. I wonder whether this woman is mourning somebody or has undergone some terrible shock, blinding her to everything around her. She sits like a harbinger of some terrible disaster. I start to worry about my father, about why he has not come for us.

"Why does it always take so long?" I say, irritably.

"Sleep," my mother says, yawning.

The taxi's seats are red vinyl just like in great-uncle Jamal's car. He is the only one in our family who owns a car, bought years ago when he went to Turkey and returned with a new car and a pretty Turkish bride. The two of them had traveled quite a bit, driving to Haifa, Gaza, Syria, and Cairo, and though now divorced, Uncle Jamal continues to drive, defying old age by moonlighting as a taxi driver for tourists. He speaks English, German, and French, and is especially popular with the ladies. But when he isn't busy with

31

tourists, he piles as many of us children as are willing into his sedan for an evening drive to the Dead Sea or a picnic in Bethlehem.

The woman jars my elbow when she moves to shift the child in her arms. Underneath her cape it is hard to tell just what she is doing, but, suspecting that the child might be wanting to nurse, I draw back. The last thing I want is for this woman to bare her breast, especially since there are men in the car. I hate it when women do that. My aunt is forever dragging my two-year-old cousin to the movie theater with us and promptly undoes her blouse whenever the child becomes bored and starts to whine. Not only do I find my aunt's swollen, brown nipple embarrassing, but it seems a miracle that my cousin does not suffocate with her face plastered against the huge breast like that.

But this woman makes no further movements and the child sleeps on. I stare out of the window, hoping that it will sleep until the end of the ride.

Once, Uncle Jamal drove my mother, father, and me to Damascus. I was very young but I remember waking up in my father's lap, just as we reached the city, to see everything bathed in a red glow. As though Damascus, in the middle of the night, was a glittering, red chandelier. Another time, quite awake, I rode beside Uncle Jamal as he sped to the hospital like an ambulance driver to get one of my cousins to the doctor. She had just swallowed the cupful of benzine that my father had left on the ground while he was fixing the garden pump and we were lucky that Uncle Jamal was at our house eating breakfast the instant that she wandered in, holding the empty cup and grimacing.

The taxi driver is humming, his right arm extended across the back of the front seat, his large, hairy hand resting behind the school principal's head. He sings the refrain of a current song, humming each stanza, but his choice is unfortunate because the refrain goes like this:

*To the madhouse, To the madhouse, He led me by the
hand and never looked back at me*

It is a popular song about a love-crazed young woman, but
mother—because of my father's time in the sanitarium—hates it
and forbids any of us to sing it. She even turns off the radio
whenever it comes on. When the driver sings the refrain for the
third time my mother puts down her knitting.

"Would you mind singing something else?"

"Ha?" the driver says, looking back when she taps him on the
shoulder.

"I said, would you mind not singing that song."

"The song?"

"I can't bear that song. A personal matter," my mother says,
impatiently. The principal, too, has turned around although his
eyes rest not on my mother but on the woman with the baby.

The driver shrugs and begins a new tune, gazing into his rearview mirror to see my mother's reaction or, more than likely, to
catch her eye. A smile hovers about his lips and I am uncomfortable. Vulgar, now impudent. I have recently been studying my
mother's face and for the first time have come to realize how
pretty she is. But she does not pay the driver any attention and
stares steadily ahead.

The woman in the man's cloak now leans forward.

"How much longer?" she says, her voice a low rumble. Again, I
am bothered by her face. It compares with none of the faces of the
women I know, and has none of the warmth I expect to find in a
woman's face. She must be a foreigner from some distant, godless
city like Beirut, or Cairo, I decide.

"Not long," says the driver, again glancing into the mirror at my
mother.

"The child is sick" the woman says.

"Shall we stop for water?" says the principal, turning around
again. But the woman draws away and shakes her head.

When we pass Bethlehem I know that we are nearly home. The

33

green fields of Hebron are gone, replaced by rocky, terraced slopes and villages built like birds' nests on hilltops—red roofs and white stone houses. The colors of the sky—blue, green and lilac—race by and merge into a rainbow outside the window. Then slowly the colors shatter, dashed into fragments of a kaleidoscope, like the fragments of our lives that my parents seem unable to piece together. Sometimes I feel I am the unluckiest person alive!

Near Grandfather's house on the Mount of Olives is a shallow ravine where, years ago, Uncle Jamal's car tipped over, spilling out my mother and two aunts. Budding, shame-faced young women, dressed in the somber black coats and veils my grandfather made them wear then, they had been so upset, disgraced before the entire village by their very own uncle! Whenever we hit a bump I think about this old story and smile.

"You look happy," says my mother.

Sitting up, I realize I've been dozing with my head cradled in her lap. She smoothes my hair with her hand, running her fingers down my wiry braid. I imagine that she is thinking of my father. Although she has silky, black hair, mine is curly and blond, like his.

We are already in Jerusalem and the market street outside the old city is crowded as it usually is at noon. The driver pulls into the taxi lot and throws open his door. He gets out and stretches, then opens the door behind him for the woman with the baby.

My mother fumbles with her own doorknob but the door is suddenly pulled open for her. I hear my father's cheerful, gruff voice and, looking up, see him standing before me. He looks handsome and so young with the sun shining down on him. He grips my arms enthusiastically and kisses me on both cheeks. Then he greets my mother. For an instant I don't know whether to act pleased to see him or not, remembering how we waited for him all week. But when I glance at my mother she is smiling and I guess that my father will have some reasonable excuse ready and that my mother will forgive him. From the way they are looking at each other, things seem to be all right.

34

Then, all at once, there is a scuffling sound behind us.

"You, woman!" a voice yells. It is the man in the front seat, the school principal, running around the front of the car. The woman with the baby is just getting out but the sharp voice startles her and she jerks up, ripping her cape on the car door.

"Stop—police! I am the police!" the principal shouts, running toward the woman who draws back, stiffening. She turns to run, seeming confused, but instead she drops her bundle which rolls onto the ground behind the car. Several bystanders lunge to retrieve it but some of its wrappings have come off and they stop. A small, blue face—barely human—is exposed.

The woman, now fighting to get through the crowd of people who have gathered, is blocked by two khaki-clad policemen, their spiked helmets dazzling in the sun.

The principal—or whoever the man is—picks up the bundle and begins to unravel it, suddenly turning his head away. The silence grows and spreads, along with the sudden stench, broken only by the distant ringing of a church bell. The principal looks back down.

"*Hashish*," he mutters. Somebody in the crowd shrieks. My mother clasps me to her.

"What is it?" I ask, already remembering the item my aunt read to us from the paper—kidnapped babies, murdered so that their bodies could be stuffed with something to be smuggled across the border. I had been angry at my aunt at the time for frightening us and for limiting our usual freedom to roam about. But now I feel sick. I tug at my father's arm. I want him to take me away from here, to wake me up and tell me it is all a dream. But my parents stand still, immobilized like everyone else.

"Hashish," the man repeats, rising, gently covering the blue-faced bundle. The word lingers, hovering above us like the smell from the small corpse, the restrained woman staring before her impassively, as we witness something more evil, more terrifying, than any of us can imagine.

35

THE LADY

It was an October morning on the Mount of Olives. I opened the garden gate and found her standing before me, her fingers curled to knock.

"Does Abu Hassan live here?" she said in slow, Hebrew-tinged Arabic.

Her lavender crocheted sweater seemed to draw in the cool breeze rather than protect her from it. Her face, a pale peach color, was powdered with tiny wrinkles. Her gray hair was braided into a bun and she stooped slightly, as though her full breasts weighted her down. Yet, she stood like a woman who knew that she was beautiful and expected to be treated accordingly. A lady.

She pulled up the collar of her sweater. "It's taken me too long to come. I don't want to upset him."

Just then, my mother opened the front door at the top of the steps and started down with the pail of bread and milk for the cats in the garden. Her wooden *kibkab* clicked against the worn stone and her slip trailed below her skirt which she had hoisted up to do housework.

"She's looking for Grandfather," I said.

My mother eyed the woman for a moment.

"Does Abu-Hassan live here?" the woman repeated her earlier

37

words to me, her accent even heavier, as though half-expecting not to be welcome.

My mother put down her pail. "My father has been dead twenty years. Who sent you?"

The woman stared at my mother, her cataract-clouded eyes hiding the myriad emotions I imagined were flooding her at this news. I glanced from my mother to the woman who seemed to be trying to piece something together.

My mother, as though realizing that the woman was not yet ready to leave, gave in. "Come, have a cup of coffee," she said, starting back up the steps to the landing.

The reason for my mother's reluctance to mobilize herself to be civil had more to do with an incident earlier that morning than with this stranger at the gate. Around dawn, the time my mother usually stirs from the discomfort of a bad leg, she had heard faint chanting in the distance. I had been awakened by it, too, and had followed her out to the landing overlooking the street.

Running up the hill towards us was a familiar group—young Israelis dressed like a squadron of boy and girl scouts. Stopping at the corner of our house, as they did each time they came at this hour, they took hold of each other's hands and began to dance, as though the spot were of some significance. Then, they continued their run through the village and on back down the Mount of Olives to Jerusalem.

Since the 1967 war, when Israel had gained control of the Jordanian-held West Bank and the old borders were reopened, we had grown accustomed to seeing Israelis among us. This familiar demonstration usually took only a few minutes and passed without incident, yet the presence of these scouts in the village was an irritant, a reminder to any Arabs who were watching that this was something that these scouts had a right to do, that this village was a place that they had a right to be.

My mother, whose family is descended from the flag-bearer who rode into Jerusalem in the seventh century with the Moslem con-

querors, considers her roots to go as deep as any olive tree's on this
mountain. People come long distances to pay homage at her
ancestor's shrine in the mosque down the road which encloses his
tomb and thread-bare green banner and headdress. It is absurd to
my mother that anybody would claim more right to be here than
we.

"Where are you from? How do you know my father?" my mother
asked, abruptly.

We were sitting in the foyer, but the woman was still shivering. I
pulled out the gas heater from behind the door but she waved it
away.

"At my age I never warm up," she said. Then, she turned to my
mother, "I live in Jaffa with my son and his family."

She sipped the coffee which I had made too sweet in my hurry
not to miss what she had to say. Then she asked for a cigarette. I
fetched the pack of Camels that my mother kept for guests in the
cedar cupboard.

Puffing, smoke rising and dissolving before her face, she said
quietly, as if both my mother and I were too young to hear such
things, "Your father was a friend."

She stared into her cup, swishing the grounds around as though
they might reveal something. When she spoke, her Arabic sounded
as strange as if it had long lain dusty on some shelf. "That was fifty
years ago. Of course, to me fifty years is nothing. Years pass like
falling leaves. To you, it's a lifetime."

"I'm fifty, myself," my mother said, impatiently.

"Yes," the woman said, appraising her. "You were an infant,
then. I meant to come many times. Your father meant much to me.
We knew each other in Jaffa before 1948. After the war I stayed
there but your father left to Jerusalem. He was an Arab. I was a
Jew."

My grandfather's house in the old, Arab section of Jaffa by the
sea had been demolished last year to make room for a new apartment building. Before that, the house had been divided among

several European Jewish families who had moved there after my grandparents had fled the city in 1948.

The woman shook her coffee cup more vigorously, tilting it to evenly spread the grounds. As she did this, a warm memory stirred within me. Fortunes are read by deciphering the intricate ridges made by the dried coffee grinds against the porcelain. When she was alive, my grandmother had read our coffee cups each morning, spying eligible young men to wed her granddaughters, white doves bearing good news, dark clouds of trouble. It had been several years since anyone had had a fortune read in this foyer since my mother neither cared for it nor believed in it.

"At first, the war brought relief," the woman said, putting down her cup. "I thought I would forget him. He was married. It was best that we separate."

I felt the blood rush to my cheeks at the woman's candor. She was about to embark on something that I was not sure I should be permitted to hear about—my grandfather's extramarital affair.

My mother eyed the woman, skeptically. "How did you come to know my father?"

"I was the 'the Delta Flower' in those days," the woman said, her sparse eyebrows lifting like a veil to reveal the past, "the best artist in Jaffa."

"Artist?" I said.

"At the *Sindbad*," the woman said.

"She was a dancer," my mother murmured.

Outside, traffic was picking up. A bus ground to a halt. Vendors called for people to buy *falafel* and fresh rolls, vegetables, ice cream. My mother waited.

"In those days," the woman continued, "a fine dancer was as highly regarded as a violinist or an opera singer. The *Sindbad* was first class. Only men of good taste were allowed in. It was as an artist that I first attracted your father. He was a serious man.

"I was good enough for him to notice me, though I was only

nineteen. I think he felt an obligation to be my protector. It was good to have a protector in such circumstances. My friends envied me one like Abu Hassan."

I glanced at my mother, then back at the woman. I thought I knew what she meant by this. My grandfather had been striking in his youth—tall, with auburn hair and blue eyes. As a decorated officer in the Ottoman army, he had been as popular with his fellow soldiers as he had been with women.

"But my father wasn't simply your protector," my mother said, crossing her legs.

Both women eyed each other. "Not everything in life turns out as you would have it," the woman said, undaunted. "Your father's intentions were honorable."

My mother leaned back in her chair. We were face to face with a woman who was claiming to have been my grandfather's mistress—my grandmother's rival. I suddenly thought of my grandmother. Sallow-cheeked and quiet, white braids hanging below a white muslin scarf tied behind her ears. She was always seated beside my grandfather, ready to prepare his lunch or dinner, his *nargila*, or to keep the younger grandchildren from disturbing him. While I never saw my grandfather reciprocate any of these favors, he had certainly seemed as devoted to her as she was to him.

All at once, I understood what the woman was here for. This was a pilgrimage back to an episode in her past, an attempt to reclaim it by giving it to somebody close to the man she once loved. I wondered how far my mother would permit her to continue.

The lady seemed too preoccupied with the past to notice any skepticism of my mother's. She gazed about the room at the faded floral slipcovers of the couch, at the iron-legged side tables, the sprig of jasmine on the television set, as though she could absorb them and somehow absorb the fifty years that had separated her from my grandfather. Her eyes rested on the bright red cover of a box of chocolates my mother had hung on the wall.

"I had a costume that color—red as blood," she said.

41

"What was it like to be a dancer?" I said.

The lady folded her hands over her round stomach. "It was not an easy life."

"You liked it, though?" I said.

"I learned to dance at school. A nun taught me."

My mother raised her eyebrows. "A nun taught you to dance?"

The woman nodded. "I was the only Jewish girl in a Catholic school in Jaffa. My father believed that the nuns taught the virtues necessary for a girl's proper upbringing.

"One of the nuns was a beautiful Egyptian girl whose parents had forced into the convent because she wanted to be a dancer. At night, after lessons and prayers, she would gather a few of us into her room and dance for us. She was the loveliest thing to us, hidden away as we were among those sullen matrons. We adored her. Soon, all I cared about was learning to imitate her every move.

"She taught me to walk like a peacock, to move my arms like a cobra, to ripple my belly like the Nile, to balance a sword on my breast." The woman chuckled, patting her gray hair, "I never had to wear a wig like other dancers."

As she sucked on one Camel after another, our foyer seemed to become the dimly-lit *Sindbad* of a half a century ago:

In strode the musicians with *tabla, kamanja,* and *oud.* Then came the wispy girl in the diaphanous skirt. Swaying to the throbbing drum, rotating her hips, her finger cymbals clinking, the girl became an extension of the music.

One moment she was a goddess, long hair braided with beads, loose strands flying from her girdled hips, another moment she was a fiery palm with a candelabra of flaming candles on her head. Expert, teasing, she would throw her head forward as though to set the cafe on fire, then catch the candelabra without toppling a single candle.

And all the while, a young man's fascinated, brooding eyes followed her—a pagan priestess—as she held him and the Sindbad in frantic anticipation. Even in his dreams, as he lay beside his wife, he would see those undulating hips, feel the sweating, velvet skin, and yearn for the moment when they would be together.

"The war changed all that," the woman said, rocking us to an abrupt stop. "There was fighting everywhere between the British, Arabs, and Jews. People were killed. There was talk of borders to be set up. I begged your father to stay in Jaffa because I was sure that things would settle down in a few days.

"One night, the British ordered a curfew from sunset until dawn. I refused to let your father leave the *Sindbad*. I was afraid for him, but more afraid for myself if he took his family away and forgot me. That night, I was certain that he had changed his mind and would stay." Her voice dropped. "It's easy to make promises in a lover's arms. It's easier, still, to believe them."

Her eyes shifted away from my mother's glare. "But, the next morning he took you and left. I might have gone to Jerusalem, too, like my friend who was married to an Arab. But I had my parents to think of. What would they do if I followed my Arab lover instead of staying with them?"

The words 'Arab lover' whistled through my head. It sounded so exotic. So reckless. Not like my austere, sedentary grandfather at all.

"But the borders were open on holidays," I said. "People were allowed to visit friends and relatives."

My mother stared at me, coldly, as though wondering what devil had gotten into me to lead the woman on. After all, the image of my contented grandparents, sitting on these very chairs in this very room, had just been shattered.

"I should have come," the woman admitted. "But I, myself, got married. I had children. I wasn't the same. I was slim as smoke when he knew me. I stopped dancing."

"You stopped dancing?" I said, in disbelief.

"I took up singing for a while, popular songs," she said, mentioning names of songs that I had never heard. "They closed the *Sindbad*."

43

I could not help feeling a certain sadness at this news, as though I had been, personally, familiar with this establishment. But I was always fascinated by anything having remotely to do with my parents' or grandparents' past.

"I suppose I should have come on holidays," she repeated, as though this had just occurred to her.

"It doesn't matter," said my mother, "he remembered you."

The woman leaned forward, alert. "He did?"

"He used to tell us of a woman he had once loved, a woman as graceful as a swallow," my mother said.

The woman grinned, her eyes melting in delight.

"Only, he told us you were Greek."

The woman's smile faded. "Greek? There was a Greek among us but your father never cared for her."

"He must have meant you," I said, quickly.

The woman picked up her coffee cup and stared for a moment at the dried grounds—layers and rivulets of the future. Then, she replaced her cup on the table, leaned heavily on the arms of her chair, and stood up.

She turned to me, suddenly, and asked, "Is there a picture of him?"

I looked to my mother, silently asking whether we could show her. Half-heartedly, my mother led the woman into the dining room to a black and white photograph of my grandfather which hung on the wall.

He was on horseback, along with a dozen other young Ottoman recruits. Tall, lean, a forbidding mustache sweeping his upper lip, he did look impressive. He sported the traditional red *tarboosh* on his head, a pistol and saber at his side, and a scowl that would intimidate the boldest of men.

I held my breath as the woman walked right up to the photograph, scrutinized it for a moment, then pointed to one of the young men. It was not my grandfather.

"There was none like him, even then," she said, softly, lifting the yellowed picture off the wall and bringing it, carefully, to her lips.

44

THE MOUSE

When it was Abu Ya'coub's turn to speak the other men sitting around the coals fell silent. Abu Ya'coub was the oldest among them and had lived through exile and wars which were to these young men only history now. His words went beyond the daily troubles of their own torn lives in this refugee camp, back to a calm that seemed almost sinister in its unfamiliarity. He began:

"It was a summer afternoon in Jerusalem. 1938. A *khamsin* wind was starting up as I walked through the old city on my way home from the Friday prayers, passing through the streets where I had played as a boy, past the old house where I had been born. I began to recall those simple days, simple, that is, compared to what we had now.

"Several days earlier there had been a general curfew and many shops were still closed. The road was empty except for other men like myself on their way home from the mosque. But, as I rounded a corner, three English soldiers appeared before me—emerging from a shadowed alley as if they had been waiting for me. One of them was Constable John Willins, a tall, blond man and despite the wind that day he was sweating so much that his hair was matted to his forehead.

"I had not seen the Constable in more than a month and was pleasantly surprised to find him here. I knew him well. He had been in Jerusalem only two years and yet we had met many times and I had guessed that he had found his job under the Mandate rather distasteful. He had asked for my advice several times and I had been glad to help him out. Some months earlier I had even arranged a truce between his police and the Jericho bedouins.

"I also liked Willins and often wondered whether we might have been friends were he not British. In other words, I trusted him and so when he took me aside and abruptly told me that he had orders from the High Commissioner to arrest me, I was shocked.

"He said, by way of explanation, that my name had been linked with certain 'insurgents' and that the situation being what it was, I was to be detained by the authorities. Although *he* knew me to be innocent, he said, as a formality I had to stay at his office overnight until he could get my release papers processed and signed the next day.

"I was to go with him now, he said, and there didn't seem any point in arguing. There wasn't much I could do about it since he was a Constable and armed. But I did insist on going home first to pack a few things and tell my wife. To this he agreed.

"His jeep was parked outside the city gate and I was ushered into the back beside another English soldier. We rode in silence through the valley and the thick walnut groves up toward my house on the Mount of Olives. We passed my brother Jamal's house and the dilapidated walls of the old fort where he kept his goats. But all I could think of were the walnut trees and the strong smell of pine along the hillside. It was practically intoxicating. It goes to show what a man will notice in such circumstances.

"The jeep pulled up in front of my house. The village street, too, was deserted except for the old man, the 'mouse,' sitting on the steps across the way. He was certainly over a hundred-years-old, then, and did little else but bask in the sun all day, telling garbled stories to the village children who gathered around him. He waved as Willins and I got out of the jeep, his white wisp of beard blowing like threads in the breeze, his mouth working absently. I waved back. Then as we started up the flight of steps to my house on the second floor, I had the absurd feeling that he knew something that I didn't.

"My eight-year-old son, Ibrahim, met us at the door and I told Willins to sit in the foyer and sent Ibrahim to fetch him some lemonade and coffee. As I went down the hall to my room to pack, I saw my wife's back as she stood in the kitchen frying something, but I resisted the urge to go and tell her just yet.

"The bedroom was stuffy from the heat and cooking, but when I went to open the window for some air I heard shuffling sounds and then the bedroom door shut behind me. I turned and had the good sense to keep silent for it was my grown son Ya'coub and my brother, Jamal, who appeared to have been hiding behind the door.

"Jamal was very agitated. He was not the sort to hide his feelings and he spoke in a barely controlled whisper that I was sure Willins could hear. Word was all over town, he said, that I and some others were being taken to a prison in the *Naqab* desert. He had come as soon as he heard, with a horse on which I was to escape to Hebron where I could hide out at our sister's until it was safe to continue on to the Lebanon.

"As you can imagine, I was dumbfounded. His words were even more of a surprise than Willins' had been. Willins had promised that I would be kept only overnight. My brother was taking this all too seriously. Willins would not have lied to me. I told Jamal he was mistaken.

"'Don't be a fool,' my brother hissed.

"'Why did they send armed soldiers if Willins trusts you so much, father?' Ya'coub said, from the window. Ya'coub was eighteen and had always been more like his uncle than like me. He was easy to incite and I could tell that Jamal had been working on him. And like his uncle, he carried a gun—illegally. I went and stood beside him at the window and looked out. The soldiers were still

47

sitting in the jeep, below, but now the 'mouse' was leaning against the vehicle talking to them. Some children had gathered.

"'I gave Willins my word,' I said, determined to stay cool. Furthermore, I simply couldn't see myself riding off on a horse, escaping like some criminal. Also, I had a wife and three younger children. What would happen to them if I deserted them? But most of all, Willins had come to my house believing me and I wasn't about to forfeit his trust.

"But my brother, equally cool now, removed his gun from his coat pocket. 'Would you rather I go into the next room and kill him?'"

At this, several of the young men around the fire guffawed in approval.

"That's the way," one of them said.

"English bastard. Liar. It was a trap, all along."

"Cowards!"

After a silence in which Abu Ya'coub drew nearer the fire to warm himself he continued:

"I stood staring at the 'mouse' who seemed to have fallen asleep against the jeep, and pondered my predicament.

"'Listen to my uncle or we'll kill him,' my son said, fiercely. They were trying to protect me by threatening me with Willins' life.

"Despite the nervousness I thought I detected in Ya'coub's voice, I knew they would do it. Jamal was no killer. But he had always been fearless, even when we were boys, and his concern for my welfare had no limits.

"I brushed past them angrily," said Abu Ya'coub. "They watched as I opened the bedroom door just enough to hear little Ibrahim's voice. He was talking to Willins, telling him some story. One of the stories he had heard from the 'mouse', no doubt. Ibrahim had been set up as a decoy. I was furious that he had been placed in such danger!

"But then I was in even greater danger, I began to realize. If

what they said was true—if I were being sent to the *Naqab* prison—
nothing could save me.

"'I'm innocent,' I said, suddenly.

"'Tell that to the prison walls,' said Jamal, unmoved.

"Willins shocked me. Why would he have lied? I was tempted to
go out and confront him to his face. But he was a dead man if I
went out there. Jamal was just waiting for a cue to send Willins to
his grave. I had to go along with him.

"I struggled, let me tell you, in those minutes between not
wanting Willins killed in my own house and my sudden, utter
aversion for him. But there was little time. I took the pistol from
my son's belt.

"The horse they had brought was tied to the drain pipe at the
back of the house and I was able to slide down the pipe from a rear
window unseen and ride down the dirt road even before Jamal and
my son caught up. In my haste, I nearly ran down an old man
shuffling ahead of me. The 'mouse' was on his way to afternoon
prayers."

Abu Ya'coub rose, suddenly. He stoked the fire with a stick,
turning his back to the others.

"Abu Ya'coub," one of the men said, "finish your story."

Abu Ya'coub went on stoking the fire. Then, he looked at the
faces of the huddled men. They seemed like mere boys to him.

"Honor. Honor," Abu Ya'coub said slowly, savoring the word as
he shook his head. "Is there any among you—you or you—who
knows the meaning of honor? Or is it simply a word you wear like a
fancy cloak?" He dropped his stick and headed into the darkness
and his own blanket.

"Where are you going, man?" someone called after him.

"It's too early to sleep, come back to the fire," another said.

"Go on with your own stories," he growled back, "I'm an old
man. I need my sleep."

Somewhere in the distance was the sound of cats screaming, the
perverse wailing of cats in heat. As a boy he had thought this to be

the sound of the wild hyenas who lurked in the village after dark. There were plenty of stories in those days of grown men, on their way home late at night, being mangled by the monstrous creatures. All along what he had heard had been cats in heat.

From around the fire came the voices of the young men. Now that he had gone, their talk would turn to women as it usually did each night after he slept. They did this out of respect. They were not a bad lot and not about to want to offend him, but he was tired of them. Tired of war, of a life of exile. Even tired of his own stories that were so old that the time between them and now seemed like layers of his own shroud.

The crackling of the fire and the murmuring voices eased him into sleep. But in that moment when he began to doze, he summoned up her image as he had not done in a long time. His wife had been dead many years but it was not she that he saw tonight.

It was Rose. Rose. Constable Willins' wife.

She had been one of the few women who had come to live with their husbands in the officers' housing in Jerusalem. But whereas the others had been thin-lipped, pinched women who looked like stubborn missionaries, Rose had been no more than twenty-five and glowed with a freshness such as Abu Ya'coub had never seen. Her complexion—the times he had been close enough to her to observe it—always looked as though the blood were being freshly drawn into it, her cheeks tinged pink as though she had just been kissed. Her eyes were blue as the Jaffa sea and she had light brown hair as fine as silk. But what had fascinated him most about her was her soft, solemn voice and delicate manner.

Abu Ya'coub had been to Willins' house several times. On occasion, the Constable had asked him to come, but one evening he had gone looking for the Constable, himself. That was the time that he was told that Willins was in Haifa overnight.

Rose had seemed happy to see him, though, and despite her husband's absence, invited Abu Ya'coub in for coffee.

Naturally, he had been surprised at the suggestion. He had no right to enter a man's house if the man were out. He started to refuse but then she asked him again, practically insisted. Because she was a foreigner and obviously ignorant of his customs, he did not want to seem rude. He accepted, sitting on the comfortable chair in the foyer, not a little embarrassed as he sipped her attempt at Turkish coffee, finding it almost impossible to meet her eyes. He gazed, instead, at the tile floor and then at her white legs, her knees just barely exposed in her short, European dress. He put down his cup, mumbling that he had to be going when, in that remarkable, unflinching manner, she asked him if he found her attractive.

Now, he actually looked at her, at those determined blue eyes, those full lips. Oh yes, she was pretty. Enough for him to envy Willins, certainly. But these thoughts found no utterance. He forced them from his head as it became clear that she was no more ignorant of what was proper and what was not than he. She was inviting him!

Because he had often thought of her, or rather of that lush body barely concealed in her thin, European clothing, he was guilt-ridden as though he had made the suggestion himself—for that was surely what it was.

Before he knew what was happening she was standing before him, pulling him up, pressing herself into the folds of his thick *abaya*. He stood a few moments, paralyzed by her ardor, by the dizzying force of her arms pulling him against her young, restive body. For a few seconds, he allowed himself the warm solace of her mouth.

Then, with a strength he found astonishing to this day, he turned and fled, blinded by his own desire. When he reached home to find that his wife had kept his dinner warm and prepared his coffee and *nargila*, he sat alone in his room and wept.

He had never told this to anyone, never said why he had acted to save Willins that day, why he couldn't have allowed the man to be shot.

51

He had never understood why or or even how he had resisted the woman, or what had driven her to approach him so openly, so confidently. He had never been with a British woman before although he had heard, from his friends who had, that they harbored a particular fondness for Arab men.

The young men would have enjoyed this part of the story. The part about the woman. But they would have wondered why he had not taken advantage of her. What she needed was a real man, they would have said. The bastard deserved being deceived. It would have been no loss even had he been shot. The British signed away our country, they would have said. One woman's virtue was a small price to pay. They would have said this because they did not fully understand about honor.

Abu Ya'coub had long since ceased thinking about his need to exonerate himself that day. He had even ceased wondering whether Willins had actually known about his visit that evening and had purposely intended to have him imprisoned. Perhaps his wife had led him to believe—God knows what. A woman like that was unpredictable.

He only knew that galloping down the road behind his house that day, heading for Hebron, meant freedom in more ways than one. He had repaid Willins. He was innocent. He would send for his wife and children when it was safe. Jamal was right. It was best to leave for a while. He had friends in the Lebanon. A brother in Tripoli. He would manage.

And as he rode, he had passed the old 'mouse' who was on his way to prayers, the 'mouse' who waved again as though he understood everything. They were, after all, running along the same track, all racing toward death while trying to live out their lives in some dignity. That was it. Maybe the old man actually did know more about the ways of men than any of them, only pretending to have shut out the world years ago.

SOLOMON AND BILQIS (SOLOMON AND SHEBA)

❦ ❦

As Bilqis, Queen of Saba', is lifted atop her dromedary to her veiled litter, four horsemen dart out of the crowd of well-wishers and fire a volley of hissing arrows that fall just short of her.

The Queen ducks into the litter, grabbing the poles on either side while her slaves restrain the nervous dromedary. Guards leap onto their horses to chase the horsemen but the Queen shouts to her retainer to call them off.

"But Highness," the Abyssinian urges, "this must be avenged." He passes a murderous shaft through the veil and Bilqis studies it. A simple wooden stick with a deadly flint head. Razor sharp. No tribal insignia. But she knows to whom it belongs. She places it in her lap.

"You won't catch them," she sighs.

"I must try, Long of Life."

"These men are Shammar, cousins of my father."

"They are assassins," the retainer warns, "cunning and treacherous. They'll be back."

"Call off your men, we're wasting time!" the queen snaps. Already the sun is lifting off the horizon and the heat will soon be searing. With a month's journey ahead, they had best get moving.

Like a sand viper roused from slumber, the caravan slinks forward in a neat, single file. Queen, retainers, dromedaries, horses, merchants, foot soldiers, handmaidens, slaves. The women of Ma'rib stand at the city gates and trill their tongues in a farewell salutation as the first overland expedition of its kind sets off from Saba' toward the Northern Kingdoms of Sinai and Jerusalem.

The litter adjusts of its own accord to the swaying strides of the dromedary, lulling the queen into a dream-like state as she sits back, eyes closed, and imagines herself a piece of driftwood on the crest of a wave. *It has passed,* she thinks. *Once more I've been lucky and Ilumquh has spared me for Saba'. Praise be to Ilumquh the Bull, God of the moon.*

Ma'rib soon grows so small behind her that it seems no more than a dew drop on the oasis, an oasis blooming in the barren desert, thanks to the genius of the Ma'rib dam. Ma'rib, now the most bountiful city in South Arabia, can boast that no man, woman, or child goes hungry. Yet for all this, her nation is plagued with fratricide; tribes descend on one another like locusts, stealing, maiming, and killing. Even her brothers, uncles, and cousins are at war. Today, she had been their target.

Yet her people are as dear to her as the children she may never have, so Bilqis is off to seek the advice of Solomon, King and latter-day prophet of Jerusalem, in a desperate attempt to bring them peace. Although she is somewhat leery—Solomon has always seemed more of a problem than a solution, a rival rather than healer—his help now is her last hope.

Also, Solomon's shipping network in the Red Sea, encroaching daily upon the coast of Saba', has been the source of much irritation to Bilqis. Ships laden with gold and precious gems that sail the Indian Ocean to black Ophir and back. Some day this king will turn his gaze towards her own rich spice lands and when he does, she must be ready. Among other things, she plans to negotiate trade concessions on this visit.

Her traveling to Jerusalem overland will impress him. Not only because it is deemed impossible in the sheer size of her caravan, but because it will display her style to full advantage. Her dromedaries' saddlebags clink with gold and gems, emanate the aromas of cinnamon, mocha, frankincense. For miles around, people will know that Bilqis of Saba' has passed through their lands. She hopes that Solomon's penchant for spices and emollients will tempt him to trade with her. His ships, combined with her caravans, could make Saba' the most powerful trade center in South Arabia.

Bilqis has meticulously planned this journey, down to the last detail this morning. Rising from the arms of the Abyssinian retainer who shares her bed, she took a fragrant bath and rub with ambergris and myrrh before going to worship Ilumquh. When she had sacrificed a wild hare, burned incense and prayed, the God had spoken to her. He had promised that her journey would meet with success and that a great temple would be named after her. Remembering Ilumquh's words, now, Bilqis forgets this morning's assassins. Even Solomon no longer scares her. *If all else fails,* she thinks, gazing fondly at her splendid robes and lithe, brown legs, *well, he is only a man, after all.*

Early one morning, a scout from Solomon's court spots the red and green banners of the mile-long procession cresting the Sinai horizon at Gaza. Reclined on his couch in Jerusalem as a slave dusts him with orange-blossom powder, the king hears the news with surprise. She had set out barely a month ago!

Brushing past the attendant, Solomon leaves the great hall, crossing the sunny courtyard to the palace stables. Whenever he needs to think, he takes a ride on a freshly-broken foal and this morning he is perplexed. About why he is so nervous, mainly.

Solomon's youthful appearance belies his fifty years. His red lion's mane and beard are oiled and neatly braided, and he wears a simple, white robe. A diligent man, he follows a vigorous health regimen, eating sensibly, getting nine hours of sleep each night, avoiding too much intimacy with the opposite sex. Monogamy, he believes, erodes a man's good nature and diminishes potency. His seven-hundred wives, proof of his thriving virility, have been like so many butterflies that he has captured, admired, then let go.

But he is confounded, despite himself, by this wanderlusting lady of whom he has heard such wide and varied reports: a lady with the feet of a goat, a lady so virtuous that no man dare approach her, no lady at all but an Abyssinian whore who reached queenship by becoming the king's favorite and then assassinating him to put herself in power. It is enough to make even him, the most rational of men, begin to worry.

Yet, he has taken great pains to make her feel welcome, even setting up her quarters with provisions for God-only-knows how many handmaidens next to his own so as not to slight her. Only her soldiers and retainers will be barred from the palace since he cannot risk possible assassins. Then, there are the beasts! Gazing over the lush Kidron valley and quaint fir and olive trees of the Mount of Olives, Solomon shudders to think what hundreds of grazing dromedaries will do. He knows he should have instructed that the animals be left behind in the Sinai which would be more to their liking, anyway. But how to do that without seeming inhospitable?

Three days later, the Sabean caravan arrives at Solomon's palace, handmaidens trilling their tongues and wiry soldiers beating drums to announce the arrival of their black-masked Queen. Bilqis' retainers, eyes blackened with Kohl, their daggers sparkling like stars from within their girdles, amass at the gate.

Water shimmers in the great hall of Solomon's court where Bilqis prepares to alight. She pauses, then daintily lifts her robes to cross the crystalline pool. Solomon, having had this marble floor polished to deceive her, now sees for himself that his guest possesses perfect, human feet.

Removing her mask, Bilqis crosses the throne room, dazzling the king with her burnished, amber face and wide, kohl-rimmed eyes, blinding him with the brilliant gold ornaments at her brow and neck. Even her black robes are spun with gold. Taking her place on the dais next to him she reaches only to his bosom, a diminutive, glittering doll.

"Welcome, Lady," he says, taking her tiny hand, inhaling a scent at once exotic and familiar.

"Long of Life," Bilqis purrs, determined at the outset that her role as queen of Saba' not be undermined, "as you see, I've completed my journey in record time and now must rest." Signaling her slaves to haul in the large saddlebags she adds, "I hope you'll accept these token gifts: one hundred talents of gold, rare and precious stones, fragrant emollients and spices."

"Your generosity is overwhelming, Lady," Solomon says, as astounded by the roomful of treasures as by her abrupt, business-like manner. "I'll await you at the feast tonight, a meal in your honor to be prepared in the manner of your own country."

"That is most gracious," says Bilqis. "Now, is there a temple of Ilumquh where I may pray?"

"A temple of who?"

"You don't pray to Ilumquh?" Bilqis' heart skips, painfully, beneath her heavy links of gold. Indeed, they had passed no shrines to the Bull along the way.

"We pray to Yahweh, here," Solomon says. "You may go to his temple."

Bilqis drops her head and shoulders, despondent. "It's not the same."

Then, gathering up her robes, she walks off amidst a tent of retainers, drawing the enraptured stares of all at court. Even Solomon is speechless for several minutes.

But later at the feast Bilqis is in high spirits. In a magenta gown with sprigs of almond blossoms in her black hair, she eats lustily from the roast lamb and sweet meats, becoming quite dizzy from the goblets of wine that Solomon intently replenishes for her. She listens while he talks of his copper refineries, his ships, his horses, his wives and concubines.

"Sovereigns should be accessible to their subjects," he confides. "I have appeased hundreds of rebellious tribes as well as the Pharaoh of Egypt and the King of the Moabites by being accessible to their daughters."

"A veritable peace-maker," Bilqis says, dryly.

"I quite enjoy the role," he says, stroking his fiery beard.

A veritable stud, she thinks. *He makes the prince of the Southern Kingdom, husband to three-hundred women, sound like a eunuch.*

Suddenly, something on his face and arms catches her eye.

"What are these spots on your face?" she says, leaning away.

His hand comes up to his face. "Spots?" Then he laughs. She must mean his freckles. "I get them from the sun."

"You should wear a mask," she says. "I hope they're not catching."

"They're not catching."

"You're sure?" She relaxes a little.

"I make it a point never to be sure of anything," he says.

"Tell me," she says, her eyes smoldering like burning resin, "is it true that you imprison *jinns* by sealing them up in bottles?"

He laughs. "Where did you hear that?"

"I have my sources," she says. Her spy network has long since penetrated Solomon's palace, infiltrating even his harem.

"I've been known to conciliate the *jinns,* Lady," Solomon concedes, amused, "but I hear that you are a mistress of riddles."

Bilqis claps her hands, delighted. "What becomes fat without eating and pregnant without conceiving?"

Unable to guess the answer, Solomon changes the subject. "I've been thinking that my fleet might be of use to us both in the future," he says, a cryptic look coming over his face.

Although Bilqis has been waiting for him to bring up the subject of commercial interests, she suddenly bristles at the mention of the long-prowed ships that arrogantly sail her waters. "Sabeans have little use for ships, having mastered overland travel," she says, tartly.

"You've never sailed?" he says.

"Never."

"I've voyaged to Ophir by ship, myself, and found it quite exhilarating."

"I can't imagine it being as thrilling as rocking on the back of a dromedary," she says, dreamily.

"Tell me, Lady," Solomon says, finally, "in your land, do women always rule instead of men?"

Bilqis raises a crescent brow, wondering what her host is getting at and whether he knows of her predicament at home. Deciding not to mention Saba' just now, she says, "Motherhood is easy to establish whereas fatherhood is dubious, at best. Does it not follow that women should rule?"

While not immediately discerning the logic of this, Solomon smiles at the queen, deciding that there is ample time to prove which of them will rule.

In bed that night, Bilqis drifts back to the year she was twelve, the year she had been presented to the aging, Sabean king as a gift to ease his passage into the next world. With her doe eyes, moon face, and sleek, filly's limbs, she had quickly bewitched the old king and became his favorite. Night after night, he sent for her, growing younger and more vigorous, enlivened by Bilqis' own youthful vitality. But on the eve of her sixteenth birthday, deciding that she had had enough, Bilqis fed her master a poisoned date. All night she sat by him, comforting him throughout his ordeal, wailing and chanting his favorite poetry. Before taking his last breath—having misread her tears of joy for sadness—the king had gratefully proclaimed her his successor.

But his sallow, contorted face often haunts Bilqis on nights when she is preoccupied and tonight, she jumps out of bed and paces the room to flee his image. *He is dead*, she tells herself, *his bones have long since turned to kohl. I am queen, now, bountiful mother.*

Becoming thirsty from the wine and spicy food she ate earlier, and finding the water jug at her bedside empty, she slips into the king's chamber to drink from his jug.

Suddenly, two arms surround her like a noose.

"How dare you?" she shrieks.

"I've been pondering your riddle," Solomon whispers, his breath a flame against her cheek.

"You're shameless—my retainers warned me!"

"I think I've got it."

"That's impossible," she says, wriggling wildly.

"Nothing's impossible. It's a rain cloud."

"What?"

"A rain cloud becomes fat without eating, pregnant without conceiving."

"A *jinn* told you," she breathes, stunned.

"No *jinn* told me. Like most things it succumbed to logic. I only had to concentrate," he says, thinking of the handmaiden he had threatened to have stoned unless she revealed her mistress' secret.

"You can't have guessed it," Bilqis hisses, incredulous.

Once again, Solomon is taken by her smell of myrrh and something else he still cannot place. He grasps a tress of her hair—thick as the sands of Sinai. Moving closer, he kisses her lips. The danger of entrusting himself to this beguiling woman arouses him almost as much as her beauty does. Her lashes flutter against his cheek like twin blades.

"This is monstrous," she whispers, alarmed by her own attraction to this ivory giant with his burly chest and strange, hairy arms, so different from her own sinuous Sabean men with their coltish thighs, their chests like taut spears.

"It'll soon be morning," he murmurs, "there isn't much time."

"Time for what?" she snaps, her conscience drumming a thousand warnings against this man.

But he is already unfastening her robe.

They stand together in the moonlight that filters in through the arrow slits of the walls.

"I am a monarch," she warns him, standing as erect as possible.

"Of course," he says, delirious, as her breasts press against him like the ripe peaches of the Lebanon. He pulls her into the shadows.

Over the next few weeks, Solomon shows Bilqis his kingdom by day, his prowess in the bed chamber at night. Everything about this desert queen mystifies him, from her knack for business to the orange *henna* on her fingertips and toes, her pert, tattooed chin, her black ringlets that glisten with camel's urine. Studying her black eyes that are at once cunning and tender, he wonders whether he has finally found a home for his restless heart. Indeed, since she arrived, no universe seems large enough to contain his happiness.

Bilqis, too, wonders if this is 'love'. Too busy for investments of the heart, she keeps only transient lovers, never losing herself in a man's embrace, never dizzy with fear that she might wake up one day and find him gone. *This must be love,* she thinks, staring into Solomon's green eyes and feeling her stomach ripple and her breath stop with longing. Sometimes, she dares not envision what will come of it.

She observes Solomon at work, intrigued by his unflagging ability to solve his subjects' woes, by the trust which he inspires. She sits through a grueling session at his court where two women fight over a baby that each claims as her own. Bilqis nearly swoons when Solomon orders that the infant be sliced in half, one for each woman. Although the child is spared and the real mother proved, Bilqis finds that she has no stomach for Solomon's concept of justice and decides to explore the streets of Jerusalem, instead.

She examines the colossal ramparts and underground passages, comparing the rough stone to the porous, sandstone walls of ma'rib. Something about the city depresses her, though. Like these fortifications, there is a stern, hard side to Solomon and his people that makes her yearn for her own vibrant Sabeans with their capricious dancing and their resplendent clothing, their passion for dromedary racing.

One night, she cries out in her sleep.
"What is it?" Solomon mutters.
"I had a bad dream," she gasps.
"What about?"

61

"I dreamed a man raped me."

He lunges for his sword. "Who?"

"I don't know. Maybe my father."

Solomon is suddenly alert, shaking off the desire to go back to sleep. "Is this customary—among your people?"

"Of course not!" she cries. "A woman's body is sacred." But she remembers the arrows fired—her uncles and cousins. Her brothers.

She shivers as she stares out the open window to the faint arc of the hills in the moonlight. "He was ugly and carried the curved dagger of the Ophirans."

Solomon puts his arm about her shoulders, drawing her to him. She soon falls asleep, leaving him to toss and turn until daybreak.

The next day, Bilqis demonstrates her skill at falconry.

"You look bored," she says, when Solomon fails to applaud her black falcon sinking its beak into the scampering rabbit.

"It's just that I've been wondering. Were there many—you know—men before me?"

Bilqis looks at him. *Men are all alike,* she thinks, *each wanting to believe himself the first, the best, the last lover in your life.*

"It might explain your dream," he says.

"If you must know, I was twelve when I took my first lover. It was on the back of a dromedary."

He stares at her.

"It was rather fun," she says, inclining her head as the bird returns to take its place on her shoulder, snapping its bloodied beak. "It took the seriousness out of the whole thing."

Several nights later, Solomon wakes up to more cries. This time, Bilqis is crouched on the floor, wide-eyed and shaking.

"Another dream?" he says, gently.

"My son raped me."

Solomon groans, burying his face in the pillow. Then, he looks up. "You have a son?"

"In my *dream* he was my son. It was the same Ophiran as before."

62

"Terrible," Solomon says, going to her, stroking her neck, wondering what had happened to the cool, abrasive woman who walked into his palace a month ago. He once read that desert dwellers were inclined to be volatile due to the harsh climate. Perhaps it is normal for Sabeans to erupt in this manner. Yet there also seems to be within her some wild thing that has yet to be tamed.

Suddenly, a dim, unsettling memory of his own stirs within him—he is still a child, free to roam his father's harem, where a pair of sumptuous arms and shoulders, pink and damp from the bath envelop him...his own mother, Bathsheba, fluffing his hair with her fingers, kissing him. The words of a long-forgotten song springs to his lips:

> *...When I found him whom my soul loves, I held him and*
> *would not let him go*
> *Until I had brought him into my mother's house,*
> *and into the chamber of her that conceived me...*

"What?" says Bilqis.

"I was just wondering whether children are secretly attracted to their parents—daughters to fathers, sons to mothers."

"Rubbish," says Bilqis.

"You might be remembering something from your childhood," he says. Somewhere, he knows, there is a plausible explanation to her dreams, to his memories.

"Ilumquh is punishing me," Bilqis says, suddenly.

"Why?"

"I've abandoned my people. It's a sign that the Ophirans will invade Saba' and usurp my throne." She turns away in a manner suggesting that she does not wish to be disturbed.

Several hours later, however, Solomon is still awake. Her dreams gnaw at him. Something about them suggests that they belong to the past rather than to the future. None of his wives or concubines ever reported such hideous dreams. He finds himself more and more absorbed by them. If he can solve them, protect her from them, she might be happy. And, he *does* want her to be happy. He has even contemplated a plan whereby their kingdoms will unite in a sort of federation—*Solomon and Bilqis.*

As the first light of dawn spreads over Bilqis' face, alighting on her closed lids like manna, Solomon is riding his favorite gray through the underground network of caves toward Jericho.

But with each passing day, Bilqis draws further and further away from him. They begin to quarrel over the very things that once drew them together—she accusing him of wanting to take over her spice industry and trade routes, he suspecting her of using him to gain access to the Mediterranean.

One night, he finds her placing a loaf of bread along with a dagger under her pillow. When he demands to know what she is up to she tells him that it enables her to think clearly while she sleeps in order to arrive at the right decision the next morning. She will not elaborate, but remembering the rumor that she had once killed another king, Solomon lies awake all night with his sword unsheathed by his side.

Bilqis, too, tires of Solomon's pettiness. Preying upon her dreams, he plagues her with questions about her childhood, about her father and mother, her brothers and sisters, as though she is some riddle to be solved through the most irrelevant details. She begins to mistrust him, fearing to disclose any morsel of information that he might use against her.

Soon they are sleeping in separate chambers. Solomon summons his Moabite wife, Bilqis surrounds herself with a bevy of handmaidens. When Solomon looks in on her one night, he finds the Abyssinian retainer sprawled beside her. Enraged by this brazenness—no woman has ever dared to insult him so openly—he draws his sword to sever the interloper's head and dangle it before her eyes. But aware that this display of jealousy will only delight Bilqis, he leaves the room, forced to content himself with the grisly fantasy.

Early the next morning, Solomon awakens to a noise like thundering trumpets. He rushes to his window, half expecting to find the palace besieged by the Moabites. Instead, kneeling in his courtyard are hundreds of snorting, bellowing dromedaries, loaded down with baggage. A single, veiled palanquin is strapped to the back of the largest beast. Sabean retainers stand at attention, restless as leopards, their daggers ablaze at their sides. Bilqis' handmaidens cross the courtyard with arm-loads of robes and trinkets, twittering like happy parakeets.

So, Solomon muses, *it's back to the barren wastes, is it?*

When she enters his throne room to say good-by, he is already at work with his ministers, scanning the text of the next year's budget. He looks up briefly, then goes back to his figures, cursing her under his breath. Today, of all days, she looks radiant, her cheeks opalescent, her hair braided on top of her head to expose a throat as smooth as a succulent oryx's.

And yet, he cannot help but feel that she has taken advantage of him, that her visit has been a flagrant charade, a selfish desire to conquer him. He wonders whether it is not this that she has wanted all along—a father. Someone to take care of her.

She climbs the dais and places a cup of steeping cardamon pods in his hand as she has done each morning that they have been together.

"We haven't much time," she says, hoping to remind him of his words to her on their first night together, a night when he had lusted for her simply as a man for a woman, when he had accepted her desire for him purely for what it was. Finally, he relents and sends his ministers from the room.

"I'm leaving," she says, sipping the hot, aromatic drink.

"So I see."

"I still don't have what I came seeking."

"I've given you full use of my seaports, what more do you want?"

"*Advice.* What do I do about insurrection and civil war?"

Solomon's stomach sinks. Despite his anger he has no wish to see her cut down. Besides, unless she reneges, he now has access to her trade routes and commodities and she could prove to be a useful ally in the future. So, thoughtfully, he says, "Beware of those to whom you do favors."

"What do you mean?"

"Don't forgive them. Crush the rebellion, kill and imprison your enemies, break their fingers one by one."

"Really?" she says, seemingly impressed by this deviation from his usual principles.

"Really," he says. "Of course there are alternatives."

"I can't take a husband from each tribe, if that's what you mean," she says.

He shrugs.

"And I don't believe any of your theories about my secret desire to marry my father. Really, Sir!"

Solomon waves this away. Coming from her lips, it *does* sound ridiculous. "I mean, you could stay here with me. Forget about them."

"Forget Saba'?" she cries, her voice breaking. "Forget my people? Forget my God? That would be like death, like losing my soul."

He sighs. "You can always abdicate."

She looks away.

"Write a book," he offers. "It will clear your head."

"You write, I suppose," she says.

"Certainly," he says.

She looks at him. "What do you write?"

"Songs, mostly. It's quite soothing."

"Lyrics," she says, suddenly aroused. "I love a good song. Recite one."

"Now?" He starts to shake his head. He will only make a further fool of himself. But when she wrinkles her brow and her eyes moisten, he gives in. He begins:

> *The song of songs, which is Solomon's.*
> *O that you would kiss me with the kisses of your mouth!*

> *For your love is better than wine,*
> *your anointing oils are fragrant,*
> *your name is oil poured out...*

As he immerses himself in song, Bilqis' eyes begin to fill. They had been happy. They could still, perhaps, be happy together. Then, something in her abdomen flutters. She laughs, softly.

"You're interrupting," he shouts.

"Sorry."

"It's a serious song."

She ignores his outburst. "In Saba'," she says, "it's customary to answer a poet's verse."

Solomon stares at her. She is truly insufferable! Whatever he does, she tries to do better. But he nods, graciously. "Go ahead."

"Let me see..." she says, closing her eyes, wetting her lips:

> *'...Your name is oil poured out...'*
> *Draw me after you, let us make haste.*
> *The King has brought me into his chambers*
> *We will exult and rejoice in you;*
> *we will extol your love more than wine;*

"You're mocking me?" Solomon growls.

"Of course not," she says, her eyes bright. The fluttering inside her starts again, a bubble gently swimming up and falling—the curious tickling of the fetus within her. Though she yearns to tell Solomon about his child, she knows that he will never let her leave if he knows.

She urges him to sing on, to drawn out the voices of her retainers in the courtyard, to subdue the quivering bubble within her.

And Solomon, though he can already imagine her back in Saba', crowing about the great king's clumsy attempts to keep her with him, cannot stop the words that leap, wounded, to his lips:

> *Set me as a seal upon your heart, as a seal upon your*
> *arm;*

> *for love is strong as death,*
> *jealousy is cruel as the grave.*
> *Its flashes are flashes of fire,*
> *a most vehement flame.* [1]

---

[1] The Song of Songs, *The Interpreter's Bible* (New York: Abington Press, 1956), p. 118, 103, 104, 143.

NARIMAN

The faint, even rattle of machine-gun fire pierced the shrill bellow of evening prayers echoing from a nearby Beirut minaret. It was a balmy summer afternoon and the three girls—Nariman, Selma and Qamar—continued to walk home from school, on past the bakery, the dress shops, the balconies overgrown with hibiscus and geraniums. Nariman broke off a flower the same orange color as the sun, a sinking flare beyond the roof tops of the apartment buildings, and slid it in between the pages of her math book. Selma, too, broke off a flower. With a sly smile, she boldly poked it down her blouse.

Nariman's face glowed from the brisk walk, drops of perspiration glistening above her upper lip and across her forehead at the roots of her brown hair. Her chest lifted gently with her panting, the swell of her breasts appearing above her scoop-neck dress. Sixth-form girls nearing graduation were permitted to wear their own clothes to school this year instead of the navy, sack-like uniforms. But while previously hidden rounded arms, slender waists and full hips were being flaunted, girls found their budding womanhood both exciting and unsettling, like vibrant flowers against a backdrop of gunfire.

The girls hesitated at the corner. Surely after last night's shooting their usual shortcut through the old, run-down alley would be intercepted by a roadblock—armed men behind sandbags, materializing out of the rubble to claim new territory. They decided on the longer, open route down the boulevard. Though never without ID cards, they were careful to avoid trouble, unlike some girls who went out of their way to mingle with soldiers on their way home.

"I didn't sleep last night," said Qamar, who was engaged to be married in the spring. Her long, black hair was swept back in a ponytail, displaying wide, beautiful eyes that were almost as dark as her hair. Qamar's clan was one of the wealthiest and best-established in Beirut and everything she did, it seemed to Nariman, bespoke a graciousness long-forgotten to most who had lived amidst the chaos of the past few years.

"Nobody slept," said Nariman. Her mother and father had been sitting on their bedroom balcony playing backgammon when the shelling started, a spray of gunfire sweeping across the top of their own building. They had had to crawl back inside on their hands and knees to join Nariman and her older brother Yousef in the window-less corridor. For two hours they sat listening to the bombs exploding, rattling the glass panes in the bookcase. When it was over, the sky was cloudy with pink smoke.

But this morning all had been calm. The doorman had removed a failed bazooka rocket from the abandoned fifth-floor apartment and swept some broken glass from the main entrance where a window had been shattered. On her way to school Nariman had passed a vendor with a cart stacked high with green mangoes and bought three of the ripe, unblemished fruit for her mother.

Only a few palm trees were left along the once-fashionable boulevard where walls were now bullet-pocked and windows were broken. Through a missing wall, a blue room with ornate molding on the ceiling was visible. Further along the street a rope cordoned off a deep, gaping trench where several razed apartment buildings had yielded a cache of ancient remains—Phoenician, Greek, Roman. Archaeologists were flying in during the cease-fires to investigate the site, resurrecting pillars, collecting potsherds.

Here the girls split up, Qamar and Selma continuing on uptown, Nariman crossing the street to her own building. Hugging her books to her chest, she nodded to the new doorman. He was the third in three months, the last, having been kidnapped and then released, had gone off in search of a job less open to attack by soldiers, thieves, or homeless squatters looking for vacant apartments.

Since the elevator seldom worked anymore, repairmen being in such demand that they were impossible to find, she climbed the four flights of steps to the second floor. She unlocked the door and stood for a moment, at once aware of certain things being out of place. The rug in the foyer was rumpled, and several pictures on the wall were askew. Her mother, too, was not in her usual place for this time of day—relaxing on the sofa, reading. Nariman called out to her as she adjusted the pictures and smoothed the carpet with her foot.

"Where's mother?" she said when Yousef appeared in the corridor on the left.

Yousef did not answer, but then Yousef always acted peculiarly lately, isolating himself from the rest of them, even eating his meals alone in his room. Their mother indulged him, saying that the confinement at home was even worse on him, a man, than on her, especially now that the University had closed down because of the fighting. A second-year engineering student, Yousef still kept up with his studies, and their mother was only too grateful that he was not out wandering the streets with a gun the way many other young men were.

But Nariman was fed up with his silence—selfishness considering what they *all* had to go through—and was about to tell him so now when a sharp sound behind her stopped her. Suddenly, someone gripped her about the shoulders and clamped a hand over her mouth. Sinking to her knees, she was yanked up again, spilling her

books and papers onto the floor, catching sight of the gray barrel
of a machine gun against her leg.

"Sss," someone hissed as she tried to pry loose the fingers from
her mouth.

"Over there," came the voice, again, and she was let go and
prodded towards Yousef. She stumbled forward, her chest throbbing painfully.

A machine gun was pointed at her by a soldier scarcely older
than herself. His face was sweaty, sun-browned. He spoke through
a broken, front tooth.

"Who else is there?"

"Nobody," said Yousef, almost as though continuing a conversation begun with this stranger before she came in. Nariman backed
against her brother. She looked at him. Her father would be at
work but her mother was always home by now. After last night she
would have gone no further than to the corner store for bread.

The soldier stepped forward and Nariman backed, further,
against Yousef into the corridor. The boy's heavy boots and uniform were dirty and his hair shaggy, but through a rip in his khaki
shirt she could see smooth, white skin.

With his gun trained on them, the boy walked through the
corridor looking from one bedroom to another and then back at
them. For a moment Nariman imagined herself marching down
the hall, holding people captive.

"You," the boy said, sharply, turning to Yousef and nodding
toward the blue bathroom behind them, "in there!" His dialect was
strange and Nariman barely understood his words.

"He's only a student," she said, quickly, not sure how to approach a soldier, but knowing that it was safe to be a student,
somebody not involved. Only those loyal to one faction or another
were killed, their bodies often burned or left at one of the over-
flowing trash heaps that littered the city.

"We're students," she repeated but the boy ignored her. He
pointed his gun at Yousef and jerked his head toward the bathroom.

"We won't tell anyone you were here," she said. "Take anything you want, anything from the kitchen, too."

She must remain calm, to persuade him to leave, but even as she spoke she realized her fear meant nothing to him.

He stamped his boot and Yousef backed into the bathroom.

When Nariman moved to join him, the boy brought his gun up against her.

He followed Yousef into the bathroom and Nariman heard a quick burst of gunfire. But it must have come from outside, or maybe she imagined it, for Yousef was still standing and the boy had merely removed the key from inside the bathroom. Now he slammed the door and locked it.

Nariman yelled at her brother to stop pounding on the door, afraid that this would anger the boy and cause him to shoot, but the boy seemed deaf to Yousef's protests and only pointed his gun at Yousef's bedroom behind Nariman. She backed in and he followed her.

Realizing that he must have killed before, that one more life meant nothing to him, she thought of escape. There was the sound of a tractor outside. If she could get to the glass doors and out onto Yousef's balcony she could call for help. Some pigeons on the balcony railing meant that their owner across the street would be watching, as usual, until they flew home. He would hear her cries. She was so close to the balcony!

Yousef's room was tidy, the beds made and the carpet spotless— her mother's diligent cleaning. On the walls were Picasso reproductions that her mother had picked out and a small, charcoal sketch of Yousef that Nariman had done for his birthday. The only mess was on Yousef's desk which was strewn with papers and textbooks, a lamp focusing on a page of diagrams.

The boy walked over to the desk and picked up a pack of cigarettes that were lying beside an ashtray. He stuffed them into his breast pocket. Then he picked up Yousef's gold fountain pen, rolled it between his finger tips, and put it down. He looked up at Nariman and said something.

"What?" she asked, still not understanding his words.

"Are you still a girl?" he said. Without waiting for an answer, he slipped the gun strap off his shoulder and placed it across the desk where it lay shining, clean and new.

"If you're still a girl," he said, coming toward her, "turn around."

Nariman stood looking at the boy's dusty face, at his lowered eyes refusing to acknowledge her. His boots scuffled heavily as he came up behind her and began to undo his uniform, and then there was the clinking of the belt buckle as he lifted her dress and pulled down her underpants.

She stood like a pillar of ice, not quite believing what was happening, unable to move, to flinch even.

Did he think this way did not count? She tried to relax. He was just a boy, a clumsy boy trying not to hurt her. Maybe he had a sister. She thought she heard him say, "Help me."

"I'll pick you up at four," her brother said, as the first bell started ringing.

"I can walk home with Selma," Nariman said, shutting the door of the silver Renault.

"No, I'll come," he said. She nodded, understanding his need to protect her. He still could not accept the fact that he had done the right thing and kept them both alive by cooperating.

It was her first day back at school after a week at home feeling humiliated and ashamed. She was tired of thinking about it and tired of her parents' pained faces, blaming themselves for what had happened. They had hardly spoken to each other all week and Nariman had been kept up at night by her mother's crying.

She would have liked to yell at them and make them understand that it would have made no difference if they had been home. They could have been locked into a room as easily as Yousef had been, her mother could have been raped, her father killed.

"We have to tell the police," her mother had said.

"What can they do, now?" said her father. His own feelings of helplessness hurt Nariman even more than her mother's crying.

"We should take her to a doctor, at least."

"I'm not going to any doctors!" Nariman had shouted from her bedroom. There were no bruises or wounds to show a doctor. Only the burning awareness and nobody could do anything about that.

"See you later," she told Yousef, poking her head through the car window.

"You're sure you want to go?"

"I'll be fine," she said, forcing a smile and following the girls hurrying through the gate to get in line for chapel. She turned once, watching Yousef drive off, thinking how relieved he must be to get away from her, to pretend for a while that none of this had happened.

She was glad to see familiar faces, even to be going to chapel for the headmistress's dreary sermon. The classroom was a flurry of activity this morning, girls calling out to her, asking where she had been. Her desk was just the way she had left it, her fountain pen and inkwell in place, texts and notebooks stacked neatly inside. The roomful of girls was soothing, their voices one big hum reaching out to her.

Then, suddenly, everyone was staring at her.

She must have screamed. Her skin was alive with goose-bumps, the burning beneath her dress erupting. Whirling around she saw Selma's pale hand and bright red nails draw back. It was only Selma, her best friend, who had touched her. Only Selma, staring at her like the rest, her green eyes wide with surprise, having merely intended, Nariman realized, to show off her new haircut.

On a Sunday afternoon in March, people are strolling along the Corniche overlooking the sea. They gather at the makeshift stalls of displaced shopkeepers to shop for stolen watches, silk scarves, French perfumes at bargain prices.

The white car rolls down the tree-lined corniche, past the old amusement park with the rusting ferris wheel and the lone "lover's leap" jutting up from the sea. Qamar is driving the car her father has given her as an early graduation present. She pulls up alongside a vendor roasting chickpeas over coals and Nariman gets out and buys three bunches of the green peas still on their stems, wrapped in cones of newspaper. She passes a bunch to each of the other two and they sit nibbling on them awhile before Qamar restarts the engine.

Driving on past the crowds they finally park along an empty stretch of highway used by drag racers at night. The sandy beach is deserted because of the water's strong and dangerous undertow and there are warning signs posted in several spots, white placard squares with red skull and crossbones.

They get out of the car and Nariman and Qamar remove their sandals and pantyhose. Selma rolls up her trousers, her athletic legs already honey-colored from afternoons spent outdoors in her short gym skirt playing net-ball for the school team. As the breeze riffles her short, bleached-blond hair she pulls out a pack of *Gitanes* from her pants pocket and offers cigarettes to the other two.

"You've postponed the wedding again?" she says to Qamar as Nariman and Qamar bend over her lighter, sucking on their cigarettes.

"Father won't let me fly to London alone," Qamar says, dropping her head back gently as she blows out the smoke. "He says that Sami has to come and get me."

"I wouldn't want to come here to get anybody," says Selma.

"He'll come," says Qamar, shrugging. "I can wait."

"Why bother getting married if you're not in a hurry?" says Selma.

"I am in a hurry. I just don't want trouble between my father and Sami."

"Come on, let's go down," says Nariman, tucking her skirt between her legs and jumping, awkwardly, down the two meters to the sand.

Selma and Qamar follow, holding their cigarettes out at arm's length. They dust the sand off of their legs and walk towards the shore, stepping around empty *Fanta* cans, seaweed, and watermelon rinds.

"Why are you marrying him if you aren't dying to be with him?" Selma presses, hurling a fistful of sand at one of the signs with a skull and crossbones. A few grains are blown back at them, flicking their faces.

"Who says I'm not dying to be with him?"

"You don't act like it," Selma says.

"How do you know how I feel?"

"I know more about love than the two of you combined," says Selma, impatiently. She is referring, of course, to her boy friend who picks her up after school in his Trans Am although her parents do not know. Nariman envisions her friend's reckless energy set free on those afternoons in the shiny car. She shudders.

"Leave Selma alone," Nariman says, now, wanting to head off the usual argument between the other two. Selma, a born rebel, is jealous of Qamar's complacent willingness to conform to her family's wishes. Nariman envies both of them, suddenly. She does not know what *she* believes any more. She does not care enough about anything to believe in it or fight for it. She simply exists, simply accepts what each day brings.

"Sami is a good man," says Qamar. "He has a good future. He's handsome."

"He's rich," says Selma.

"He's my cousin," Qamar says, undaunted. "We've been promised to each other."

"You don't love him," says Selma.

"How do you know? Love comes later."

Selma rolls her eyes. "I'd love to get out of here, to go anywhere. Last night I thought the thunder was a bomb."

With the cease-fire still holding after a month, people have begun to sleep again. Still, it is easy to become alarmed by a sudden noise. But to Nariman, the silence is all the more frightening for what it might bring.

77

She had faced this strange silence again several days ago on her way home from the dry cleaners. One minute it was as if the entire city was holding its breath; the next, a soldier behind a sandbag was yelling for her to get down.

Obeying, she ran into a doorway to hide, watching as the rifle inched above the sandbags and let loose a volley of bullets into an alley across the way—as though it had a life of its own.

Two men in pajamas ran out from an apartment building, machine-gunned both the alleyway and the sandbags, then disappeared. When it was quiet again, Nariman picked up her just-cleaned clothes, stepped out of the doorway, and started home. The man who had shouted out to warn her was slumped over the sandbags.

"Did you hear about Julie?" Selma is saying.

"The journalist?" says Nariman.

"She was raped," says Selma, picking up a smooth stone and hurling it into the water. "She and her husband were stopped at a roadblock one night in the mountains. Lucky they weren't killed."

"I haven't seen Julie in ages," says Nariman, shoveling up sand with her toes.

"I saw her at a disco the other night. She acted as if nothing had happened," says Selma.

"You went to a disco?" says Nariman, unable to hide her envy. It seems like years since she has been out for any fun.

"Foreigners are all the same," says Selma, "too curious. Would *you* think of driving into the mountains at night?"

Nariman wades into the water, swishing her feet as a school of minnows dart back and forth to avoid her. "The water's cold," she says.

Selma is smoking another cigarette and Qamar is stretched out on the sand with her head on Selma's lap. With her wind-swept black mane and face misty from the sea air, Qamar looks like some shipwrecked goddess. She seems so whole, so pure.

Nariman cannot imagine Qamar being forced into what she had been.

"I'm going to Paris next month to see my sister. Maybe I'll find a job there, or a husband," Selma says, winking at Nariman. Qamar smiles, benignly, at this goading.

"I think I'll be going to the University in London," says Nariman. "I've submitted my papers." She will be graduating in June with honors, easily assuring her of a place at either of the universities here, but that might mean spending a year out of classes as Yousef has. Besides, she needs the change. She needs to escape the memory and bouts of nausea. Anywhere will do, so long as there is no chance of her ever hearing that dialect spoken again. She has come to recognize it on every street corner and in every taxi cab and bus as though she were deaf and can suddenly hear.

Some distance down the beach are several boulders and on one of them sits a man, watching them. Nariman noticed him when they first jumped down to the sand. Now, she wonders whether he has been watching them all this time, seen them smoke, kick up sand, wade in the water. She wonders whether, having heard their loud voices and laughter, he might be thinking that they are the sort of girls who have become hardened and reckless from war, girls to whom little is sacred anymore, who don't mind giving a man a good time.

"See that man?" she says.

"Where?" says Selma.

"Over there."

Selma looks to where Nariman is pointing. The man is beginning to walk toward them.

"What about him?" says Selma.

"It's time to go," says Qamar, standing.

"He's all the way over there," says Selma.

"It's not safe," says Qamar.

"Don't be silly," says Selma, surprised. "There's one of him and three of us."

"No telling what he might be thinking, he's been there a long time," says Nariman, suddenly sure that he has been watching them. "My mother worries if I'm not home by now."

"Your mother always worries," says Selma.

Nariman looks at her friend sharply though she knows that Selma does not mean anything by this. She bends to examine a torn, yellow sandal that looks like it might have belonged to some girl who had drowned in the undertow. When she looks up, the man is still walking toward them, casually, as though it is quite normal for a man to approach three girls on a deserted beach.

"I'm going," says Qamar, starting across the sand to the sidewalk.

"What's wrong with her," says Selma. "A man's free to walk on the beach. At least let's wait for the sunset."

Nariman looks at the sun, at the flaming sea below, then back at Qamar who is climbing up a rock to get to the car on the sidewalk. They can all be safely on their way home if they hurry, but Nariman does not move. Suddenly she says, "I have a knife."

"A knife?"

"I always carry it," Nariman says, retrieving from her pocket the slim, silver switchblade she had taken from Yousef's drawer.

"You're as bad as she is," sighs Selma, shaking her head, dousing her cigarette in the sea. "All right. Let's go."

But Nariman stands still. No longer afraid, she will wait for the man to get close enough and then she will go to him. She knows what he'll be thinking. He'll be pleased.

She turns to Selma. "Are you a virgin?"

"What?"

"Are you?"

"What sort of question is that?" Selma says, staring at the blade in Nariman's open palm. "Let's go."

Nariman closes her fingers over the blade with her thumb on the switch, having often practiced flicking it open.

"Nariman!" Qamar is calling, waving to them.

Nariman looks back at her and at the waiting car. She does not move even when Selma shakes her arm. *This will only take a minute.*

"Nariman!" Selma snaps.

Nariman takes a step forward.

"Nariman," Selma pleads, her voice faltering.

Nariman can already feel the man's soft flesh yielding to the knife. She closes her eyes. Out of the silence she can hear the soft, faraway croons of the pigeons on the neighbor's roof-top beyond Yousef's balcony.

Then she remembers the boy, how he tried to be gentle, how he had left her intact. For an instant she is amazed. What kind of boy does that?

She fingers the knife again before slipping it back into her pocket. This man thinks she is waiting for him, willing and eager. But he should know better. There are warning signs everywhere. *Beware of the sea. Beware of the woman.*

FLIGHT

❧ ❧

The plane has been airborn two hours before the old woman sitting in the window seat turns to Samia and asks for the time. Samia looks at her wrist.

"Half-past seven," she says, noting the expensive gold watch on the old woman's own left wrist.

The woman says nothing, but her beaked, stringent face appears confused as she resumes gazing out of the window.

Samia, too, looks out at the velvet carpet of clouds below, wondering when they will get to New York. Her bulky frame is wedged somewhat self-consciously between this old woman and the man in the aisle seat. It was two hours ago that they left Beirut—ten more hours to go.

Ordinarily, Samia would not mind. She likes long plane rides, likes being suspended like this with nowhere to go and nothing she has to do, with her thoughts flowing backward and forward freely as though not fixed in any particular time. Back to the last few years, to the pain, the fear, then forward to when she will see her brother Ahmad and meet his new American wife, Claire, and to the things they will talk about, the things they will do together. She has brought Ahmad a specially-ordered box of baklava from his favorite bakery although he has assured her he can get everything he wants right in New York.

Today, though, from the moment she stepped through the plane door into the smell of stale cigarettes and something like boiled cabbage, Samia has wanted to have the flight over with. Even before that, when an airport security guard sniffed her open suitcase for drugs, when a security woman took her into the curtained cubicle and ran her hands over Samia's body, squeezing her breasts for any concealed weapons, Samia has had second thoughts.

She glances at the 'fasten seat belt' sign which has just come on again due to the turbulence, then at the bobbing, blond head of the French stewardess a few seats ahead who is trying to pour coffee.

It has been a shaky flight since they left Beirut and Samia worries that the plane has not been well-maintained. She imagines screws coming loose, parts flying into the icy stream outside. She sees herself and the other passengers crashing to the ground in a flaming heap, fried in their seats. Part of her is afraid that they will never land. Part of her dreads landing in America at all.

She has trouble swallowing the dry dinner that is served: a roll, a slice of salami with pistachios arranged in it making it look like a face with two eyes and a nose, a foil-wrapped triangle of *La Vache Qui Rit* cheese, a large green apple, a banana. She eats the cheese and salami and nibbles on the roll; bananas give her a rash. The apple she will save—the famous Lebanese apples her brother cannot get in New York.

The old woman who asked for the time burrows into her roll with her fingers, emptying the soft dough onto her plate, chewing on the crusty outer shell.

Samia looks back at her apple. It looks strange, somehow, a little too fresh and beautiful. It is perfectly round, a polished green with a blush of pink on one side. It is the kind she used to buy from roadside stands in the mountains on her way back from the Cedars. Before she can pick it up, smell it, reassure herself that somewhere in some high, mountain village men and women are tending and harvesting an apple crop safe from the clatter of gunfire, the apple rolls off of her tray and onto the lap of the man in the aisle seat next to her.

The man is about her age, fiftyish, with silver lighting up his stiff, brown hair and a day's grey stubble on his cheek. He carefully picks the apple off his lap and hands it back to Samia.

"They used to serve hot meals, even during the fighting," the man says, the first words he has spoken to her, as though the incident involving the apple is cause for contact between them.

Samia nods. She does not want to talk, not with this man, not with anyone. The humming of engines is all the company she needs. She talks enough back home. There is little else left to do anymore but talk.

"Airline food must be a low priority," the man goes on. "The staff must be busy just keeping the airport functioning when it's open."

"The kitchen is probably shut down," Samia says, hoping to end the conversation.

"Or there aren't any good chefs. My cousin is a chef and he left to open a restaurant in London."

Samia taps her fingers on the thin, plastic coffee cup. She has asked the stewardess for a refill.

"The old hostesses were a lot better," the man says. "They were prettier, and they smiled." His own lower lip spreads in a lush smile as though to illustrate his point.

This, at least, is true. The last time Samia flew out of Beirut on Middle East Airlines was five years ago to go to London. The stewardesses had all been young, Arab women who smiled politely when summoned. The one serving their section today is a middle-aged French woman who seems in no hurry to please anyone.

"But when you travel as much as I do you learn not to be choosy," the man says, patting his breast pocket out of which juts his plane ticket. "We're lucky to get a female at all. Most women won't work out of this airport anymore."

The stewardess arrives with the pot of coffee. Her eyes glow

85

within the cobalt blue eyeshadow that highlights the wrinkles underneath and the crotchety look on her face. Her make-up is too bright, as though it has been applied in a rush, or without light.

At the moment of take-off, all the plane's lights had been shut off to keep it from being a target for ground fire until they were safely over the sea. There had been several gasps in the pitch black cabin, passengers jumpy at the thought of more danger. But Samia had found the dark peculiarly soothing, as though she were sailing into outer space, smothered in a vast, impenetrable void.

Doing without light, of course, is something she has gotten used to from the years of power cuts they have had to live with. On a good day there is electricity for two hours in the morning, two hours again in the afternoon and from six to nine at night. Just enough to keep the refrigerator cool and the water hot for a daily shower. More and more, though, they have had to do with cold baths and candle light.

Samia thinks of the children that she has left behind. Not her own, of course, she is still single. An old maid. She is thinking of the children in the refugee camp and in the slum behind it that attend the United Nations school where she teaches third and fourth grades. They are at home now for the summer. In a month, however, if the fighting calms down, they will return to classes expecting to find her there. Only the American school Principal, Mr. Conolly, had been skeptical when she told him that she would be back, that she would be gone only a month to visit her brother.

"New York," he had repeated after her, as if it were a place so remote that she could never be expected to get there, much less to return. Other teachers had left after similar promises and never returned. Why would it be any different with her?

She had reminded him, though, that she was the school's oldest teacher, had been there twice as long as he, himself, in fact. How could she not return? She, a daughter of this city, born and raised in this downtown amidst the busy shops and markets, the blaring of the Koran from the mosques and the hollow ring of church bells. This was her only home. The only place she knew.

But she knew that she no longer belonged here. She had left his office feeling like a traitor.

Two hours later, Samia is having her third cup of coffee. This one is surprisingly fresh and flavorful and since the plane is gliding smoothly now, she is able to enjoy it. It is a miracle to drink such good coffee on an airplane. She thinks of an article in the newspaper she had read not long ago about a coffee machine designed for jet fighters that was guaranteed to brew good coffee even after the plane exploded and all aboard were killed.

"Excuse me." It is the old woman on her left, again. "What time is it?"

"Nine forty-five," Samia says.

"Thank you."

Samia glances at the gold Rolex on the woman's thin wrist. "You have a watch, yourself. Why don't you look at it?"

The woman looks at Samia, startled. "I . . . I can't see without my glasses."

The man on the aisle mutters, "She probably can't tell time."

This has not occurred to Samia. She glances at the woman who appears not to have heard. The woman pulls down her sleeve to cover the watch.

Several minutes later, the woman tugs at Samia's sleeve. "Could you tell me where we're going to?"

Samia wonders if she has heard correctly. Then, she hears herself say, "We're going to hell."

The old woman stares at Samia, uncomprehending.

"We're going to America. Where else would we be going?" Samia says, as stunned by her own sarcasm as by the woman's question.

"America?" the woman says, still looking bewildered. "What sort of place is this America where the sun never sets? If it's nine forty-five it should be dark. It was nearly dark when we left."

"We're gaining time," Samia explains patiently. "It's still morning in America."

"Oh," the woman says, looking relieved. "I thought they might be taking us to that place where the sun never sets."

"That's Norway," Samia says.

The old woman reminds Samia of her mother. It is that constant need to be reassured of things—the exact time, their destination—the need to tie in to reality when the pull of the unknown, of death, is stronger than ever.

In the last months before her death, Samia's mother had been unduly anxious, as though she were preparing for a journey she did not want to take, as though she were saying goodbye. Samia had often wondered afterwards whether her mother had felt her life coming to an end. Her death had come as a complete surprise to Samia because her mother had seemed healthier in those last few months than she had at any other time in her life.

Yet each morning she had asked Samia, "Are you going out again?"

And each morning Samia had replied, "I'm going to school, mother. You know that."

"What about the kidnappers?" her mother would say.

"I'm too old and fat to be kidnapped," Samia would reassure her, kissing her mother's silken forehead and handing her a small cup of Turkish coffee with a cookie to dunk in it.

Samia had worried, at one point, that her mother was going senile the way she kept asking the same thing. Yet she could also keep track of every item of news on the radio, know exactly which streets had been bombed the night before, which faction had taken control over which district, even the exchange rate on the Lira.

"They kidnapped Jarodian," her mother had said on that last morning as Samia was leaving for work.

Samia had paused at the door. "How do you know that?"

"It was on the radio."

Samia had hoped it would not be announced on the radio. Jarodian, a short, balding Armenian, had been their jeweler for years. They had both been very fond of him, his face almost as round as his horn-rimmed glasses, his shrewd eyes always twinkling like the ready cache of topaz and amethysts in his desk for his special customers.

It had seemed like yesterday, although it had been several months earlier, that Samia and her mother had attended Jarodian's daughter's wedding. It had been held in a posh hotel—posh, that is, under the circumstances, for the dazzling Phoenecia and Saint George had practically been pulverized. The bride's finery had been ordered from Chanel, the bride's mother had confided a bit too loudly when Samia and her mother had gone up to congratulate her. Indeed, the wedding dress glimmered with what looked like real pearls and a diamond-studded kerchief was twisted boldly around the bride's forehead. Even Jarodian had looked younger that night, puffed up proudly beside his wife's emerald-green wrap of ostrich feathers.

It had all been so beautiful—the latest fashions, the finest food, and everybody smiling despite their haggard faces, everybody wanting to stay a little longer, to sniff the perfumed air and admire the flowers, to delay forever their return to the tattered city outside.

Then, several weeks later, men had broken into Jarodian's home where he had been keeping his merchandise since the fighting, and taken him and his wife hostage. Word had spread that it was his assistant, the quiet boy whom he had taught to solder gold chains and polish gems, who had led the men to Jarodian's goods.

Nobody had seen the family since, no one knew whether they were alive or dead. Only the boy had been sighted driving a new, silver BMW.

That last day Samia had gone to school, anyway, locking the door with the six locks to keep out intruders. It was later that evening, as she sat in the kitchen rolling grape leaves by candle light, that the shooting began.

A storm of bullets had pelted the concrete buildings, spraying red-hot into the black sky. She had quickly scrambled to the floor and called out to her mother to stay in bed. A few minutes later, when she had crawled to the bedroom, Samia found her mother still in her bed, her eyes wide open and her mouth gaping. Shaking her, searching for blood, Samia found nothing. Only an old woman apparently dead of a heart attack. No tears, no farewell, no mess. Just like that.

For an hour or so it had seemed like the end of the world. What could she do? Who could she go to? Her telephone had not worked for several months. She had a niece across town but how could she get to her? Anyway, both her niece and her husband were rather estranged from her and she did not quite trust her niece's husband, suspecting him of working with some subversive group. Certainly, she never talked politics around either of them. She had thought of going to her boss, Mr. Conolly, who had been by to check on her earlier; but by now he would be back at his home at the school and it was too late and too dangerous for her to go there.

She had covered her mother's face with the blanket. Then she had blown out all the candles in the apartment. Finally, she had put on her black dress of mourning and, lying down on her bed, had pulled her own blanket up over her head.

The next morning, with the help of her neighbor downstairs, Samia had washed her mother's body, wrapped her in some new muslin she had bought to make a tablecloth, then buried her with the help of the doorman in a nearby cemetery. It was not a Moslem cemetery, but it was too dangerous to travel across town to their family plot.

The man on the aisle is removing something from under his seat. He reaches between his feet, searching, his chest against his knees. He twists, fumbles. Samia hears the sharp zing of a zipper.

Samia feels herself falling away, as though she might faint. Her feet seem frozen. Somehow, she knows that it is a weapon the man is retrieving, some sort of handgun that he will aim at the pilot to hijack the plane. For an instant, she wonders what she should do. She turns to the woman at the window who is staring out, her eyes set in an oblivious glaze.

Before Samia can utter a word, though, the man slowly pulls up. He is holding something in his hand—a thick, folded newspaper. She can make out the title: *Le Monde Diplomatique.*

The man looks at her, perhaps sensing her stare. "This is the only newspaper I trust. It's good we can still get it." He shakes it open. "Would you like to read it?"

"I don't know French," Samia says, at once sensing that he is Christian.

"I'll tell you what's going on when I'm done," he says.

She turns toward the window to let him read. It is a kind enough offer. It would be nice to read something trustworthy for a change instead of having to sift through the three of four local newspapers as she does each day to glean something of the truth.

But today she wants to read nothing and hear nothing. They can all go to hell. She wants to immerse herself in this insulated vacuum in the sky until they land. There will be plenty of time to talk when she sees her brother and Claire.

A bell chimes. The seat belt sign is on again and the plane abruptly lifts and drops. Seats rattle. An overhead compartment jolts open and pillows drop to the floor. Samia's heart lurches.

A teenage boy across the aisle is smiling strangely, like a child, obviously enjoying the bumps. He catches Samia's gaze and stares back at her. Then, he suddenly draws his finger across his throat as though to slit it, laughing silently, his mouth spreading open gleefully at this announcement of doom. Samia looks away. The plane shudders once more then settles.

The man on the aisle says something.

Samia looks at him.

"I said, ten years ago who would have guessed it would go on this long," he says.

91

She shrugs.

"Where are all the fun-lovers, the theatres, the bikinis," he says, rolling his eyes. "I remember when a bad time meant that the disco was closing early," he laughs. "We used to spend the night at the Disco during curfew rather than go home early."

He is right, of course. She still cannot understand the violence or how her people came to have the desire or the endurance to fight so long.

"Did you go to Ba'albek this year?" the man says.

"To Ba'albek?"

"To the festival."

"No, no, I didn't go. Was there a festival this year?"

"Of course. It was sold out, too. I heard a concerto by Dvorak. Something by Brahms. You should have gone."

"I sometimes do," she says, thinking of the sweeping view from the top of the mountains when Zahle, Ba'albek, and the green fields of the Bekaa' come into view; the town of Chtoura where she stops for a light dinner of yogurt and cheese sandwiches before continuing on to the festival. She always enjoyed the folklore show performed on the ruins of the giant temples of Jupiter and Baccus— the crooning of Fairooz amidst the stomping of the *dabke* dancers, the men in baggy, black trousers and gold vests, the women in chiffon pantaloons like fluorescent moths.

"You don't really believe it has anything to do with religion do you?"

Samia looks at him. He is talking about the fighting but she does not know whether he is asking her or telling her.

"Moslem, Christian? Druze, Jew?" the man says, his face intense. "Why this sudden preoccupation? Live and let live, I say."

Despite cheeks that are a bit puffy he is rather handsome, his hands slim and strong, reminding her uncomfortably of hands that had once slipped an engagement ring on her finger.

"In the old days telling a good joke was a sign of manhood," the man continues, "not all this strutting about with guns."

Yes. Samia remembers those days, too. Days that had been filled with the laughter not only of her and her beloved, but the laughter of everyone. Those days before her fiance had left her, before all this trouble began cutting people off from one another.

Her fiance. Paul. It has been ten years since she last saw Paul. Most days she hardly thinks of him, yet some days she thinks of nothing else.

He had been a teacher along with her at the school. He had been Christian. It had broken her mother's heart at first to learn that her only daughter wanted to marry a Christian. Samia had waited this long, forty years, her mother had cried, to marry a *Nisrani?* Yet, she had succumbed to Paul, once she met him, just as Samia had.

Paul had been cordial, handsome, and just enough older than Samia to make her look young at her wedding. Best of all, he made Samia feel beautiful. Although she had never been slim, he made her aware of her waist, narrow like the neck of a vase, of her full breasts, the breasts of a woman ten years younger, never ravaged by suckling infants.

The fighting had only just started at that time and only in certain areas of Beirut. The prospect of being hit by a sniper's bullet or being kidnapped was still remote enough to make one brazen rather than fearful.

They would leave school together in the afternoons and Paul would drive up to the mountains where he would find a deserted spot overlooking an orchard or field of wildflowers. He would take her breasts in his hands, fondling each through her blouse, inhaling them, as though he were buying fresh melons. How Paul had loved her soft, rounded flesh and how she had learned to love it, too, on those fervent afternoons, waiting for him to stop the car and knead her thighs through her skirt. The more ravenous he was for her, the more yielding she became.

The wedding they had planned together—a simple ceremony with a Moslem Sheikh and a few friends—now seemed merely a formality intended to postpone their final union, to augment their desire.

Then, several days before the wedding, intensified fighting between Christian and Moslem militiamen caused the school to close early. After the children had left, Paul waited in his car, as usual, to drive Samia home. Then, as though on some devilish inspiration, he veered away from the usual route to her apartment building and took the road leading up to the mountains. Although frightened at first, Samia knew that the fighting was only in the city. The mountains would be quiet, crisp and serene.

From their spot overlooking the terraced slope and bright sea, they could hear the crackling guns below like some distant New Year's celebration. The absurdity of their rendez-vous so far removed from the city, seemed to move them both. They kissed hungrily, their passion spurred by their dread of losing each other. To Samia, it suddenly seemed as if they had very little time left.

The more they whispered their fears to each other, their disdain of the growing hatred between Christians and Moslems, the more reckless they became. Suddenly, Paul was tearing at her clothes and she was helping him, opening her blouse, spreading her legs. She shrieked. His ferocity made her helpless. All she wanted from the world was Paul ripping into her, cleaving to her.

Samia twists in her seat, now, suddenly uncomfortable with the memory of her moans that afternoon in the damp car. She tries not to think of her white arms and breasts tinged pink where he had crushed her.

Paul had driven her home, afterwards, had taken her right up to her apartment where he had greeted her worried mother, then left Samia, her body blazing, with the promise to pick her up the next day to check on the order for the wedding cake.

That had been three days before the wedding. Samia had not seen him again.

She had called the school, called his apartment where he lived with a cousin, but was told that he had left town. She had had to call the wedding off, of course, telling her mother and friends that Paul's elderly father had taken ill. At first she worried that he had been kidnapped or hurt in some way—several days earlier, a man had been sewn into a sheet and dumped from a seventh floor balcony. Yet, somehow, she knew that Paul was alive and well. Perhaps, she had reasoned, he was frightened at the prospect of marrying a Moslem women in view of all the difficulties they would face. Some differences were just too deep and too great to be ignored. Finally, however, she faced the truth: Paul had simply taken all he wanted from her.

"Somebody's getting paid," the man on the aisle says.

"What?" Samia says, startled. She has not allowed her memory of Paul such free reign in a long time.

"Money," the man says, rubbing his thumb and forefinger together.

"Oh, yes." Samia realizes that he is still talking about the war. "Must be."

"Gangsters and smugglers growing fat operating those illegal ports. They're up to their necks in shit if the fighting stops."

Samia stiffens at his cursing.

"They have a vested interest in keeping the war going. They fan the flames. Did you hear about those two they found near the airport?"

Samia shakes her head.

"Those brothers. Baroudis. Missing for weeks."

Samia nods vaguely.

"They found them near the pine forest. Shot. Their—excuse me—their balls stuffed in their mouths."

Samia jerks, as though a rod has just been rammed up her spine.

"They're a malignancy," the man says, picking his tooth. "There's no stopping them now. The other night I had to pay 5000 Lira to hire an ambulance to get me safely home from a party."

It is almost midnight Beirut time, a relatively peaceful period of the night when Samia usually sleeps well. The bombs and machine-guns start around two or three a.m. when she wakes up abruptly, whether she actually hears them or not.

The stewardess has closed most of the cabin windows so that the passengers can sleep. Some people, probably too edgy from the previous days, have reopened their curtains to the light outside.

Are you going anywhere besides New York?" the man next to her asks.

"Just New York," Samia says.

"A visit?"

"My brother lives there." She does not feel like explaining that Ahmad, a surgeon, had finally left Beirut after one too many operations performed at gun-point for some militia or another. She looks out over the head of the old woman on the left to the clear skies beyond the window—blue threaded with layers of lavender, pink, and yellow.

"I'm stopping overnight. Then I'm off to Chicago," the man says.

Samia is silent.

"So, you'll be going back?" he says.

She looks at him.

"To Beirut, I mean."

"Where else would I go?" she says.

"A lot of people are leaving. There's only so much one can take."

"Are you going back?" she says.

"Oh yes. But I don't have to stay. I travel quite a bit. Every few weeks. It's not like having to live through it all the time."

"Why don't you just stay away, then?"

"Business," he says, as though this should be evident to her. "I need to be there." He turns slightly in his chair to face her and Samia spots, for the first time, a patch of green in one of his brown eyes. She recoils, inadvertantly, never having seen an eye like this before. She looks away as though the imperfection might curse her. How can there be a two-tone eye? For a moment she wonders if it is false. A glass eye.

"My mother was French," the man says. "She used to say that she gave me a field from France in the speck of green in my eye."

Samia glances back at him, embarrassed that her discomfort was so apparent.

"I've never seen anyone else with an eye like mine," the man admits.

"God be praised," Samia says. "Anything from God is a blessing."

"How long will you be staying in New York?" he says.

"Maybe a month. I really don't know. I haven't seen my brother in three years."

He nods. "The war has separated everybody."

"Excuse me." It is the old woman. "How many hours are left?"

"About seven," Samia says.

"Is it always this long?"

"I suppose so," Samia says, watching the woman smooth down her cuff over her wrist.

"They said it would take twelve hours but I didn't know it would feel so long."

"It's my first time," Samia says, hoping the woman will stop asking her questions.

"My son lives in New York. He wants me to move there. I told him I would come just for a visit. At the last minute I almost changed my mind but he would have been too upset. I haven't seen him since my daughter died."

Oh God, thinks Samia. *Please don't start.* But out loud she says, "I'm sorry. Was she living in New York too?"

"New York? I wish she had been in New York," the woman says, staring at the seat in front of her. Samia can see the woman's eyes mist. She is sorry she asked.

The man leans forward to see the old woman better. "What happened?" he says.

"She was standing on my balcony," the old woman says. "She had just made us both tea and was waiting for me to join her. It was such a pretty day, late February, nearly spring. She called me, but I had to answer the phone. 'Mother,' she said, 'today I'm going to plant some new geraniums in your pots. These are dying.'

"I didn't pay much attention to her since I was trying to hear the voice on the phone. That's when I heard the crash." The woman's voice almost disappears.

The man on the aisle clears his throat.

"My windows were gone. I looked out at the balcony but my daughter wasn't there. It was so strange. The ringing is still in my ears. I went to the balcony and looked over. I saw her dress in the street below. Then, I realized it was *she* lying there." The old woman looks at Samia. "She was blown off my balcony."

"I'm sorry." Samia feels she is suffocating. She is shocked despite having heard worse stories the last few years.

"My balcony," the old woman says. "It should have been me."

"Don't say that," says Samia. "What's written is written. It was God's will."

The man sits back in his chair. He looks away.

"It was God's will," the woman echoes, looking unconvinced.

"God be merciful to her," Samia says.

The woman moves her arm and slowly turns up her cuff to expose the gold Rolex. "This was her watch," she says. "It's like new. Only it doesn't work anymore."

One night a week ago, after getting ready for bed, Samia had slid open the glass door of the dining room and walked out onto the dark balcony in her bare feet. She had heard sounds, the sounds of a dog howling.

Not that this was unusual, since there were more than enough stray dogs roaming the ruined buildings and littered streets scavenging for a meal. It was that the howling seemed to be everywhere, vibrating through the winding alleyways, climbing the walls of her building. They had seemed so close and she could hear the small yelps mixed with the huskier, deeper barks.

Then she saw them. They were all the way down the street, twenty or thirty dogs racing across the moon-wet pavement, their howls like the screaming of women and children scrambling for cover, like the wounded and maimed, the orphans, the machine guns.

Samia, again, thinks of the children. Sometimes she writes about them in her spare time, her theories of teaching. It is her way of reassuring herself that her life has some meaning, of remembering the peace and beauty that she had once, absurdly, taken for granted. It has been ages since she has written anything, though, and she sometimes worries that she will never write another word in her life. She worries that her thoughts, lying lifeless in the pit of her stomach, will rise up and choke her because she cannot allow herself to focus on them.

She used to take her notebook to the apartment of a friend who lived on the Corniche, sit on an iron swing on the balcony overlooking the sea, and write. She would watch the colors of the seaside cliff change as the sun moved across the sky—bright yellow, ecru, green, then purple. Sometimes the colors had been so sharp Samia had wanted to cry. But she had written—page after page—quickly filling the entire notebook, draining her soul like a catheter.

But as time passed, this had become increasingly difficult. Her friend's apartment was broken into and occupied, first by Christian militiamen, then by Israelis, then by Shiites. The windows were shattered, furniture ruined, feces smeared across the walls. Three homeless families now lived in the barren rooms and Samia's friend had left for the United States where she was filing for permanent residence.

But even more important than the loss of this retreat is the fact that Samia's very subject matter—the children—have changed so much from the war that it seems that all she has written, all the things she once knew to be fact, are now irrelevant, ridiculous. The children of ten years ago that she set out to write about are not the children of today whose first look at the world drills them in hatred, whose first steps are amidst the blaze of burning houses and the ring of bullets and death. She is too frightened to even contemplate what goes on in the minds of such children.

In her own fourth grade is an eight-year-old girl, Mariam, whose black lashes are so long and curled that they almost touch her eyebrows when she looks up. Mariam saw both her father and uncle killed last year, their throats slit like sheep. Recently, Samia sat by the beds of children who had suffered burns after tiny packets dropped onto the streets by Israeli planes had exploded when they picked them up to play with them. Then there were the two little boys who had killed a girl with a stone and made a game out of showing the police where they had buried her body. Who could say what made a child do something like this?

One day, recently, as Samia walked home from the doctor's office, a militiaman had appeared from behind a pyramid of sand-bags and blocked her way. She had reached in her purse to re-trieve her identity card, but instead of taking it, he had placed the barrel of his gun firmly against her waist and asked her if she knew of any woman who wanted a man between her legs. Samia had instinctively looked behind her, half expecting to find the woman he was referring to. Then she had looked back at him, realizing that he meant her. He seemed no older than fifteen or sixteen, and for an instant, she thought she recognized the face of one of her former students above the cartridge belts glittering across his chest. "No," she had uttered weakly. She felt she was going to vomit all over his machine gun and worried that this would make him angry. But just then, the boy had stepped aside for her to pass.

"How long did you say you would be in New York?" the man next to her says.

Jarred back to the present, Samia tries to remember. "A month," she says.

"Not very long," he says, folding his paper. "I thought I might come to visit you at your brother's."

This time he has caught Samia by surprise. Another thing the war has done is bring together people who have nothing in common. Since when does a man take the liberty to propose such a thing to a woman he has just met? To assume that she is not married? Or that she would even welcome such a visit?

"I have to return to work," Samia says.

"Oh?" The man looks surprised.

"I'm a schoolteacher."

"Where do you work?"

"I teach third and fourth grades," she says. To give the location of her school would be to label herself.

"A schoolteacher," he says, musingly, as though it were some rare, long-vanished breed. "Not a practical profession these days. Still, you might find a job in New York."

"Work? I'm not going to New York to work."

"You could teach Arabic," he goes on. "You have to do something in America or else you'll go crazy. Nobody has time for anybody else. Not like us, afternoons in the cafes, wasting our lives."

He reaches over and gingerly pats her arm. She lets his fingers rest on her skin. When he lifts his hand, she feels a sadness, like a weight, left on her arm.

"I'm going back," Samia says, almost to herself.

"Why?" he says.

"Because," Samia pauses, "because I need the land, the water."

"Ah," he says, "of course." He settles back in his seat looking rather cynical. "Of course the sea is a great inspiration."

"Well," the old woman says, leaning toward Samia with a confident smile, "you'll soon be back by the sea."

"I'll visit you in New York in a month's time," the man says, lightly. "You'll have changed your mind. America is like a vacuum cleaner—it devours you."

Samia looks straight at the man. His eyes express a certain logic.

101

He does not seem to care what she thinks of him, does not seem as though he is trying to draw her or impress her. Despite herself, she warms to this directness, something that she has missed in people lately. Yet she is unable to respond to him in his same easy manner, cannot even tell him that she will be happy to receive him at her brother's house in New York. She is drowning in the image of the young militiaman, of Paul, of the mutilated brothers the man has just spoken of.

It is one o'clock Beirut time but it is still light in the sky, as though the fact of Beirut has ceased, the only reality being here and now in the sky. The old woman is fast asleep, snoring lightly above the rumbling engines. The man has left his seat and not returned for half an hour. Samia sees the top of his head next to the blond tufts of the stewardess's hair near the rest rooms. Samia stretches out her legs, resting her arm on the man's arm rest.

Some moments later, the stewardess comes down the aisle, for once looking amiable, as though someone has just paid her a compliment or made her a proposition. Samia feels a cold sting of anger. This man is like all the rest. But the anger flows out of her, leaving instead a bitter calm. Nothing is worth her fury any more.

"Miss," Samia says, suddenly.

The stewardess focuses her painted eyes on Samia.

"I need a glass of water."

The stewardess stares at her before turning to go back up the aisle. Samia waits. In a way, she has been afraid of this moment.

She fishes in her bag for a pen, then collects the three shiny, white airsickness bags from the seat pockets in front of her and begins to write. First she writes the address and telephone number of her brother and tears it off. She will decide later whether or not to give it to the man. Then, she writes anything, anything that comes into her head, her hand scrambling to keep up with her thoughts.

The stewardess returns with the water and Samia puts the glass on the pull-out table where she is writing. When she looks at it, she feels she can see right through the water to the source, to that place deep within herself that she has closed off for so long.

She drops her face in her hands. Her shoulders shudder. Then, she wipes away the tears with her palms and starts to write again, this time evenly and confidently, even optimistically. Water is the beginning. Water is life, soothing as the womb.

She pours a few drops of the water into her hand and suddenly her thoughts emerge, her hand races. She stops, wets her hand again, and she is off, recording, reacting, reaching.

Eventually she will get to the children. Eventually she might even get to Paul.

She calls the stewardess for another glass of water. Now she is free, free to dig beyond the devastation and pull it all out. If only she can just keep going until she finishes, before the man comes back, before the old woman wakes up to ask the time. She hopes, although she is still fearful, that if she persists long enough it will all become as tangible and as clear to her as the water in the glass.

SKIATHOS

As Dimitri's plane approached the island, he cursed himself for again doing what he swore each year he would not—take the morning flight from Athens. Invariably, the island was windy at seven o'clock, the turbulence playing such havoc with the aircraft and his stomach that he almost wished to get it over with, to be dashed like an egg against the hills rather than set down on the runway a few feet ashore.

It was his guilt, no doubt, that brought on this giddiness each time he came to Greece. His mother's homeland. His father had been Turkish. Though Dimitri had been born and spent much of his seventy years in Istanbul, he had lately developed a curious yearning for his mother's country. Like a child craving its mother's bosom. He had spent the last ten summers in Greece, most recently on this island, Skiathos. He liked the *Sporades.* The olive groves, pines, and white-washed houses that mounted the hillsides were distinctly Aegean, yet the islanders were oriental enough to assuage his Turkish loyalties.

A month ago he had been offered an appointment as Assistant Minister of Tourism in Istanbul. Although it would be the highlight of his diplomatic career—not many men seventy years old could hope for such an opportunity—Dimitri was not keen on accepting it. For one thing, he doubted that he still had the stamina for all the traveling, for the tedious social functions and glasses of *Rakki.* And it would also tie him down to Istanbul. After years of civil service in other parts of the world, Germany, England, Bolivia, Chile, he had grown accustomed to living abroad, to an independent life. In Istanbul he would be surrounded by his family—sisters, cousins, nephews—which would mean a greater involvement with them than he had ever desired.

He stopped himself. He would not think of work now. He would make the right decision as to what to do when the time came. He always did. Now that he was in Skiathos he would abandon himself to the pungent smell of the pines, the embracing azure of the Greek skies, the festive vigor that animated the island—and his spirit—each summer.

The one-room airport was jammed with travelers waiting to take the plane back to Athens. Golden-thighed Germans and Englishmen in shorts and rumpled hair slumped sleepily on black vinyl chairs. Gaunt tourists like himself. Only he was just starting his vacation whereas they had the bleak look of the departing. He found his suitcase and walked to the blue mini-bus that was collecting those passengers staying at the *Pelias.*

"Mr. Dimitri—nice to see you again."

"Andreas," Dimitri said, nodding at the receptionist. Andreas was a slim man in his mid-thirties with a brown mustache like a blade and freshly-combed hair. Despite his frequent appearances in the company of some attractive female guest, Dimitri suspected Andreas of being a homosexual. His gestures were overly precise, and he had a way of leaning close to confide the most benign triviality.

"How's the weather in Athens?" Andreas asked.

"Humid," Dimitri said, signing the register and glancing at a handwritten sign in German posted on the wall behind the reception desk. There were instructions about meals and entertainment.

"More Germans this year?" Dimitri asked. Skiathos had been an English outpost ever since he started coming here seven years ago.

106

"They're everywhere. The English are pissed," Andreas said, winking. He was a transplanted Austrian himself, like so many Europeans who had come to run the tourist facilities on the island. His real name was Wilhelm.

"Business must be good, then," Dimitri said.

"Excellent," Andreas said. Then, as though the question had been meant as a personal one, he whispered, "I've an old flame visiting."

Dimitri stared at Andreas, wondering what "old" could mean at his age. "What's the forecast this year?" he asked.

"Thirty thousand, but not until August."

Dimitri winced. Skiathos' population the rest of the year was only five thousand.

"Time to look for another spot," he muttered, scribbling his initials at the bottom of the page and snapping the pen shut with emphasis.

"Telephone lines out are terribly jammed," Andreas warned him.

"I've no calls to make."

"There is some good news though. No jellyfish expected," Andreas called out as Dimitri followed the boy carrying his suitcase across the breezy reception hall.

Still the same homespun decor: coarse, linen curtains over the open windows, stone floors with hand woven wool rugs, antique chests. The whitewashed walls were hung with brass trays—Turkish trays—and blown-up photographs of the island.

The *Pelias* was beginning to stir. In the dining room a waiter folded crimson napkins, and a few guests, probably British, were already reading newspapers on a terrace surrounded by pines.

Dimitri descended the white-washed steps to the garden. The hotel seemed to have aged since last summer. The swimming pool, which was still being filled, had long cracks along the inside where a fat pipe was pouring greenish water into it. The faint stench of sewage permeated the garden, mingling with the cooking smells coming from the kitchen vents.

Across the garden were more steps leading down to the bungalows. The *Pelias*, with its splendid but impractical sprawl of bungalows and steps along a hillside, tended to remind Dimitri of a
mammoth about to become extinct. It took over ten minutes to
climb from the beach to the main building at the top of the hill,
ultimately alienating the selective tourists it had once hoped to
attract. To avoid the back-breaking climb, Dimitri had reserved a
bungalow mid-way between both. His row was 'Calypso'.

The rooms had not changed either—a mattress on elevated,
white-washed concrete, a pine dresser and several stools, more
linen curtains embroidered with roosters, jugs, and grape vines.

Dimitri tipped the boy, then opened the wooden doors to the
small balcony. The hotel bay was visible through the pines, water
that was still a morning grey but would turn a translucent turquoise in a few hours. It was dotted with motorboats. Though he
often took a taxi to the more picturesque *Koukounaries* beach further along the coast with its popular, American-style hotel, this
beach was fine for days when he lacked the energy. Besides, he
liked the *Pelias*. It was a discreet hotel. The guests were mostly
middle-class British and Germans who came in groups and kept to
themselves.

In a while he would change and walk down to the beach to take
stock of this season's material. A lot of single women would be
sprinkled in among the couples, women in search of some rare
romance to remember Greece by. Not that he was interested in
such an affair for himself. Although to many women a man of his
maturity and generous pocketbook held substantial charm, he was
content to leave them to the younger Romeos. But he did enjoy
observing the dalliances that often unfolded under his nose. It was
a simple enough diversion that seemed to alleviate some of his
secret terror of having to live out the rest of his life alone.

But it was still early, only a quarter to eight, and he had not slept
well last night. He opened his suitcase and removed the small
bottle of sleeping pills. He put one in his mouth and lay down on
the bed. It was ironic to be so fearful of airplanes considering how

indifferent he had become to living. More than once, lately, he had contemplated taking his own life—with these same pills—rather than continue to grow old alone. He doubted that he would ever be able to reconcile himself to that. For the first time in his life he was beginning to regret not having better prepared himself in his youth by marrying and having children.

At those times, it was all he could do to remind himself how lucky he was to have had this freedom to travel and live in so many exciting places, to have pursued so many women, to have known so many interesting people because he had not been consumed by a family. In those days, forty years ago, you were not considered for a foreign posting if you had to drag along a wife and a half-dozen children. Dimitri would force himself to remember that there had been those who envied him then, even some who envied him now for this freedom. One reason he was still vigorous enough to be in demand at the Ministry was due, no doubt, to his not having led the burdened life of most married men.

Moments later, a cock crowed from somewhere down the hill, as though to warn him that his time was up. But Dimitri, sinking into his mattress as though into quicksand, was unable to rouse himself.

Later, as he stood in his swimming trunks surveying the crowded beach, he saw that he was not alone in choosing to come in June. Not only were there twice the number of speedboats lolling along the shore, but the bay was being sliced by windsurfers from every direction. He watched them glide by, novices who flopped onto their backs in the water bringing the mast and sail crashing down on top of them. He ruled out swimming for the time being.

The sand was fine and white as salt, flying about as he trudged through the rows of young bodies turning a deep, nut-brown or flaming red. He breathed in the heady, coconut scent of suntan oil. Most of the women were topless although Dimitri found this somehow less satisfying than seeing them in full bathing suits. It was also tiresome to be continually averting one's eyes from a pair of bare breasts, especially when they belonged to a woman his own age. His favorite style had been the suit, some years ago, that offered up a woman's breasts in a 'help-yourself' way that he had found particularly endearing.

Snatches of German conversation spilled into the air. He loved to hear German women speak, the way they sucked in their breath as though caught by surprise. It used to drive him wild all those years ago in Frankfurt when he worked in the Turkish Consulate. That had been during his twenties, a decade best remembered for his enslavement to passion. But that was long ago. Even those *frauleins* he had loved then had long since been compartmentalized, reduced to tidy labels in his mind: tease, domineering, mysterious, bitch.

Dimitri chose a large pine tree at the far tip of the crescent, unrolled his straw beach mat and sat down to read the Greek newspapers he had taken from the airplane.

Then came those breathless, German voices again! Three girls in loose, pastel shirts were walking toward him. They came right up to his tree and, without a word to him, began to undress.

He looked back down at his newspapers, pretending not to hear the swishing sounds of their clothes being flung to the sand. Out of the corner of his eye he could discern pale buttocks and slim thighs. Unripe breasts. When they sauntered down to the sea in bikini bottoms, flaunting the fact that he was no threat to them, he felt deserted, as though he had known them briefly. They began to toss a volleyball back and forth, leaping and lunging like startled gazelles. He sat under the tree with their discarded clothing and dry pine needles—part of the landscape.

Breakfast was the only meal Dimitri ate in the hotel since it was the same everywhere on the island: eggs, crumbly fruitcake, juice, coffee. In addition, there was a particularly good apricot preserve with the crunchy hearts of the pits in it, the way that his mother used to make it.

It was almost nine o'clock the next day and the guests were suddenly climbing up the hillside to catch breakfast before the dining room closed. They could have been the same group as last year, the men tall and scrawny, their hair stiff and unruly from the sea. The women were always plumper, with wanton white arms that were streaked red and beginning to peel. Some of the guests looked dazed, as though they had not slept well on the hard mattresses or were beginning to wonder what they were doing up so early. Perhaps *Greichenland* had not met their expectations. Perhaps they found the *Pelias* wanting.

Dimitri, on the other hand, liked the *Pelias'* spartan accommodations. The creaking shutters, the bathrooms with the mirrors rusting from the salt air and with only drainpipes and plastic curtains for showers. It reminded him of his childhood home outside Ankara. Too much of his adult life had been spent in modern homes with sterile, air-conditioned rooms. Istanbul had become so congested with traffic that he had to change his shirt from the pollution whenever he came home from work. Even his apartment was suffocating, cluttered with expensive rugs and antiques, cared for by servants. He came to the Pelias to be free of the trappings of his formal life, to soak in his thoughts amidst the simple, intimate surroundings

After breakfast, he stepped out to the terrace to see what people were watching down in the pool area. A string of humans, clinging to one another's waists, were hopping and kicking their legs in time to the jarring music from a loudspeaker. Directing this convulsing serpent was a tall, slender woman on the edge of the pool wearing a straw hat with yellow flowers. Hopping and kicking, she yelled out instructions in English. Now, placing both hands on her knees, she drew her legs in and out, in and out, causing the serpent in the pool to disintegrate to copy her.

Dimitri was impressed by their utter abandon. Grown men and women participating in something so silly! It was so like the British. Yet, in a way, their surrender to the foolish was touching. When the instructress bent over her knees and began to flap her arms, her audience mimicking like lunatic mosquitos, Dimitri burst out laughing.

That afternoon on the beach, he saw the instructress again. He recognized the hat first, then the sinuous caramel back, the shapely, slightly bowed legs. She sat gazing at the sea.

The hat gave her a certain well-dressed appearance although she wore only a bikini bottom. Except for the tip of her nose and her chin, her face was hidden beneath the straw. He followed her gaze. The sea was choppy, and only the expert wind-surfers were sailing. Perhaps one of them was a boyfriend of hers and she was on the look-out for trouble.

But maybe he was wrong in thinking that she was watching someone, for all at once she stood up, tied a flowered wrap about her, and started for the steps. Dimitri stood too. He wanted to follow her. But what would he say to her? Anyway, by the time he caught up with her he would be out of breath and look ridiculous.

Late that night, returning from dinner in town, he stopped on the deserted terrace off the dining room to glance at the panoramic view of the glittering town. The *Pelias's* guests generally slept early, and except for the night manager at the desk, Dimitri seemed to be alone. Then, all at once, he sensed something moving down by the pool. A mere shadow, at first, it dipped and twirled in the dark, leaping one minute, squatting the next, finally crystalizing into a woman in dark slacks and blouse—the intructress of the morning. A tiny glow, the tip of her cigarette, swam through the dark as she undulated her arms. She seemed to be practicing the next day's exercises.

He stood silently watching, dazzled by the heat that suddenly coursed through his veins.

Watching her brought back the memory of a long ago night in Germany when he had driven to Hamburg after having just broken up with a German woman he had thought himself in love with. He had had too much to drink to be driving, and he had sensibly pulled off to the side of the road to take some fresh air. Suddenly,

112

from the thick of some nearby trees, there had appeared a grey stag.

As he had stood mesmerized, wondering what tricks his groggy, unhappy mind was playing on him, the stag had turned and began to canter down the road a bit. The fluid agility of the beast had bewitched Dimitri. Suddenly, he had lifted his arms and was galloping behind the animal, exulting in its beauty and in his own new freedom. He was suddenly airborn, like the stag, alive with youth, and lust, and the serene knowledge that there was a new woman waiting for him somewhere.

The woman cavorting beside the pool, now, was like that stag, drawing him out of himself and into life once again. Dimitri wanted to lift his arms and cry out, as he had that night outside Hamburg, loping tipsily after the wild, elusive animal.

"It's not wise to wear a hat in this hot sun, you know," he said to her the next afternoon.

She was lying on her side with a magazine and looked up as though she half expected him. Her face, revealed at last, was round, offset by an upper lip which rose to a point in the middle like an inverted V and by a delicate, pointed nose. Her eyes were a plush brown, the color of her ponytail, tapered at the outer corners like huge teardrops. She looked about thirty and up close her rosy-brown skin was the color of fresh-baked *kadaifi*.

"It's true," he said. "Heat trapped on the head can be extremely dangerous."

He admired a healthy skepticism and the look in her eyes seemed to say that she did not believe a word he said.

"Dimitri Mustafa," he said, extending a nicely-formed hand, the part of his anatomy he always took pride in.

He could not remember when he had first become aware that he no longer attracted women the way he used to, when he realized that there were more younger men about than ever before. Now, he was suddenly conscious of his sagging breasts, the white hairs on his chest where once had bristled a curly, black forest, of

113

his belly protruding like a squash. His bare feet were stuck in grey, suede shoes that were streaked with salt. But women admired his hands, as well cared for as a surgeon's or a pianist's.

"Nice to meet you," she said, unflinching, placing her hand in his own as though she expected Skiathos to abound in decrepit, old men. "My name is Helen."

She was British, of course. There was a twanging lilt to her words. Manchester, most probably.

"You work here, Helen?"

"Yes."

"Doing—er—dancing—"

"Dance exercise."

"I watched you at the pool. Fascinating."

"Come join us."

He shrugged. "Next time, perhaps. Is this your first trip to Skiathos?"

"Yes."

"But it's not your first time in Greece. I can tell. You seem quite at home. Except for the hat."

"The hat?" Her fingers touched the rim as though to check whether something was wrong.

He went on. "Skiathos is haunting. The Argonauts passed through this channel to get to the Black Sea, so did the armies on their way to Troy. Have you been to the *Koukounaries?* You mustn't miss it. The most beautiful beach in Greece."

Though considered a talented speaker, often asked to lecture on foreign affairs at the University, Dimitri knew he was rambling. Yet, he was almost glad to see that a beautiful woman still had this effect on him.

"Are you from Athens Mr.—"

"Mustafa, Dimitri please. My mother was from Athens. My father Turkish. I live in Istanbul. But Turks don't know how to enjoy life as the Greeks do so, once a year, I come to remember how good life can be."

"Greek and Turkish," she said, smiling, curious.

"Dangerous combination. But they were good for each other—my father and mother."

There was a black mole above her right breast like a tiny spider. Her breasts were lovely, neither large nor too small. Yet Dimitri was not lustful. He took an interest in them as a painter or sculptor might, with a fascination beyond desire. He congratulated himself on finally being able to distance himself from women.

"Don't think I always go up to strangers and spit out my life story," he said, quickly, embarrassed that his eyes had strayed from hers. "It's probably the mood here, a little different from each year. Had you been to Skiathos before you might notice it—far too many people. Too many Germans. But you will enjoy it. Don't worry. Only I notice the difference."

"It's more crowded than I thought," she said, nodding. "It's becoming like everywhere else—commercial. But its still decent. Guests are wholesome, if you know what I mean. Mykonos—" he said, dismissing his old haunt with a sharp wave of his hand.

"It's expensive," she said, almost sadly.

"Oh yes," he said, feeling a certain edge. This, at least, was to his advantage.

"I was promised free room and board if I taught during my stay," she said, squinting up at him. "Now they're making me pay for all the meals."

"They always do. They want you to think you're getting a bargain. But, of course you mustn't waste your time eating here. In fact, I know a pleasant taverna overlooking the port where the lobsters are as juicy as grapes."

She raised her eyebrows, slightly.

"If you're not busy, that is," he added.

"I'm going shopping in a little while. Perhaps afterward—"

"The Kingfisher. It's only a few minutes from the shops on the upper level of town. Ask anybody how to get there," he said, then started back for his tree before she could change her mind. When he glanced back at her a few minutes later, he saw that she had taken off her hat.

115

When she had left the beach, Dimitri ventured down to the shore. The windsurfers had left as had most of the swimmers. The water was cold. The salt stung a scrape on his leg. It was all he could do, at first, to splash it on his arms and thighs. The sea seemed to be offering itself to him, yielding to his feet, the seaweed twisting about his ankles; even the pink and green pebbles were round and smooth beneath his toes. He plunged in and began to swath the water with brisk, expert strokes. He continued back and forth several more minutes, giving himself to the pull of the tide, the salt water lashing at his face like tears, until he had to stop from the familiar spasm in his chest.

"The home of Alexander Papadiamantis, revered writer," Dimitri said to Helen, pointing to a lone villa across the harbor, on a sliver of land jutting into the sea. Strewn with white light bulbs, like a bride's skirts, the villa seemed to be floating in ink. Dimitri cracked a lobster claw and extracted a shred of milk-white flesh while Helen, who had finished hers, smoked a cigarette.

From the clematis-covered balcony above the town, they watched people strolling along the waterfront in a great mass, like the ebb and flow of the tide. The sidewalk cafes and souvenir shops were crammed with tourists while the locals strolled along the water, the old men with their hands clasped low behind their backs as though they had all the time in the world. But Dimitri felt as detached from them as from the other restaurant patrons. Tonight he was a God among mortals.

Pulling away the napkin he had tucked into his collar, he called for coffee.

"Do you always ask for "Turkish" coffee in Greece?" Helen said, an amused smile lighting her lips.

"Habit," Dimitri sighed.

He watched as a little boy cleared the table, sweeping up the empty bottles of *Robollo* wine and the half-eaten plates of fried *kalamaris*.

"Each time I come, a new child is working here. As soon as they're old enough, they join the family business. Father cooks, mother cleans up, even the older sons who have other jobs come back in the summer."

"It must be a good business," she said.

"The best."

"Why don't you open a taverna?"

"Me?" he said. "Why? I've no sons to help me or to leave it to."

"But you've been coming here a long time. You must know someone who would go into business with you..."

"I only come on vacation," he said, surprised at his own abruptness. "I come to rest and forget. I don't meet anyone, really."

"To forget?" She said it slowly, in a way that made him wonder whether she, herself, was trying to forget something.

"And you?" he asked. "Have you something to forget?"

She smiled, then, finding no ashtray, put out her cigarette in the narrow vase of carnations on their table. "More like a decision to make."

Dimitri's eyes sought the curve of her cheek where the shadows hit—buffed marble through the last traces of smoke. The creases at the corners of her eyes belied the sadness that had just clouded her face. She was a woman who obviously smiled a lot, a woman who *should* smile.

"Have you ever been married?" he said.

"No."

He breathed deeply, freely, for the first time this evening. "I never married," he said. "But that's not to say that I won't. My nieces are ever hopeful, introducing me to this old spinster or that widow who they say will make me an excellent wife. When I refuse they accuse me of keeping a seraglio of girls here."

Helen stared at him.

"But you can see for yourself, it's not true. No woman comes here alone. She comes with a husband, a boy friend—"

He was rambling again. Was she not here alone?

117

He got up, pulled a cinnamon scented carnation from the vase on the table and placed it at her fingertips.

They walked down cobbled steps to the wharf. A ferry had just come in from *Skopelos*, tanned young passengers streaming onto the sidewalks. Greeks were hunched over backgammon boards in the caiques moored along the dock that brandished large signs for day trips to *Lalaria*, and 'any beach on Skiathos'. Donkeys were tied in a row outside a tourist agent's office with similar signs, presumably for those who preferred to ride. The bright street lamps gave Helen's shoulders a burnished, copper luster below the thin straps of her sundress.

Unable to find a taxi, Helen flagged a white jeep headed out of town.

"He doesn't look old enough to drive," Dimitri protested of the blond boy with hair like fresh-cut grass at the wheel. But Helen, already in the back, beckoned to him gaily. Realizing that it had been at least twenty years since he'd ridden in such a contraption, Dimitri none-the-less climbed in, trying not to think about the heartburn he would get from all the bouncing.

Back in his room at the *Pelias*, eyeing the pajama-clad figure in the mirror, Dimitri was surprised to see the same white-haired man as this morning.

He took his nightly pill, accidentally scattering the entire contents of the bottle onto the dresser. The pills lay there, tiny, dull pearls. Pearls. He began to gather them up, thinking how the ancients had believed pearls to endow one with everlasting life.

For the next five days Dimitri courted Helen. He met her on the beach after lunch and invariably invited her to dinner in the evenings. He would say goodnight to her at the front desk since she liked to sit in the lounge and read, and he would walk down to his bungalow and lie in bed, nursing his memory of the evening as he stared at the sky through the slats of his shutters.

In town, she walked with the easy abandon of a woman who knew that she was beautiful, a woman accustomed to being deferred to. This was all the more appealing since there was nothing lofty in her attitude toward him. Once, in a souvenir shop, she fancied an antique Ottoman mother-of-pearl chest. The olive wood had been eaten away with age, but the embedded pearl and silver filigree shone smooth as ice under his fingertips. He bought it for her on the spot despite her protests. When they were out of the shop she turned to him, her eyes suddenly wild.

"Dimitri—"

But he had not allowed her to finish. "Don't begrudge me this small pleasure."

"It's just that you're too good. It's not right."

He caught her hand and brought it to his face. The joints of her cool fingers were barely visible, the tips tapered like the fingers in a Renaissance painting. Her nails were bitten, childishly.

"You'll never know—" he began, his voice cracking as he brought her fingertips to his lips. His lungs felt too full for his chest. Then, he stopped. Her eyes had settled on his softly, unafraid. He gently released her hand. The last thing he wanted was her pity.

"If we were in Athens, tonight, I would take you to the Acropolis to hear Beethoven," he said to her one afternoon, as they sat on the beach at *Kastro*, the ruined fortress city on the crest of a cliff. They had come by boat from town since there were no roads to this far side of Skiathos, and Dimitri had patiently waited on the shore while Helen and the other boat passengers climbed the rocky ascent to the lookout to hear how the islanders had fought off invaders and pirates from that very spot for five hundred years. When Helen returned, sweating through her pink T-shirt, looking as exhilarated as if she had just visited another planet, Dimitri thought of the Acropolis.

"You've never heard Beethoven until you hear him at the Acropolis," he said, his eyes locking into her own. "Last year I went to his Ninth. I sat on the very top step, put up my feet, and shut my eyes. When the chorus began the finale, I felt that the stars were going to reach down and grab me."

119

She was rinsing her face and arms with sea water. The sea was rougher here than on the other side of the island. Even the pine trees strained to one side, their trunks permanently warped from the perpetual east wind.

"I feel dizzy," she said, suddenly. "I need to cool off."

She pulled off her shirt. Her waist and hips twisted like taught elastic as she tugged off her jeans. Her skin tightened in the breeze, her brown nipples growing. There was a blue mark near her left hip bone above her bikini—a bruise, a love bite? Dimitri flinched as he sensed its tenderness. He imagined pressing his hungry mouth against it, drawing the pain into himself. He saw that she was gazing down at him, steadily. His hands quivered. He could feel his hair fluff about his skull.

Suddenly, seeing her eager, determined face, her body bold and ready for life, Dimitri was engulfted by the acute bliss he had felt that night at the Acropolis. The banality of the world disappeared before the sublime beauty of a woman like Helen, before the sheer magnificence of Beethoven's notes in that grand temple.

He thought her eyes dimmed, suddenly. "You're a special man, Dimitri," she said, and with a gentle, almost sad sag of her firm shoulders, she flung herself into the surf.

"Someday I'll take you to hear Beethoven there," he said, as they followed the others back to the anchored boat. Some of the passengers were going to be dropped at the nude 'banana beach' and were in a hurry to leave.

The announcement for 'Bouzoukia night', the event of the week, was posted at the reception the next morning as Dimitri left by taxi for a business appointment in town. Noisy affairs, these musical evenings, since the British were always getting drunk. Last summer there had been an ugly fight when someone pushed a woman into the pool.

He was on his way to see the agent he had hired to find him a villa. It had not occurred to him before. But Helen's companionship these past few days had started him thinking about renting his own place where there would be more comfort and privacy. Helen could stay with him and not have to bother with working at the hotel. They could make friends with the other vacationers who regularly rented and he could even entertain friends from Istanbul—not the old ones who didn't know what to do with themselves anymore—but nieces and nephews, anyone amusing. He would surround himself with life. Not too long ago, he had set a challenging pace in Istanbul society.

He planned to telephone his housekeeper in Istanbul to join him when he got back to the hotel. He had told Helen that he had come to rest. Now, rest was the last thing in the world that he wanted. When so much life seemed within his grasp, again, he had to live it. And suddenly, he could not imagine himself without her.

In what capacity he was to enjoy her company, he was ashamed to admit even to himself. Not as a daughter, certainly. Yet he could not bring himself to say 'lover', although he had certainly been that to her many times over in his dreams these past nights— dreams that were as carnal as they were passionate and in which Helen, supple and eager, proved as reckless as he. It had been too long since he had last felt this brutal urge to plunge himself between a woman's thighs. He would awaken quite shaken, even scared. In his dreams he impaled her again and again, until the rattle of the dawn wind against the shutters and the crow of the rooster dragged him to safety.

The dirt road leading to the main street into town was narrow and the taxi suddenly swerved to the side, flinging Dimitri hard against the car door. There was a sharp pain where the door handle dug into the soft flesh of his shoulder. Dimitri cursed the driver loudly, rolling up the window against the rising dust. Then he saw the red *Fiat* in the middle of the road, its driver trying to maneuver it back into the right lane.

It was Andreas, and someone else bobbing alongside him as he drove by without so much as a glance in the taxi's direction.

"Faggot!" Dimitri hissed, a bellow in the closed-up car. If Andreas

121

spent half the time at his job that he did on romance, this road might have been paved years ago. Dimitri would be sure to tell the Austrian off for this negligence as soon as he got back. Only his urgency to get to town kept him from doing so right now.

But he did not get back to the hotel until eight that evening and by then Andreas was off-duty. The agent had taken up Dimitri's entire day before finally showing him something even remotely suitable: a three-bedroom villa in *Kalamaki* that was a close enough walk to the beach, had a bit of garden, and could be occupied in a week. It was cause to celebrate! Dimitri had bought a bottle of wine to invite Helen for a drink in his bungalow where he would propose that she move with him to the villa. All very proper, of course. She had nothing to fear from him. He was already thinking ahead to showing her Istanbul, introducing her to the Bosphorous, the Topkape. He had to call his housekeeper.

The sound of the *bouzoukia* was coming from the bar where two men sat before microphones strumming for a group dancing the *sirtaki* in the middle of the sitting room. The bus driver who had brought Dimitri from the airport was leading the dancers, waving a white handkerchief above his head. Holding his hand was Constantina, the pretty, middle-aged chambermaid, still in her black blouse and skirt, who had just this morning scooped up the sheets from Dimitri's bed and shared a cup of tea with him on his balcony. He remembered her surprised glance when he had not attempted to prolong her visit as he usually did simply for her company and for the soothing sight of her crossed, slender ankles and the surge of her breasts below her gold crucifix. This morning he had impatiently dismissed her as he wanted to get to town. Beside Constantina was an obese German and his wife, then an English couple with their three children whom Dimitri recognized from breakfast. At the other end was the boy who had carried his suitcase the day he arrived, then Andreas, then a tall, dark youth Dimitri had not seen before.

Round they went in a circle, the ever serious Greeks doing the rapid steps forward and back, side to side. Now and then they would snatch the hand of some game-looking guest to join in. All at once, Andreas caught a woman's hand and dragged her after him. It was Helen!

Dimitri stood, transfixed. He had never been any good at dancing—he had trouble discerning the rhythm. But he liked to watch and could not help admiring the Austrian's sure-footed agility.

The guests began to break away from the circle so that only Andreas and three other men—the bus driver, the bellboy, and the dark-eyed youth—were left. Dimitri studied this debonair stranger who looked so out of place among the islanders. He was undoubtedly Athenian at that height, with his fine jaw and black hair cut, fashionably, without sideburns. *An old flame.* He would not hesitate to wager that this was the one—Andreas' old flame. He looked faintly familiar. Dimitri was certain that it was he who had been sitting beside Andreas in the Fiat this morning.

The men swayed slowly, their eyes closed as though in prayerful meditation. Then, they leaped and vigorously stomped their feet. The dancing moved Dimitri. He almost wished that his mother had never left Greece and that he had been born here, a fleet-footed Adonis. He was amazed, gazing across the floor, to find Helen staring at the men as spellbound as he. Not wanting her to see him so disheveled after his long day, Dimitri slipped away to his bungalow to shower and change his clothes.

"I need to call Istanbul," Dimitri said into the room telephone, anxious to contact his housekeeper. He could hardly hear the voice of the receptionist from the noise but it sounded like Andreas.

"How long will it take?" Dimitri said.

"I'll call you back," said the voice.

He showered with the bathroom door ajar so that he could hear the ring but nobody called. He dialed again.

"I must call Istanbul," he said.

"There are no lines."

"Can't you go through Athens?"

"There are no lines out," said the voice, curtly.

"But you said you would call back."

"There are too many people on the island to take everyone's calls," came the irritable reply.

"Is this Andreas?" Dimitri snapped, just as whoever it was hung up. He buzzed the reception again. No one answered.

The main building, noisier and more crowded than before, was filled with guests returning from town or from the beach who were helping themselves to platefuls of food from the buffet in the dining room. Dimitri, more comfortable now in a starched, blue shirt and pressed slacks, began to look for Helen. They would go out to dinner. Then he would tell her about the villa. She could see it tomorrow morning.

Helen was not in the hall or dining room. The dark young man, the Athenian, was teaching one of the Germans a dance step. The bellboy was behind the bar serving drinks. Dimitri asked him whether he had seen the English lady who had been dancing earlier.

"Andreas' friend?" the boy asked.

"Who?" Dimitri said.

The bellboy shrugged.

When the *bouzoukia* started up again, Dimitri walked down to the garden. The dark water of the swimming pool danced under the light from the flickering torches on the terrace. He stood where Helen did each morning when she gave a lesson, picturing her posed on the concrete edge, flailing her arms like a wounded duck. Only such a beautiful women would dare adopt such an ungainly posture.

He went through the pine trees and down the white-washed steps—a milky way against the dark hillside. In the space of an hour he had climbed up seventy steps and descended them twice. It could be lethal. It made him even more determined to take the villa.

He turned at 'Calypso' to fetch the bottle of wine from his dresser. Helen's row, 'Aegisthus', was further down.

For a moment it felt like he was falling asleep, minutes stretching into hours as his feet tapped lightly down the steps, his thoughts sliding into dreams. It felt like the old days in Hamburg where the *frauleins* had gone crazy for his flamboyance and his sharp, Tartar looks. Some of those women had been quite wonderful. There had been the blond who spoke with a slight lisp, the delectable way her tongue was forever flicking her upper lip. Then there had been Bolivia. He still thought the women of Santa Cruz the most beautiful he had ever seen.

Suddenly, there was the sound of laughter and a door slamming shut. In a flash, Someone brushed past Dimitri, leaping up the steps as stealthily as a moonbeam.

Dimitri stopped. He turned around. He stared after the arrogant back, those narrow shoulders.

There was a cool, deep silence. The shadow had disappeared into the trees without so much as rustling a leaf. Dimitri stood holding his breath, not daring to step any closer to Helen's bungalow. *An old flame.* Andreas' words to him that first day. Yet, Helen had never said anything about Andreas, never even mentioned his name.

Dimitri's breath seemed lost somewhere, trapped within his ribs. Somehow he gasped, drew in air as though through a straw. Had he been a fool all this time, spending his money on her, taking her to dinner, getting caught in some bizarre triangle?

Had it been Helen in the car with Andreas this morning, the one who had kept the Austrian's mind off the road so completely that he had nearly collided with Dimitri's taxi? *An old flame!* Had Andreas brought her here?

Dimitri stared at the door of Helen's bungalow. It seemed to reverberate from the force of Andreas slamming it. He looked back up the somber hill, hearing a thread of bouzouki melody, wondering why Andreas had been in such a hurry.

He, Dimitri, would knock, demand the truth from Helen, demand to know why she had made such a fool of him. What had he done to deserve this? Again, he groped for breath, trying to still the shudder in his breast. He reached before him as though to knock on her door, but stopped. Despite himself, he began to remember her ducking into the waves as she had that day below the *Kastro*—a supine siren, heavy with the sweet vulnerability of youth.

Suddenly, he cracked the wine bottle against a giant pot of geraniums. The red liquid trickled down the white steps, seeping into the dirt around the clipped rose bushes and hybiscus. His hand was turning red, too, but not from the wine. It was blood. He had cut himself with the glass. Strangely enough for so much blood there was little pain, only his awe at this oozing from his palm, only his own marvelous realization that he could still bleed so. A soothing relief came over him.

He reached out, impulsively, and touched Helen's bungalow door, blotting his bloodied hand. He stared at the grisly imprints of his open palm. Pilgrims used to signify their safe return from Mecca with red paint on the doors along the streets of Istanbul in this way. He remembered being horrified by them as a child, thinking that someone had been butchered behind the closed, blood-stained door.

He reached out now, fumbled through the blinding night, and blotted his hand again and again until all the blood was off. His knees buckled, plunging him onto the wet, pungent soil. He was safe, home from a hazardous pilgrimage.

At the airport the next morning the flight from Athens was just landing. Bus drivers were waiting for their passengers, smoking cigarettes, collars turned up against the morning breeze. The Pelias driver, lithe dancer of last night, was checking his wheels. He stood up and yawned, glancing at Dimitri without recognizing him. Soon he would be letting new guests off at the *Pelias* to be charmed by the wind-blown halls and the rough, peasent curtains. Andreas would sign them in, as usual, having taken over from the night shift, and mumble something that would sound like an intimacy. Dimitri had left early, purposely, to avoid him.

He bought a cup of Nescafe from the stall, sat down, and imagined going wherever the next flight out of Athens was headed—to Corfu where he had not been in years, maybe to some less frequented island like Santorini. *Santorini.* He had never been there. It gave off a lively, vibrant ring like the wine bottle of last night.

He took a breath to stop the sinking in his chest. Helen would soon be leaving her bungalow to have breakfast. Dimitri thought of the look on her face when she saw the door with its grim bloodstains. His blood. It was so unlike anything he had ever done, before. Yet, it had been his pilgrimage. It had been he who had allowed her to crack his iron-clad heart.

He pushed himself up, forced his leaden legs to walk. Such a blow as last night's would have surely shattered a much younger man, would have crushed his heart like beans in a mortar. Yet last night, for the first time in months, he had slept without a pill. Without a pill and without a dream. He would cradle this ache in his chest for a while but then it would ease, grow dull, slowly be absorbed back into his body. He could see that an ego was a mere trifle in the greater scheme of things. As insignificant, really, as hearing Beethoven in the Acropolis.

The Turks were stringent believers in destiny. "What is written on the brow the eye will behold." Helen was not to be his fate, after all. His destiny was awaiting him back at the Ministry in Istanbul.

He would start his vacation anew with this thought. This, and the memory of the shattered wine bottle as its essence spilled into the earth along with his blood. It had given off a lively, vibrant ring. Like the sound—Santorini.

JELLYFISH

"Billy!" Suzanne cries, opening her eyes and rising up onto her elbows.

"What?" says Billy.

"Nothing," says Suzanne, remembering that her son Billy, six, is splashing in the shallows beside the boulder on which she is sunbathing. It was only a dream, almost a daydream, in which something terrible happens to Billy. In the three weeks they have been in Greece, especially since arriving on this island, Hydra, she has had to contend with a horde of menaces—minotaurs, cyclops, medusas—that invade her dreams to attack her son. In this dream Billy had tumbled like Icarus from the sky on wings that she, his mother, had fashioned.

Perhaps it has something to do with her and John's attempts to get Billy to overcome his fear of the sea, although she suspects that John is as content as Billy to swim in the hotel's sweet, chlorinated pool—to Billy like the familiar community pool in New York. Suzanne loathes pools with their filmy surfaces, their smell of bodies. To her, nothing compares to the sea's vast purity. She is exasperated that neither her husband nor her son share this devotion.

This remote cove on Hydra was her idea. She cannot believe that they have the spot all to themselves—a shore of tiny, white gravel that crunches underfoot while myriad stones the color of lapis and jade shine through the water. There are pungent pines and olive trees with twinkling, lime-green tops planted in rows like toy trees on a game board. The scratching of cicadas is punctuated only by Billy's contented splashing and the rumbling of occasional boats on their way to and from the island.

It is just the place to tell John.

Suddenly there is more splashing. John is coming ashore, snorkel on his forehead, fins slapping the water.

"I told you to play on shore," he says to Billy who is in waist-deep water.

"I'm catching crabs," Billy says, hoisting up a plastic cup.

Although Billy can swim, Suzanne knows that his repugnance for salt water might make him panic. She should have been watching him more closely.

"You're not allowed to swim alone," John says, removing his fins.

"How's the water?" Suzanne asks John, not wanting to arouse Billy's fears now that he is venturing into the water on his own.

"I caught these myself," Billy interrupts, "I nearly caught a shrimp, too. You can see right through him!"

John stoops to look into Billy's cup. Next to their son, her husband is a colossus: six foot three, full chest and arms from daily workouts, firm belly. Having recently lost all remaining baby-fat, their son looks vulnerable as a molting bird. Squatting, now, his thin arms and legs look like wire triangles as he pats the walls of the sand castle that he has decorated with shells, pebbles, seaweed and part of a starfish. He places the cup of crabs in the middle.

John climbs onto the boulder next to Suzanne and uses her towel to dry himself. "There are jellyfish out there," he says.

"It's too early for jellyfish," she says. "It's only June."

"The fellow at the hotel says a girl got stung the other day."

"Did you see any now?"

"I saw something that looked like a man-of-war," he says, sounding annoyed at her doubting him, at her presuming to know more about the sea than he does.

He rolls up the towel, places it under his head, and shuts his eyes. Suzanne gazes at the short, black lashes, the eyes moving underneath the closed lids, the line of his nose and mouth like the chiseled, marble faces in the Acropolis museum. She leans down and brushes her lips against his, but he quivers and brings his hand up quickly, as though brushing off a fly. Opening his eyes he says, "Do we have any ammonia?"

"Ammonia?"

"For jellyfish stings."

They met here on Hydra eight years ago. John was a vacationing bachelor at the Surf Club hotel where Suzanne had a job teaching scuba-diving. She would lecture groups of sun-burned tourists before leading them, weighted down with equipment, into the shallows to practice. John had done a lot of water-skiing, slaloming across the water like a dragonfly skimming the surface of a pond. She had watched him, fascinated, certain that he was an American.

It had taken a week for them to finally meet in the sandy bar one afternoon. It turned out that he was a New Yorker like herself, a banker. She was an expatriate from Long Island teaching scuba-diving in the summer to pay for art classes on the island in winter. She had promised to look him up when she visited her parents in October, never dreaming that she would marry him and exchange her white-washed rooms in the artists' colony on Hydra for his East Side apartment. Then, Billy was born. They have not been back to Greece since that summer nearly eight years ago.

Suzanne is surprised at how little John actually enjoys the water. The Mediterranean. Water-skiing, he will circle the bay twice and then swim ashore without even getting his hair wet—as though the point is simply to stay above water. He refuses to take wind-surfing lessons because it entails falling into the water a lot. The one time he did try he drifted out so far that Suzanne and the instructor had to rescue him in the speedboat, trailing the board and sail back to shore like some huge, dead fish. Even in this beautiful cove today, John has been swimming with a mask and fins.

John had not wanted to go to any of the islands after hearing of the outbreak of typhoid on Kos.

"But we can't not go to Hydra," she had said, practically in tears.

"It'll be full of tourists and queers."

"They're on Mykonos," she corrected him, dryly.

"They're everywhere."

"That's only because the men are so pretty, here," she had retorted.

She finally won. They had taken the hydrofoil from Athens, her heart soaring at the sight of the Napoleonic mansions on the island hillside and the freshly-painted white houses along the quay.

This morning, they had walked through the town and taken a path along the mountain to this cove Suzanne remembered from having snorkeled over the reef.

She gets off the boulder and walks across the gravel to where Billy is rebuilding his castle. He looks up at her through black bangs fringing his eyes. His face is brown as pumpernickel.

"Where are you going?" he says.

"Swimming."

He leaps up. "Can I come?"

"Not right now," she says, feeling guilty at refusing him, yet needing to be alone.

She wades into the Mediterranean, clear as cellophane, her red toenails like watermelon against the smooth rocks. She plunges into the cool water like an eel, swimming over the reef, around the bend of the cove. After several minutes, tired, she swims up to a large boulder. She grabs hold of the rock, but something moves against her hand. Two nude girls are sunbathing. Embarrassed, she floats away on her back, catching sight of a nude man further off. He is climbing the rocks, lean and graceful as an Apollo.

In the distance, John's voice is calling from the shore, shouting at her to come back.

132

Billy has amassed another starfish, a purple sea urchin, some pine cones. He has a similar cache, smelly and faded, on their hotel balcony which he wants to take back to New York. The thought brings a twinge of nausea to Suzanne as she stretches out on the boulder beside John.

Raising one tanned leg, then the other, she stares at her flesh, newly firm from swimming. Unlike John, she does not work out at home or at a gym, preferring swimming and snow skiing to stay in shape. If they lived in Greece she would look this good all the time, spending summers teaching diving again or wind-surfing when she got good enough. She might even paint again. She thinks of raising a baby here, perhaps a girl, who will take to the sea naturally.

"Doesn't being here make you want to have another child?"

John surveys the cove, the cobalt sea. "No."

"It does me," she says. "Everything is so beautiful. People love children here."

John shrugs. "We don't live here."

"I know. But I like this feeling."

"If we had a baby we couldn't travel like this. Billy goes everywhere with us now. Our life would change."

"But the *feeling* is important. The feeling of wanting a child. It means you have faith."

John is silent a moment. Then, he reaches over her to pick up his fins and mask. "Billy and I are going exploring in the next cove," he says.

Suzanne watches him disappear with Billy into the pines. John is forever on the move—on the subway to his job, flying off on a business trip, descending to his basement darkroom to spend hours developing film—forever avoiding sensitive issues, leaving her with the acute sense of their unit being constantly fragmented.

What she likes about Greece is the continuity. The sound of the cicadas in the pines is like a bridge connecting the centuries. These same sands of Hydra had harbored Odysseus' ships and spawned Aphrodite and Calypso. She closes her eyes and lets her mind drift, thoughtless, into the harmony of the cicadas.

But it is not the cicadas vibrating, now. It is something further away. She lifts her head. A yellow speedboat is rounding the bend of the cove in a white froth of water. It seems to be coming toward her, but then abruptly turns and continues out the opposite end of the cove.

A few minutes later the noise returns. This time, a woman's voice floats across the water, then a child's. Again the boat approaches, not turning as it did before, but coming right into her beach. The sound of the motor grows softer. Finally it stops, completely.

They are quite near now. Two men, two women, and two children sitting in the bobbing boat. Suzanne sits up and stares at the strangers to indicate her presence, to keep them from invading her spot. But it is too late. The children are already in the water, squealing their way ashore. If John and Billy were here they might not have come. They probably think she is alone.

The men drag the dinghy onto the gravel several yards from Suzanne. The women get out, carrying towels and a small cooler. Like herself, they appear to be tourists, nordic, fair-haired. They glance at Suzanne as they walk over to the pines on the other side of the boulder on which she is sun-bathing. Perhaps this is their spot. Her side is the larger of the two and it must seem ridiculous for her to be taking up all this space by herself. But she does not move to give it up.

The two children playing in the sand next to the beached dinghy are older than Billy—about nine or ten. One is a girl with waist-length blond braids. Both wear only bikini bottoms. They are a deep bronze, like the woman who now joins them, rubbing her thighs and arms with the sea water several times before submerging herself to her shoulders, holding her chin up stiffly.

Suzanne looks at her watch. John and Billy have been gone over an hour. She feels another wave of nausea. She is hungry. She gets down off the boulder to get lunch ready.

The two women sitting across the boulder sip drinks, exposing bare, uniformly-tanned breasts to the sun. Suzanne squats down and spreads a towel. She sets out the *feta* and *kiseri* cheeses, the *tarama*, black olives, tomatoes, and a loaf of crusty bread. She sniffs the bread. It smells of honey, just like the bread she used to get from the bakery when she lived here. Putting down the bread, she uncorks the wine and drinks straight from the bottle. Those almost forgotten days! She had swam topless—though it was far from being the norm then—and had crossed the Peloponnese on a motorcycle, island-hopping through the Aegean and painting pastel villages. Once, drunk on *Retsina,* she had made love to a Greek in a roomful of sleeping friends.

"Dad caught a squid!"

Billy's shrieks pierce the hum of voices across the boulder. He runs out of the pines and up to Suzanne carrying John's dripping mask. He shoves the mask under her chin, spilling water onto her thighs.

"Billy—" She shrinks from the sight of the minute head and tentacles that dart from one corner of the mask to the other.

"It was hiding under a rock," Billy says, jiggling the mask. "Dad made it swim right in."

John is behind him, his face red and his fins hanging across his shoulder. He turns to the voices behind him.

"Don't stare," Suzanne whispers. Billy turns around to look, also. "They got here a while ago," she says, as though it is her fault.

John drops his fins and sits down across from her, his back to the people, a frown crossing his brow.

"Do I have to eat this," Billy says, looking at the food.

"You have to eat something," Suzanne says.

"What's that?"

"*Tarama*—cream cheese and caviar."

Billy makes a face although he does not know what caviar is.

135

"You like *feta*, I can make you a sandwich in this nice bread," she says, tearing off a piece from the loaf and making a deep groove in it.

"*Retsina*," says John, picking up the bottle. "What's the occasion?"

Suzanne shrugs. "I thought we were going to be here alone. I wanted to talk. What's it like on the other side?" she says, thinking that it might be more private.

"Here's nicer," John says.

"Way nicer," says Billy, biting into his sandwich. He removes the cheese and chews the bread.

John dips a piece of bread in the *tarama* and eats it, the dry salt at his temples moving as he chews as though his face were about to crack.

"Do you remember the first time we shared a bottle of *retsina?*" Suzanne says, filling two plastic cups.

"When?" he says.

"You don't remember?"

"On Hydra?"

She doesn't answer.

"At that beach club?" he guesses.

"You complained that it was too vinegary," she says, making herself a *tarama* sandwich. Billy takes the mask to the sand castle and pours the squid into the cup with the crabs and shrimp.

"What did you do that for? It'll suffocate," John reproaches him, loudly.

"Come back and eat, honey," Suzanne calls, brushing off pine needles from Billy's bread. But Billy is in the water again, hunting. Near him, the two other children are taking turns diving for something underwater.

"No wonder he's so skinny," says John.

Suzanne takes a deep breath. "Can't you say something nice for a change?"

"What do you mean?"

"You haven't said one nice thing all morning."

He is silent, looking surprised.

"What's on the other side?" she says, trying to be pleasant.

"Garbage."

"Garbage?"

He shrugs. "Coke cans and old flip-flops. There won't be any tourists left if they don't keep their beaches decent."

Across the boulder, one of the women stands and calls to the children in the water. A word—*plage*—pronounced with a thick 'l' reminds Suzanne of the Bulgarians and Yugoslavs she once camped with in the Peleponnese. The woman adjusts her bikini bottom to cover an arc of white skin. Her broad back and calves, ever her ample breasts, are athletic-looking rather than sexy.

"Do you think they're Bulgarians?" Suzanne whispers.

"Bulgarians?"

"John," she says, "Do you think we could live here?"

John is staring at the woman's back. "Where?"

"Here. I mean in Athens. You could get a good job."

He pulls aside the towel with the food, then stretches out on the pine needles beside Suzanne and lays his head on her lap.

The woman turns to face them for an instant before sitting back down, disappearing behind the boulder.

"Don't *stare*," Suzanne says, smacking John's nose lightly. "Did you hear what I said?"

He looks up at her. "The Greeks are out to lunch. The country's bankrupt. Why would we want to live here?"

Suzanne is wind surfing, the taste of salt water sharp on her lips. Her board rises and dips to a familiar *Buzookia* tune. Somehow, she knows she is dreaming, again. Below her, a shadow like a giant kite begins to sweep across the white sand. Suddenly, a shark's fin surfaces next to her. She hears a scream.

"Damn!"

She opens her eyes and sits up. Something is surfacing in the water in front of her—large, brown shoulders and a hand yanking at a blue mask.

"Damn!" shouts John, smashing the mask against the water and twisting to look over his shoulder.

"What is it?" she says, still shaken from her dream. Her leg tingles as she hobbles toward this scowling Poseidon.

"Jellyfish—don't come in," he shouts, scanning the water in front of him.

"Are you all right?" she says, the wine clouding her head.

"It feels like I've been speared," he mutters.

Carefully, Suzanne wades in. The sky has turned overcast and there is a cool breeze. She shivers. John turns for her to see where he is running his fingers. A raised patch of red skin has several welts protruding from it.

"It looks like a jellyfish," she admits, afraid to tell him how big the mark is.

"Damn. We should have brought ammonia."

Billy is beside them, staring at his father's back, his fears of the water suddenly confirmed. He starts to laugh at the sight of the scar.

Suzanne says nothing, grateful that it was not he who was stung. She touches the amoeba-shape scar with her fingertips. "Maybe you should sit in the shade."

"It scraped my back just as I found this. I've been searching for one all morning," he says, holding out a pearly, white chunk of coral.

She reaches out and touches it. He had given her one when they first met at the Surf Club. It had been a kind of joke, then. She was the diver but he was the prospector. It seems, now, through this symbolic gesture, that he has somehow felt what she has been keeping from him these past few weeks.

Something suddenly touches Suzanne's back. She whips around.

It is the blond woman from across the boulder, oiled and smelling of almond flavoring. She is holding up a fistful of sand and gesturing toward John's back. Seeing Suzanna hesitate, she pats some on John's back, herself.

"Hey," John says, starting to turn around.

"Wait, honey," Suzanne says.

The woman is gesturing for her to do the same. Across the boulder, the woman's companions are watching.

Suzanne scoops up a fistful of sand and pats John's back. He cringes but does not turn around, obviously aware of and avoiding the stranger's nude torso. Indifferent to her own nakedness, the woman moves her hand over the blazing scar, over the welts, smoothing on the sand like a salve. Her breasts sway fearlessly with her movements, the nipples stopping just short of John's skin.

"Does it hurt?" Suzanne says.

John arches his back. He seems helpless to defend himself against their fingertips.

"John," Suzanne says, emboldened. "I'm going to have a baby."

The water is teeming with the small, round jellyfish, now, their lavender and pink tentacles floating on the surface like earthworms. The blond girl and boy have brought a net and are scooping some up and flinging them on the shore.

John, his back perfectly still, turns his head enough to see Suzanne from the corner of his eye.

"I'm pregnant," she says, feeling slightly foolish, slightly lightheaded, as though revealing the secret has left her physically lighter.

The blond woman stands back and clicks her tongue at the darkening scar. "Bad," she says, in heavily-accented English. "Very bad."

"Yes, it's very bad," Suzanne agrees, surprised that she feels so good, so elated.

All at once, she is ashamed for having shunned these people all afternoon. She turns to the woman. "Are you Bulgarians?"

"Yugoslavia," the woman says, looking at Suzanne from heavily-lidded blue eyes. She glances at the water and clicks her tongue at a bobbing jellyfish.

"Suzanne and John," Suzanne says, realizing only too late what she has done. John, still with his back turned and with his hands folded over his chest, will now have to turn around and acknowledge this pear-breasted woman. He will have to shake her hand, or something, have to confront her nakedness. Suzanne looks away to avoid witnessing his embarrassment.

The hillside has turned gray, olive trees starting to sway under the breeze that must have caused the currents to wash ashore the jellyfish. Closing her eyes, she tries to understand it all: the new child in her belly already beginning to claim her, Billy on the brink of separating from her, her own mystifying love for John despite his being so vexingly disparate from her.

She listens, waiting for his anger at her for having put him on the spot with this woman and for the reckless, absurd way she has just announced her pregnancy to him.

But, to her surprise, John does not do this. Instead, he is talking to the woman, thanking her, telling her that his back is better. Suzanne hears the woman invite them both for a glass of wine. Suddenly John is saying yes. Suddenly, to Suzanne's surprise, he is even asking the woman her name.

THE WEDDING

Oh henna, oh henna, henna Oh syrup of dew.
For fear that his mother will come searching for him, I'll
place him in my eye, oh henna, and draw kohl over him.

The girl watches from the window of her second-floor bridal chamber as the old women—hired especially for the wedding—beat their heavy tambourines and sing the lulling love songs into the hot night air.

Sitting in the dirt road, against the walls of the white-washed, mud-brick house in the seaside town north of Dubai, they sway from side to side as though they are the impassioned ones themselves. Now and then they ululate shrilly, rapid 'lolololeeee' off their tongues, to commemorate the occasion: a man taking a wife. The same cry that celebrates the birth of a son, or men riding into battle.

The women's tinseled gowns and veils, their golden masks, the silver rings on their gnarled fingers, catch the moonlight and flicker. Occasionally they stop singing long enough to sip the bitter coffee and the sweet tea brought by a servant of the house, draining the dark liquid below their masks. Soon they will eat from large trays of saffron rice and boiled lamb: the wedding feast.

Sara, the bride, is seventeen. Her thick, black hair is fanned across her back like a peacock's tail and glistens with coconut oil. The palms

141

of her hands and soles of her feet are painted, stencil-like, with orange henna; her skin is scented with musk.

She goes back to sit on the wooden marriage bed, a fragile novelty that creaks under her weight. More inviting to her are the silk cushions against the wall and the smooth, straw mats and wool rugs that cover the floor. In her father's house, she and her family sleep on cotton mattresses on the floor. In summer, when not even the tall wind-towers draw a breeze into the house, these are carried up to the flat roof to sleep on. It is an honor, this elevated bed, a sign of her groom's wealth.

Her pink, sateen wedding dress swishes as she draws the bed sheet over her. The translucent gown on top glitters, the gold threads that her mother cross-stitched into it pricking Sara's skin right through the dress underneath. But she is proud to wear the gown—to show off her mother's proficiency with a needle—and only hopes that the bridegroom will notice the hours of work that went into it and not tear it off her as some men were known to do.

The pearl earrings, gold bracelets, and a necklace of gold links that fits snugly round her neck and comes down to her breastbone like loose armor, are gifts from the groom, a well-to-do pearl merchant. Sara could look forward to a comfortable life from now on, her mother had boasted, so long as she obeyed her husband and gave him no cause to send her back to her family, or to take an additional wife. Sara's beauty is credited to her having been sought after by the merchant's family, her beauty and her family's good name. For although her father is not wealthy, he is a pious man and his reputation is without blemish. His wife and daughters spend their days at home instead of out gabbing with other women and none of Sara's three older brothers frequent the coffee shops, smoke, or patronize the few discreet harlots of *Jowhara* Street.

"Firm as apples," her mother had boasted, cupping one of Sara's well-formed breasts as the other women kinfolk helped prepare Sara for the wedding. "Remember," her mother warned, "a man is never so aroused as when his bride defends herself."

"Remember the screams of your cousin," her aunt added, "—try and outdo her." Sara knew that this was meant as a joke. Aisha's screams had been excessive and the poor groom ended up with a black eye that made him the butt of light-hearted ridicule rather than a proud husband.

"Think of your father, your brothers. Where can they show their faces if your struggles aren't heard?" said another aunt.

"Don't let him suspect that you like it," her mother warned, shortly before she and the other women left the room, "not the first time."

Sara knows to let out the expected bellows, the screams for mercy that will prove her virtue and make her father proud among the towns-people. But she does not think of her reputation now, or of her beauty: high breasts, taut belly, wide, gazelle's eyes. She is thinking, only, of blood.

She remembers watching her father butchering lambs on feast days, seeing how meekly the animals surrendered to her father's knife even though they scuffled feebly as the steel bit into their throats. They would shudder and kick as they bled and when she had cried the first time, her father and brothers chided her. It was blessed to sacrifice, they told her, and the animal doesn't suffer since it is over with so quickly. Ashamed of her fear, Sara had stood by as they went to work cutting through the skin, fleecing the carcass neatly, disemboweling it for the spit. She had been sickened but had stood there anyway. Now it is this same sickness that creeps into her stomach.

No one is forcing her to marry this man. She accepted his proposal herself, even when her father asked her a second time—just to make sure. Her friends tried to argue her out of it telling her it was foolish to give herself to so old a man, that he was almost forty. She had turned down all the other proposals that had come her way since she left school five years ago. Why had she suddenly chosen this man when she could have had someone much younger? She had not been able to tell them why.

She had been one of the best students at the small *Saqr* Road school until she turned twelve and her father decided it was time she stayed home and learned women's work—something she could use in the future.

"Now that you can read and write, it's enough," he said, and she had not protested. He was a good father. He loved her. She knew that he would not force her to do anything she did not want to do, or give her to any of the women who besieged their doorstep with marriage offers the instant the rumor spread that she was eligible. Although the younger the girl the more desirable as a wife she was because her character was so much more malleable, Sara had no desire to move in with a strange man and his family, to grow round and ungainly in childbearing, to lose her youth so soon.

At the sudden twist of the doorknob she turns sharply toward the noise, taking in the strange room again as though for the first time. There is a basket of dates in one corner, the smell of ambergris from a glass vial at the window, melodious crooning from the street:

> *For fear that his father will come*
> *looking for him,*
> *I'll place him in my hair, oh henna,*
> *and braid it round about him.*
>
> *Oh henna, oh henna, henna*
> *Oh syrup of dew...*

The tall man enters the room and shuts the door with a finality that makes Sara squirm. He resembles an angel in the white *abaya*. Like her dress, it is embroidered with gold at the neck and down the sides. During the wedding ceremony, when he had arrived at her home with his male entourage and taken his place beside her on the pedestal, she had scarcely looked at him, afraid that he would be an old man. But she saw enough, now, to know that he stood as straight as any young man and was relieved that her friends had been wrong about him. She had trusted her father's description of him—that he was neither old nor young, quite tall, a good man—and knew that he must have accepted *her* on his mother's judgment because they had never met.

When he comes forward now, to look at her, probably to decide for himself whether or not she pleases him, she accepts his gaze with lowered eyes. She studies his sandaled foot on the ground next to the bed, the folds of his *abaya*, his large hand against his thigh.

> *For fear that his sister*
> *will come searching for him,*
> *I'll place him on my breast, oh henna,*
> *with a pearl to cover him.*
>
> *Oh henna, oh henna, henna*
> *Oh syrup of dew...*

The man turns toward the sound of the voices. He goes to the window and peers out, then draws the glass panes together, bolting them shut. Though the lyrics had annoyed Sara, they had distracted her. Without the intruding voices, she is suddenly filled with her own thoughts. Why is she accepting this loveless union? How can she respond to the touch of this stranger? She feels each twitch of her body as though she is a sand castle ready to crumble and be swept away at the onslaught of a wave.

She watches the man at the window slip off his *abaya*, his white headdress and black *gutra*, the lacy, white skullcap. He hangs them on a hook. His hair is cropped short, unlike that of some of the younger men who grow their hair to their shoulders in a reckless sign of manhood. This man will be different, perhaps. Wiser. Gentler.

Her mother told her that not all men undressed the first night— that some men were apt to be modest and consider a young girl's feelings. Sara hopes it will be so with this man for she feels weak again at the prospect of confronting a stranger's naked body. She does not want to be embarrassed, or attracted even. But most of all, she does not want to compare this man to the other man whose image now tugs at her heart more violently than when she held him in her arms, whose face is before her once more, eyes teasing her, teeth biting her neck.

Suddenly, the bridegroom steps out of his sandals without undressing and slips, wordlessly, under the sheet next to her.

The other man, whose image comes to her so readily, had been only nineteen. Othman was his name and he was the brother of her best friend, Jamila. Though Sara and Jamila were the same age and had been classmates at school, Jamila had married early and was now nursing her second child. They were still good friends and Sara would go visit Jamila in the mornings, walking through the market after the men had done the grocery shopping and gone off to work.

One day, six months ago, Sara had arrived at Jamila's house and found a young man in the foyer. Of course, she immediately excused herself, it being forbidden for men and women to mix freely or for a woman to reveal her face to a strange man. But noting the surprised look on her friend's face, Jamila told Sara that it was only her brother, Othman, and that he was just leaving, so Sara could come in. Several weeks later, Sara was going out of the wooden door of Jamila's courtyard, when Othman came up behind her, grabbed her arm through her black *abaya* and forced her into the garden, away from the street. While he held her arms, restraining her, he told her how he had watched for her in the mornings when she came to visit, how he used to see her walking home from school with his sister when she was younger, how he had waited so long for this moment.

Sara stood, terrified, as Othman told her how he had seen only her eyes at first but how he had not been disappointed when he had watched, through his sister's window, as she removed her long *abaya* and mask. She was, he told her, as beautiful as he had imagined.

"I want to marry you," he said.

Confused, staring at his lightly pock-marked face, and trying not to listen to the wild words that came from his lips, Sara was unable to pull herself away. Although Othman's dazed look frightened her at first, she realized that it was only his own fear that they would be discovered together that made him stare at her like that. She let him pull her into a corner of the garden where a few pink oleanders shielded them. Then, as the desert wind blew against his face, ruffling his checkered headdress and his long, curly hair underneath, he pressed his lips to her eyes through the holes in her mask.

"I knew from the start that you would love me. We will marry and have children," he said. She felt faint, wanting him to go on yet knowing that this was not right.

"I have a father, and brothers," she managed to say. "If you wish to marry me then go to them and ask for me."

"That is difficult right now—," Othman said, placing his warm palm on her breast.

"We are crazy to stand here like this," she said, pushing his hand away. "Go and ask for me."

"Soon. Soon I will meet with your father."

"What about Jamila," Sara asked, suddenly eyeing her friend's window.

"She knows, don't worry." He had confided in his sister, he told Sara, and Jamila had encouraged her visits for him.

Sara could not believe that Jamila's friendship had been extended for her brother's sake, or that Jamila would expose her to such danger. Like Sara, she knew the risks of such meetings. Still, Jamila must love her brother and might have done so out of this love. The pleasure that seeped through Sara, now, when Othman touched her made her not begrudge Jamila this. Long after she had walked home, she still felt Othman's hands hot on her arms.

She was afraid to answer any of the messages Othman sent her through Jamila over the next few weeks. Only when Jamila told Sara how desperately he needed to talk with her did she finally agree to see him. Just once, she repeated to herself.

During this meeting Sara sat beside Othman nervously, sweating beneath the mask and *abaya* which she refused to take off, allowing Othman to hold her hand only through the silken cloth while she counted the minutes until Jamila returned with the baby. But other times followed and soon Othman persuaded her that love had no taboos and that even in the old days a man was free to spend an entire night with an unwed woman so long as his sword lay between them to ensure her honor. Sara began to love Jamila for absenting herself those few hours and for not questioning her when she saw her.

When Sara finally removed her mask and *abaya* and undressed for Othman, allowing him to love her, it seemed perfectly natural. Afterwards, as they lay beside each other and she asked him when he would go to her father he refused to answer, pulling her to him roughly, as though it was his right. She rested her head on his chest, her hair covering them both, and her lashes brushed his skin as she tried to blink away the tears in her eyes. Less than an hour before he had spoken to her so fervently.

She took his restlessness as a sign of his troubles elsewhere. She knew that he had been fighting with his father over their *dhow* which carried cargo between Dubai and Delhi and that the old man had recently cut Othman out of his share of the business.

One day Sara waited an hour without Othman showing up for their appointment. She was about to leave when he finally tapped at his sister's door. She ran to him but he stood, impassive. When she asked him what was the matter, tugging at his arms for him to hold her, he said that they could no longer meet. He had learned that they had been seen together.

Alarmed, Sara waited for him to say that he would now, finally, approach her father but instead, Othman seemed to accept the fact that he would no longer see her as though he had expected this to happen all along. That afternoon, as she walked home through the deserted market—empty shops sealed like catacombs—she turned around every so often to see if someone were following her. She scanned the high walls on either side of the narrow streets, the ornate windtowers above the houses, the alleyways where old men sat or napped in the shade. She found no one. No one had ever seen her with Othman, she knew.

At night she lay awake studying the constellation through her window, tracing the lines of the scorpion, the silver arc of the crescent moon amidst the clouds. Othman had said that he would contact her when things cooled down but she had not understood what "things" meant. She knew, however, that something was bothering him, something which had to do with her. Had she been a fool, all this time, for going to him? Was that what he was punishing her for? He must be thinking that she would go with another as easily as she had gone with him. She would see him, somehow, and tell him that it was not so. She could never love another.

But a few weeks later, news spread through town that a young man's body had been pulled ashore by fishermen's nets. A knife wound—like a palm frond—was gashed across his chest. Suicide, they said. Nobody had to tell Sara that it was Othman.

Sara's mother, though she had not known him, wept at the news, telling neighbors that he had been the brother of her daughter's best friend. What a pity, she cried, but all life is in the hands of Allah, may He preserve them from such evil. It took a full morning for Sara to absorb what had happened. By afternoon she gathered the strength to pay the required condolence visit to Jamila, someone with whom she could share her loss. But when she got there, entered the all too familiar room and met her friend's reddened eyes from across a throng of mourning women, Jamila got up and walked out, refusing to see her.

What had she done, Sara wondered, to deserve this? Hadn't it been Othman who had wanted her? He knew the penalty of their act. Could it be that he had never intended to marry her? Had discarded her and taken his own life rather than face marriage or execution?

Sara could think only of how to take her own life. She could stab herself, as he had done, wander into the desert until she dropped from heat and thirst or was mangled by hyenas, or she could drown herself—she had heard of other women doing this, the black *abaya* found first, floating like a large blackbird in the sea, still clinging to the victim's arms. But each time she resolved to go through with it the hateful will to live stirred within her.

Finally, having no one else, Sara told her mother. She had anticipated this moment for days but had not expected her mother to react so violently by slapping her, beating her and pulling her hair, as though to mar her daughter's face and body.

"Why couldn't you have been ugly? Whore! Better that than this shame! Why? Merciful Allah, why?"

"He said he would marry me," Sara whispered.

"Marry you? After *what?* You should have died before letting him..."

"What am I to do?" Sara sobbed. He had ruined her.

"How do I know what you should do? Why didn't you think of that before? Do you know what your father will do to you? To both of us?"

Her father? He would kill her, drag her through the street by a noose round her neck to show people how he dealt with a shameless daughter, avenge the disgrace she brought on him and on her brothers and cousins, on her entire family.

Finally, exhausted, her mother turned away. For three days she did not speak to Sara. Then, she went to her and said:

"You will have to marry."

"Marry? How can I marry now?"

"It must be soon. What if you're pregnant?"

"I'm not...I know I'm not..."

"You can't be sure. It's a wonder you've lasted this long."

"But he'll know, mother. Any man will know. How can I risk that?"

Their gazes locked together for an instant. "I'll have to think," her mother said, suddenly nervous. "I need time to think."

In the bridal chamber, this new husband puts his hand to her shoulder and begins to stroke her. He puts his hands around her neck and unclasps the heavy necklace, placing it on the floor. When he turns back to her it is as if to say, *now is the time to do the expected.*

Sara looks at the man's face. It is rather broad with a strong nose and a full mouth. A face like any other, not unpleasant. Nothing in it to love or hate or even to fear. When he pushes on her shoulders she acquiesces, lying down. Again, a memory lights up within her—the warm weight of another body on hers, demanding.

"You are not frightened?" the bridegroom asks, kissing her neck.

"I am," she answers, quickly, remembering her mother's warning, but the man does not seem to notice that she lies. He kisses her jaw, her ears. He touches her hair. He moves closer and she feels his legs through their clothing, her skin hardening.

She shivers, wanting to be done with it, wondering why he does not simply thrust himself into her and then leave her alone. Men know it is agony for a girl the first time and a good husband would not impose himself on his bride too long.

She hears Othman whispering to her, describing her own beauty to her, and she can almost see him coming toward her now, eager. It is *him* she wants to show, not this man, what a joy she can be.

But this man will not leave her alone. His face hovers on her neck, nuzzling her above her sparkling gown. His lips drift further down her breast to her stomach, then he brings his head back up to hers and covers her mouth in a kiss. His tongue enters her mouth and she is so surprised that she spits, bringing her hands to his chest and pushing him back, angrily.

He seems fascinated by her anger. He kisses her again and when she begins to fight him, he thrusts his knee between her legs. She begins to yell, calling for her mother and father but this only draws a smile from him. The more she screams the more he seems to relish her, coaxing her softly as he would a wild horse.

When he breaks into her, she bites his hand in pain, feeling something trickling down her legs. All at once, the thought of the white sheet stained red relaxes her and she is quiet. He draws back sharply, rising, staring at the blood that speckles the sheet and penetrates his own robe. Then he bends and tugs at the sheet.

"They're waiting," he says, and Sara thinks he smiles at her, gratified.

She gets up and smoothes down her gowns as he removes the sheet, takes it to the door and thrusts it out into the hall. She hears the whispers outside the door and knows that his sisters have retrieved it to display over the walls of their courtyard. The entire town will share in their pride tonight.

The man lies back down on the bed and, turning away, tells Sara to sleep. She understands that he means to give her privacy. His consideration means that he is a good man and will be a good husband. She climbs into bed beside him, no longer afraid, imagining that the face buried in the pillow beside her is Othman's, that the body stretched alongside her is Othman's. When he wakes up she will show him that only he can satisfy her and that she will never leave him. Maybe then he will love her.

Only a mother, she knows now, truly loves. Her mother, who had given her life, had given it to her again tonight. Those clever fingers that wove the beautiful rugs and mats in their home, that had stitched the dainty designs on the wedding gown, had perfected Sara's wedding night.

Just this afternoon, she and Sara had snared the bird—a small sand-colored sparrow—and Sara had watched her mother slit its throat and drain its blood into a small, yellow sac of sheep's gut. This she then sewed shut, just loose enough to break open at the right time, and tucked into her daughter where the bridegroom would enter. It was, perhaps, her greatest gesture of love, and it had worked.

Sara gets out of bed and reopens the window. Outside, the voices of the women reach out to fill the town:

> *Walk with me, walk,*
> *lead me over the flowers,*
> *on the wings of my happiness,*
> *lead me to my beloved,*
> *walk with me, walk.*

Why do you celebrate? she whispers, hating the old crones, despising their songs. She wipes her eyes, the tears and *kohl* staining her knuckles black. She wants to raise her own voice above theirs, above the highest wind-tower and minaret, above the grunts of the sleeping man on the bed. But instead she whispers to them, pityingly, "What do you know of love?"

KUWAIT 1956

I was six years old and sitting beside my mother in an airplane, searching out the window for the giant sandbox my father had promised me. We were flying to the Arabian Gulf from New York, after an hour's transit in Cairo. To make the move away from our green suburban neighborhood and my friends in New York more tolerable, my father promised me the biggest sandbox I had ever seen. I looked for it, scanning the endless beige ridges thousands of feet below the plane, hoping to sight the little wooden-framed sandbox like the one in my school back in White Plains.

Kuwait. I said the strange word over to myself, just as my father taught me. Kuwait was the name of our new home.

Again, I felt the pulling at my scalp. I whipped around but was not quick enough to catch it. I looked up at my mother, but she only smiled at me benevolently, above it all. I took another quick glance behind me through the crack between our seats, the same crack that the thing passed through to grab my hair.

The thing turned out to be a hand, although at first it seemed like a claw the way the thin fingertips were tinted orange and the brown skin was wrinkled and dry. Behind me, in a previously empty seat, sat midnight. Black-rimmed eyes were surrounded by a black, satiny mask, covered by a gold-flecked black veil. A black cloak held securely at the chin covered the hair and body.

"Is it Zorro?" I asked my mother.

Twice, so far, the fancy Zorro reached between my mother's seat and mine and pulled at my hair. Twice, my mother whispered to me not to worry, that it was only because my hair was red, and the woman probably never saw red hair before, that she wanted to check to see if it was real.

My mother was American, with hair even redder than mine and eyes that were a watery blue. My Arab father had rich, brown eyes and black hair. I looked like my mother but my eyes were green. For a long time, because of my mother's blue eyes and my father's brown ones, I assumed that blue and brown made green.

"Give her a jelly bean," my mother said, nodding to the paper bag of candy in my lap that we bought in New York just before boarding.

I looked at my mother, despairing at the calm she could muster in any situation. I did not want to give up my jelly beans, certainly not to the night rider behind me.

"Give her one, Isabelle," my mother insisted.

Reluctantly, I turned around and pushed the bag part of the way through our seats. I saw, through the woman's veil, her eyes darting from my face to the bag and back. As I waited, her orange fingers emerged from within the silken, black folds. She reached into the bag and retrieved a red jelly bean.

I turned away, glad to have that over, hoping that would keep her occupied while I resumed my search from the window for the long-awaited sandbox.

The desert was hotter than anyone could imagine. The first few days were an endless sandstorm, tiny needles flaying my arms and face and enveloping the entire landscape in a beige cloud. When the air settled, the August sun scorched whatever grass and trees were spared by the storm. I believed it when several British and American women, the expatriate wives of employees of the oil company my father now worked for, told my mother that the concrete got hot enough to fry an egg.

It fried the soles of my feet when I stepped outside the front door to contemplate the endless dunes, the flat, disappointing sandbox that my father promised. I never quite forgave him for tricking me, nor had I forgiven my mother for going along with his joke and for smiling when my father confessed that this was it—the desert was the sandbox. It was as though it had not occurred to her that what I really wanted was a simple wooden sandbox with just enough sand for making pies and tunnels. The desert was more sand than I could fathom. What would I do with it all? Where would I begin?

There were no English schools in the desert except for a small correspondence school run for the children of expatriate employees. My mother, with characteristic bravado, enrolled me not only in that school but also in the Arab girls' public school in *Shuaiba*, a fishing village three miles up the coast, so that I might learn Arabic and have the benefit of a real school.

On my first day there, in the dilapidated school, a tall girl with a black ponytail tied with white elastic and protruding breasts under her green-checked uniform, paraded me about, showing me off to her friends, to the teachers, to the two black cleaning women in gauzy pantaloons and white veils. All the while, she held my hand and smiled at me, feeding me cookies from a box of glazed animal crackers.

"I won't go there any more. It's ugly and they speak only Arabic," I grumbled to my mother when I got home, half sick from the heat.

"Well, you'd better learn quickly or you're going to feel stupid," my mother said, standing at the stove frying chicken.

I stared at her back, shocked that she would actually contemplate sending me back to that frightening place where there were only a handful of fair-skinned girls, and where I was the only redhead.

Despite my balking, I returned to the Arabic school the next day and the next. After the third week, we moved from the dilapidated, gypsum structure with crumbling wind towers to a brand new pink and turquoise cement building with latticed balconies that over-looked the sea. It was the most beautiful building I had ever seen. Aqua, yellow, azure, mauve, and yellow again at the sandbars were the colors of the Gulf just beyond the playground. The brilliance of the water as it echoed the harsh sun was enough to sear the eyes. In this new, and certainly more attractive, setting I began to adjust.

Sea gulls circled above the playground in the mornings before the bell rang as groups of girls walked arm-in-arm, memorizing the day's lessons or playing hopscotch in the sand, hopping and flick-ing a flat rock from square to square with their toes. I usually joined in a game of Wolf and Mother where a train of girls, led by a mother sang, "I am the Mother who will protect you," to the opposing train led by the wolf who retorted, "I am the Wolf who will eat you," the object being for the wolves to grab as many persons as they could from the mother's train who then turned into wolves themselves.

We would gaze over the low school wall at the waves slapping the shore, the translucent water turning into a murky froth of shells, sand, and bubbles as it broke. Girls were not allowed in the water and did not swim. Only the boys from the school next door were permitted to strip down to their black trunks and hurl themselves, oblivious, into the waves as the girls shouted in fear and envy.

At lunch time we sat at long tables as Omar, the broad-bellied cook, ladled lentil soup into our mugs. One of the cleaning women, a heavy silver ring in her nose below her velvet eyes, passed out hard-boiled eggs and cheese sandwiches.

It was at lunch that I first noticed Hala S. I remembered her from class, a girl with milk-white skin and black, marble eyes. Hala: a moon's halo. I was intimidated from the start by the girl who smirked rather than smiled, by her flashing eyes and black, unruly pigtails, by her taunting pink lips.

She stared at me. "I am Lebanese," she said fearlessly, announc-ing that she too was different, not like the others, at the same time pushing away the plate with the egg and sandwich.

Weeks passed and the new school routine took over. When the bell rang, we lined up two-by-two, according to class, to do arm exercises and jumping-jacks, sing the national anthem, and lower our heads to recite the Muslim *fatiha.* Afterwards came inspection time. Each girl would stand in her crisply-pressed uniform and starched hair ribbon—the work of Shuaiba's pressing shop, since most of Shuaiba's modest houses had few electrical appliances—then pull out a folded handkerchief to hold in her orange, hennaed hands as a sort of backdrop to display clean, short nails.

If it was a Monday, hair was checked for lice. Using two pencils so as not to soil their hands, the teachers poked through each girl's scented, oiled hair in search of the offending parasites. The obviously well-scrubbed girls, such as Hala and myself, were often passed by. Others were doubly-scrutinized and sometimes led away, first for a haircut, then to sit, sobbing, in a corner of the bathroom while their hair was fumigated with DDT and wrapped in nets.

School ended at one o'clock, ten minutes before the boys' school next door so that the girls could get home without mingling with the boys. Girls who were seen dawdling in the road were sharply reprimanded by the teachers the next morning. I was the only one allowed to remain at the gate after school because I waited for our driver, who came in a white car to take me back to our compound.

Sometimes, though, the driver was late, and I was still standing at the gate when the boys were let out. With their heavy satchels and gray uniform jackets, their hair shaved to a bristle, they looked like small soldiers. They stared at me as they passed, at my red hair, my freckles and green eyes. They would smile, baring crooked yellowed teeth, calling out, "*Quitta!* Cat! Meow!"

From Shuaiba, I was driven straight to the compound's English school for another two hours of work with the expatriate children. We were fifteen girls and boys, ranging from first to seventh graders, in a single room of a building originally built as a commissary. We worked individually, under the guidance of an English woman named Mrs. Potter, who sent off our monthly exams to be graded

157

by an assigned but faceless teacher in London or Baltimore, depending on whether one was following the British or the American curriculum.

I usually arrived at the English school in time for the midday break and a game of Farmer in the Dell or Red Rover. When we were a little older, it was often a heady game of Spin the Bottle. Of course, I never mentioned to the girls in Shuaiba that I participated in something as unthinkable and vile as kissing some strange boy.

Those first few weeks and months in the desert and in my new school were marked by two lingering images. The first was our garden clothesline forever strung with brown underwear—men's, ladies', and children's white shirts and panties tinted the brown of the brackish water forced out of the shriveled earth. All the houses in the compound looked much the same from the backyards! The other image was the glistening, honey color of the locusts that besieged us that September.

To those living in an expatriate compound intent on bringing some semblance of Western culture into the inhospitable desert, the locusts came as a sudden, unwelcome sight. My mother and I dashed about the patio clanging kitchen pans to scatter the horde that descended hungrily on our new trees and on the patches of soil that my mother was determined to turn into flower beds. Still, by the end of the day, the zinnias were gone, and the oleander and frangipani leaves were whittled to stubs.

The Kuwaities, however, like other desert peoples who had faced this scourge countless times before, dealt with the locusts in a different manner. In school the following day, these dreaded pests were cause for a manic celebration. Fried up crisp and golden, they were brought from home in jars or oily paper bags for the mid-day snack. With mouth-watering abandon, girls dangled the delicacies into their mouths, gingerly crunching them down. I shrank from an invitation to taste and was nauseated the next few weeks as school seemed to take on the locusts' dripping, amber hue as they were sneaked out of desks to be shared between classes, just as the teacher's heels could be heard rounding the corner.

Hala lived in Shuaiba, near our school. One day, in the fourth grade, I told my mother not to send the driver for me after school because Hala had invited me to go home with her. I had never visited Hala at home but I knew where she lived because my driver had given her a lift after school on several occasions. The best part about going to visit her was that I would walk home with her and the other girls.

We left school together that day and headed down the empty dirt road toward the marketplace. The boys' school next door was not dismissed yet so there was still a lulling, intact quiet pervading the afternoon. I was jubilant and yet ambivalent at the freedom to walk in the streets, as though I suddenly had been let out of prison with no idea where to go or what to do. We walked with the other girls past the small shops, past the steaming pressing shop where Indian men in *dhoties* and what looked like pajama pants stood pressing the long cotton men's *thobs* and girls' and boys' uniforms, past old men squatting, asleep in shady alleyways. From one ornately carved wooden door, left slightly ajar, came faint kitchen sounds and the smell of hot bread and saffron.

We finally came to a light blue, wooden door that Hala kicked open. She led me down a dark corridor to a sunny courtyard surrounded by rooms. Several stools and a table stood against one wall of the patio and in each corner was a large rusting tin, the sort used to store olives in, blooming now with petunias and jasmine.

Water streamed onto the patio from inside the house where swishing noises accompanied the shrill singing of a woman on a radio. All at once, a torrent of dusty water landed in a puddle at our feet.

"Mama!" Hala shouted.

A woman, her cotton house dress hoisted above her knees, emerged from a door and stood looking at us, broom in hand, a scarf wound tightly about her head.

"So, you've brought her," she said, looking pleased.

"Mama, we're hungry," Hala said, flinging her satchel into a corner of the patio.

Her mother continued to stare at me, smiling, wiping her brow with the back of her plump hand.

"You must feed her," she said.

"Sit down," Hala said, pulling out a stool for me.

Minutes later, she came out of the kitchen holding two bowls of rice and a stew of green beans and tomatoes. She gave me a spoon and we sat in the warm courtyard and devoured the meal, I savoring the beans' greenness, the onions and cinnamon, the tomatoes as sweet and ripe as Hala's mother.

Hala had two brothers. Sameer, two years older than we, arrived home soon afterwards from the boys' school. Tall and brutish, Sameer looked nothing like Hala or her mother. Bilal, the baby, however, did have the white skin and dark, dancing eyes of his mother. Being an only child, I was fascinated by Bilal. I stood him up and coaxed him to walk on his curved, unsteady feet. That made him squeal with laughter and soon Hala was annoyed that all I wanted to do was play with her brother.

Later that afternoon, Hala's father came home. He was short, with a heavy belly and a mustache. He brought a guest with him and Hala was sent to the kitchen to make coffee. I watched, impressed, as she boiled the dark powder in the small pot, the froth bubbling away, then poured the coffee into tiny cups on a tray. At home I was not considered old enough to be of much help around the kitchen.

Hala's mother appeared in the kitchen to take the tray to the men in the next room. Her eyes were freshly painted with kohl and green eye shadow, her lips rouged, her full bosom puffing out of a low-cut, shiny dress that whistled when she moved. Her hair, earlier hidden under the scarf, now bounced about her face in brown curls and she smelled like her pungent garden, like jasmine.

Sometime later, as Hala and I sat out in the courtyard playing cards, Hala's mother entered an inner room of the house alone with the guest. He was much taller than she. She had to bend back just to smile up at him, opening her mouth enough for her gold tooth to flicker as the man slipped something into her hand.

At the end of the fifth grade, two things happened that awakened me to a reality that I could not quite believe in. First, I overheard my father telling my mother that there had been a terrible accident, that Hala's house had caught fire and the baby died. After my initial numbness, I started to scream. Bilal!

The fire was put out by the time we arrived at Hala's house, but the walls were streaked with black as though someone had attacked them with a piece of charcoal. I heard Hala's mother's screams from another room, a terrible howling. Hala, herself, seemed to be more interested in the chocolate cake my mother brought than anything else, stuffing chunks of it into her mouth and then vomiting it up as she suddenly remembered what happened. I stood uncomfortably, trying to keep out of the way of the men carrying things in and out as though the family were simply moving, trying not to hear the muffled voices of Hala's mother and father in the next room.

Hala did not go to school for almost a week during which I had nightmares of riding my horse, *Hidiya*, and coming across the stiff, charred remains of Bilal in the sand. I could not forget Bilal's chubby face and his fat, squat legs, his ringing laughter.

The next time I saw Hala's mother was at the end of term during our yearly school play. She sat among the other mothers cloaked in traditional black *abayas*, herself in a black dress of mourning, her face wan without her usual make-up. She sat through the play as if by force, her face blank despite Hala's exceptional theatrics, not once smiling her beautiful, glinting smile.

Then, on the last day of school, we had the second shock to take with us through the summer. Aisha Rashid, a Kuwaiti girl who surpassed both Hala and myself in our studies and thus usurped the coveted position of first place in the fifth grade, left school to

161

be married. It was whispered that the groom was old and already had another wife. That absorbed the older girls and the teachers, clouding the usual euphoria of report cards and early dismissal. The absence of the studious, gentle Aisha only served to confirm the awful truth.

Aisha Rashid's father was a wiry pearl diver and except for her long braids and docile eyes, Aisha could pass for a boy herself, with her lean body and brown-speckled teeth. Although physically not inspiring, Aisha was like the mother of us all in the fifth grade, almost ancient in her wisdom and kindness. It was unthinkable that her father would give her away in marriage to an old man when she was smarter and better than any of us. I was horrified when I pictured her toiling under the burden of several children and a husband, suddenly realizing how unimportant all her hard schoolwork was and how selfish I had been to compete with her.

Yet Aisha Rashid's marriage had been only the beginning. As though drawn by some mysterious call, girls faded from our midst one by one over the next two years to get married or to help their mothers with work at home. By the seventh grade, of the original thirty, our class was down to ten.

For a long time afterwards, the memory of Bilal's death and Aisha's leaving were intertwined, as though they were the same— marriage and death.

At the end of the ninth grade, we had to take state examinations to enter high school. There was, also, of course, another exam to graduate from high school. Both tests were held for everyone in a central location, on a specific day.

There were only seven of us girls from the Shuaiba school going on to the new high school in *Fahahil.* Three were Kuwaiti, two were Egyptians, then Hala and myself. We were transported by bus for an hour along a tar road that ran like an endless spool of black thread toward the main city.

The sun beat down on the tar, sending waves of heat across the road before us, as though the bus was driving through water. It was easy to half close my eyes and imagine that the bus was traversing the sea, the end of which was the distant horizon where the waves really did look blue. All around us the sand was like the ocean floor—pure, yellow, enveloping infinity.

We were quiet in the hot, un-airconditioned bus. Some girls reviewed their textbooks, Hala dozed against the half-opened glass window as the wind beat against her face, and I stared out at the scattered villas that appeared, signaling the beginning of the city limits.

The habitual desert drabness and years of black, goat-hair tents and gypsum villages must have inspired the builders of this new place to use the brightest, most iridescent colors possible. Unlike the pale pastels of the prefabricated houses of our compound— softly muted colors intended, no doubt, to blend into the surroundings—the new Arab houses of the city shouted out to be noticed. Like our pink and blue school, these colorful, multi-floored structures were intended to inspire in their own vivid, distinct fashion. A green wall here, a yellow there, a pink veranda, a blue door, all wrapped into one confectionery delight. There were flat roofs and sloping roofs, a speckled tile facade on one side of a house, surrealist dots and squares on another, like siblings in a large family, each building demanding attention, each trying to outdo the other. Ever since I could remember, I wanted to live in one of those delicious houses.

As Hala and I began our first year in high school, we became acutely aware of ourselves as young women. Our high school was in Fahahil, a town built around an oil refinery but better-known to us as the place where everyone did the weekly grocery shopping at the covered food market. The endless rows of food stalls smelling of fruit, spices and fish were usually jammed with black-*abayad*, slippered women and men in *thobs* as well as an assortment of Europeans and Americans lugging heavy baskets full of groceries.

The girls in the new high school came not only from Fahahil and Shuaiba but from other villages in the vicinity and the school

had a fleet of six buses. Hala now rode a bus to school from
Shuaiba while I still came by car. I would have liked to go by bus
but I could not, since we lived in the compound, but Hala hated
the bus and its cranky, old driver.

"Why is it that I have to end up with an old man for a driver
when I could have had him?" she asked once, indignant.

I followed her glance to the young man in blue jeans and red T-
shirt. He was slim and muscular, handsome, with a mustache growing down the sides of his mouth. We both watched as he crouched
to fix something on the bus's front tire, the way the muscles in his
arms flexed as he worked, hardening and quivering with effort. All
at once, he stood, frowned, and kicked the tire with his foot. Hala
giggled sharply and the man turned to us, briefly, before climbing
onto the bus.

The next day in class, during the history lesson, Hala leaned
toward me and whispered, "He wants to see me."

"Who?"

"The bus driver."

"How do you know?"

"I saw him looking at me this morning when he was parking the
bus. He has *eyes.*"

I copied a few notes from the blackboard because the teacher
was looking at us.

"He's married," Hala whispered. "He has a baby, too," she added
jabbing me in the ribs, as though a child was sure proof of his
virility.

The teacher raised her voice in a stern falsetto. "Hala and Isabelle,
move apart."

Hala stared at the teacher a moment longer than necessary,
before she gathered up her books, bending toward me as she did
to reveal a folded piece of paper stuck between her breasts at her
unbuttoned uniform collar.

"Take it and wait for me after school," she whispered, then
trudged to the back of the room and flopped down noisily at an
empty desk.

164

While the teacher resumed charting the course of the Islamic conquests under Tariq bin Ziyad, I unfolded Hala's note. Scribbled hastily were three words: "Thursday at seven."

Later, as we came out of the high school gate, the young bus driver was leaning against the bus, arms folded, as though waiting for us. This time, instead of scowling, he looked Hala in the eye and winked.

"That means he wants to see us," Hala said.

"What do you mean?"

"Did you read the note?"

"You wrote 'Thursday at seven'."

"*He* wrote it. A girl from his bus passed it to me. He wants to meet me here before school on Thursday morning, when the drivers come to get the buses."

I knew the man had to be foolish to write such a note. If Hala reported him, he would be fired immediately, perhaps even jailed.

"I'm going to do it, Isabelle. Will you join me?"

"Of course not," I said.

"I just want to see what he wants."

"We know what he wants, Hala."

"What?" she goaded me.

"I guess he wants to kiss you or something."

"Yes," she said, "he probably wants to kiss me."

"But he's married."

"So?"

"You don't care?" I thought of Hala's mother, and of the men who visited her.

She shrugged, puckering her lips slightly. "I feel like being kissed. So what if he is married. If he doesn't care, why should I?"

Her hedonism, her eagerness to be kissed, fascinated me.

"Have you ever kissed anyone, Hala? Any man?"

"Only my father—and my brother. But that's different."

Kissing and sex were still mysterious to me and Hala's desire to be kissed seemed like an attempt at being adult.

"You want to know what it's like, don't you?" Hala asked, her eyes flashing. "Well, now we'll know."

Perhaps it was the lure of the dangerous—defying parents and the school's tyrannical teachers—rather than the actual kiss that intrigued her. Hala's pouting lips did not fool me as easily as she thought; I did not believe she hungered for this man's lips, but rather for knowledge. That's why I agreed to help her.

The only problem was how to get to school for the seven o'clock rendezvous, when her bus and my car did not get there until eight. It was too far for her to walk from Shuaiba, where she lived. If I asked my driver to pick us both up that early, my parents would be suspicious.

As usual, Hala found a solution. She suggested we tell our parents that we would be spending the night at a friend's house, to study for an exam, and actually stay overnight at school.

"Sleep here?" I said.

"Why not? We'll sleep in the infirmary or in the janitor's quarters."

"How will we get in? Aren't those rooms locked every afternoon?"

"We'll hide inside and they can lock us in."

"How will we get out? They don't reopen before seven."

I pointed out that the kiss had to take place some time between 6:45 when the bus drivers arrived and 7:15 when they started off on their routes.

Hala nodded. "There's only one thing to do. We'll sleep on the bus."

I began to protest, seeing the bus driver's kiss as nothing more than a silly experiment.

"Isabelle," Hala said, taking a breath, as though preparing me for a great blow. "We must do the best with what we've got. If I am beautiful, then I am meant to be admired and kissed by men. It's my destiny. I'm not saying that everyone should; it might even be wrong for some. Besides," she added, "my mother says that in love there is no shame."

166

In my dream on the bus that night, an endless, humid night that seemed to linger on, minute by minute, just to spite us, to punish us for the deception, I heard Hala's mother laugh deeply, as she used to before Bilal's death.

When I opened my eyes, Hala was already awake and staring into the bus's rearview mirror as she thrashed a comb through her short black hair. My watch showed 6:15. The sky glowed with the pink of dawn but the sun was already bright, the heat seeping in at us through cracks in the bus window. I watched Hala a moment from the back row of seats where I had stretched out, finally having fallen asleep on the sticky vinyl, wishing I were actually at Basma's house where I told my parents I would be.

"It's time," I said, patting the wrinkles of my bunched green-check summer uniform, wondering how to explain my disheveled appearance at school. Then I heard the crunching of tires across the sandy school parking lot.

Hala looked away from the mirror, her lower lip dropping.

"Oh, God," I said, recognizing in the small car below the young man's red T-shirt. "What are we going to do?"

"Is he alone?" Hala whispered.

"Did you expect his wife and baby?" I was suddenly furious for having gone along with the plan.

"Don't worry. You stay on the bus. I'll be back." She glanced at her face in the mirror, then slid open the bus door and hopped down the steps.

I watched, horrified, as she disappeared, as though once the sand enveloped her she would be gone forever, or else regurgitated back as something unrecognizable.

I went to the front of the bus and looked out. No one was in sight. I jumped down the steps, just missing a wriggling black snake with a yellow neck. I backed away, watching it slither under the bus, its skin glittering like diamond chips. Then I remembered something the girls often said at school—that black snakes with yellow collars brought good luck.

167

I walked to the back end of the bus and peered around it. Then I went from bus to bus. Hala was nowhere.

The bus driver's small, empty car was parked against the school wall, and the blue school gate was open. I assumed that Hala and the driver were inside. I hesitated, then headed for the gate, afraid of what I might see and yet determined to protect Hala if she needed me.

Inside the gate, again, there was no one. The school had a docile, tranquil appearance in the absence of the stern authority of the teachers who were probably still upstairs in their quarters. It could have been a museum or a park with its vast, sandy grounds, scattered water fountains, and trellised corridors. I enjoyed the fantasy of a park, which dissipated my fear of being found by one of the teachers.

Then someone grabbed me. I opened my eyes. It was the bus driver, his hand clamped over my burning wrist.

I smelled sweat, an acrid, manly smell combined with a sweet scent of palm oil from his hair. I stared at him, at his unflinching dark eyes, the mustache.

"What are you doing here?" he hissed.

I opened my mouth to cry out, then stopped.

"Who are you?" he asked, relaxing his grip a bit.

"I came with Hala."

"Hala?"

"Yes."

"Hala?" he asked again.

"Hala. You were here to meet her."

The bus driver dropped my wrist. I stood and stared at him because my legs would not move. They were fixed in the sand as though I were buried—buried alive like the infants long ago—afraid to move, also afraid of being touched again by this stranger.

He stared at me without a word, as though trying to make up his mind what to think of me, of my unwashed face, my loose ponytail, my pale eyes and freckles, which he seemed to be counting one by one.

He took a step toward me, and I stood, waiting for whatever would happen, watching him lower his head slowly, hesitantly, until his breath scarred my cheek and his warm mouth touched mine. I did not move away or make a sound when he tugged at my lips, only waited for him to finish, hearing Hala say, "In love there is no shame."

I did pull back finally, remembering my own notion that sex was vaguely violent and unpleasant. I pushed the bus driver away and, pressing my skirt pocket against my thighs to keep in the pens and erasers that jingled as I ran, I fled out the school gate.

Although the driver made no attempt to restrain me, I felt that he had enjoyed it. Somehow, in the end, that seemed important.

Hala stood at the bus door looking visibly shaken. Her eyes narrowed when she saw me running toward her.

"Where have you been," she demanded.

"Looking for you," I said, feeling that Hala could read every line on my face, every pore, and knew that I was lying to her.

Instead of reprimanding me, though, she lowered her eyes and the familiar smirk appeared.

"I got scared and hid in the watchman's room," she said.

"You what? What about the driver?" I shouted.

"I don't know. I didn't see him."

"But we waited all night. You mean we did this all for nothing?"

"What's wrong with you, Isabelle? This had nothing to do with you," Hala said, impatiently.

"Nothing to do with me? You wanted me to be with you. You asked me to. We went through all this for nothing!"

"Not for nothing," she said. "It just wasn't the right time. Someday you'll know what I mean."

"You talk too much, Hala," I said, tears suddenly flooding my eyes. The night's sleeplessness, the fear, the guilt of lying to our parents, and finally my first kiss—totally unplanned—was too much for me. I felt like a small lost child and wanted to go home to my room, my horse, to rush into my mother's familiar arms.

Instead, it was Hala who embraced me, looking frightened at my hysterical outburst.

Patting my back, she crooned, "Don't cry, Isabelle. Someday you'll understand. There is no shame in love, really there isn't. Someday you'll understand."

HALA

One summer we arrived in Kuwait, a place so hot and vast, yet seemingly invisible to the rest of humanity.

The "we" who arrived from Zahle, our lush village in Lebanon, were myself, my mother, father, older brother, and my barrel of a grandmother who always smelled—no matter how frequently she washed—of sweet, rotting pears.

Only weeks before, this fleshy, wrinkled old woman whose white hair crawled below her back in a curved braid, this woman who could cajole me into her arms with a croon or terrorize me with a single pout, was the woman I believed to be my own mother. I even called her "Mama."

She was the woman who had appeared before me ever since I could remember, the one whose presence filled my every waking hour and my turbulent dreams, who fed me with her fingers bread and oregano when there was nothing in the house to eat, bathed me in the metal tub of water in which she had just washed our clothes because water was scarce, rubbed my body with oil to make my bones strong. She was fearless—once catching a mouse with her bare hand as it scurried up a curtain. I wanted to be just like her—strong, harsh, and brave.

Then, one day, Aida, the pretty young woman I thought of as my

171

cousin, came to the house. She had waves of chestnut hair and skin as white as the frothy cream my grandmother skimmed off the top of my boiled milk each morning. I liked the way she smelled, deep, aromatic, and mysterious. After giving me her usual loving pinch and peck on my cheek, she told my grandmother to start packing because we were all leaving Zahle.

Zahle. White stone houses with red roofs and flowers sprouting from every window and balcony, carts stacked with peaches and green apples the size of melons, terraced orchards across the valley, crisp morning air that slapped our faces when we opened the windows. How could we leave Zahle?

Of course my grandmother argued with Aida. As a rule, she resisted anyone's telling her what to do. I stood on a stool in the kitchen listening to the women and gazing through the purple vine outside the window at a man who leaned against our garden wall. He wore a crisp suit and smoked a cigarette, and I was sure that I recognized him as the brother of crazy Issa, the village dimwit.

That night, my grandmother rocked me to sleep against her breast, telling me that we had to leave our home to go with Aida. She explained that it was Aida, not she, who was my mother. The man who waited outside was Aida's husband, the man who should have been my father, but was not.

She told me the truth that night—that I was not the child of my mother's husband even though I should have been since they were married long before I was born and even had a son, Sameer, who was my older brother. My grandmother was neither delicate nor indulgent and did not spare me the detail that I was Aida's bastard daughter. Yet I held her no grudge for this. Although her methods of showing it were occasionally extreme, she was utterly devoted to me, and she made sure that I knew it.

So, I was a bastard. This was shocking, yet, in a strange way, exciting news. I was different, special in an odd way. Not that I comprehended the extent of this shame or its further implications. At six, I only knew that something drastic had changed my life.

Gone was the cozy polarity between me and the old woman. Instead, an entirely new galaxy appeared on the horizon consisting of a mother, a father/stepfather, and an older brother—the last I did not know nor want to know. It was thrust upon me like a piece of broken glass, this new family, as though I was supposed to absorb it into myself, just like that.

The reason for this sudden revelation, my grandmother explained, was that my new father/stepfather was moving us away from Lebanon to another country where he would make enough money for us to live like kings.

The fact that my grandmother was being hauled off along with me was the only, albeit small, consolation in the face of this terrifying news.

Our first days in Kuwait, in the dusty, damp city, were so hot that only my father ventured outside. I smelled the wetness in the air, smelled the heat that made me want to tear off my clothes simply in order to breath. Having lived only in the cool of mountains, none of us had confronted humidity before.

I was sick and drowsy those first few days, my discomfort compounded by my worrying that I was not presenting myself in a favorable light to my new family. We were staying in the crowded apartment of relatives who had agreed to put up my father before they knew that he was bringing along a wife, two children, and a mother-in-law. Unfortunately, Aida quickly grew grumpy when she realized that the full rewards of our uprooting were not going to materialize as quickly as she had imagined. For the time being, squeezed into a bedroom with her husband, son, mother, and sick daughter, she had to help out with the cleaning, cooking, and caring for the several small children of our hosts. I overheard her say more than once that she had not given up her own daughter all these years to run after someone else's brat, while my father suffered the hundred-degree heat to find a job.

The few times I ventured out of the apartment building with my grandmother in late afternoons did not allay my fears. Construction was everywhere. Cinder blocks were piled carelessly as though a child had stacked them, rickety planks of wood bridged holes and tunnels that were being dug by dark men in ragged turbans and red and purple smocks the colors of the distant sunset. There was a disheveled, transient look about the place that suggested that it might all be gone tomorrow, buried beneath the deep sand.

I recognized only a few familiar words of Arabic around us while the rest was gibberish: the Urdu, Hindi, Farsi, Swahili used by the workers—Pakistanis, Indians, Baluchis, Somalis—who, like us, I would later learn, had come in search of a new life.

The Arab men of Kuwait strode about in long, white *dishdashas* and sheer, white headdresses which were held in place by a black cord or else folded back as one would a towel over wet hair. Women, enveloped in silky, billowy, black *abayas* seemed to glide down the streets as though on silent wheels.

Finally, we got lucky. By the end of the third week my father found a job as a welder for an oil company and with it came a small house several miles from the refinery in a village by the sea. With our belongings strapped on top of a taxi, we rode out of the baking city along a lone black road into mile upon mile of boundless desert. The ride seemed interminable. We might have driven all the way back to Lebanon! When it seemed that we could drive no further, that we would be marooned and swallowed up by the blank, soft sand, I saw it. We all saw it—a thin, blue ribbon across the horizon in the distance just above the car's hood.

I stretched up to glimpse better what everyone else seemed so excited about. It was barely discernible from the cloudless sky—yet it was a darker, richer blue than the sky, quickly growing into another vast space. It was water. We had reached the village by the sea. We had reached our new home—*Shuaiba.*

We settled in quickly. Our small house was surrounded by a maze of narrow lanes with high, mud walls that were punctured by occasional doors. Some of these doors were of dark wood and were so short that it seemed they had been made expressly for children. Other doors were large and carved in minute detail with zigzags, arabesques, and even flowers. Ours was a plain door of blue-painted wood that seemed to relieve the intense heat that reigned throughout, as though one had come upon a dazzling lake.

Several days later, I ventured into the road to face whatever might be of interest. There were other girls in the alley—slender, copper-skinned, with eyes as wide and dark as plums. A few, about my age, would suddenly pop out of one of the doors in the walls and run to the market or carry a baby about for a walk. Some of the girls wore the blowsy, black sheets of the women over their long dresses, often with long, embroidered white pants underneath. Some even came up and spoke to me in their strange dialect, but most of them simply stared.

Soon, though, word must have spread that there was a new girl about, for entire bunches of girls began to stroll into our alley where I spent a lot of time in front of our door to make myself available for questions such as where did I come from, and what was a mountain, and was there really such a thing as snow? In time, we became friends and I spent the last weeks of summer mostly in the road outside our blue door playing hopscotch and tag.

Among the Shuaiba girls I now set a standard. They began to think me sophisticated with my strange accent and my knowledge of places other than their flat desert. Often the older girls would say, "Wait for Hala," if there was something of interest about to take place.

Even my new family seemed less alien, now. My grandmother seemed reconciled to relinquish control over family matters to Aida, and my step-father, in a special effort to be friendly, taught me to play backgammon and cards after supper. Were it not for Sameer, I might have soon become as happy in Shuaiba as I had been in Zahle.

It was strange having a big brother. Sometimes Sameer seemed to be cruel, screaming at me for no reason, even spitting at me if I did something that displeased him. Other times he was protective and even kind, allowing me to play with wire cars that he fashioned for himself to play with in the streets with the other boys. I mostly ignored Sameer, however, and he was just older and taller enough than I not to have to pay me too much attention. Yet, this brother, the true child of my mother and her husband, must have resented me. Aida made him buy me cookies and the pink, coconut candy I loved from the Shuaiba market since I was a girl and too young to go out in the streets. At night, when it was time to wash for bed, Aida washed my feet in the pail before Sameer's so that I always had the fresh water. Although ambivalent about him, I was not too concerned by Sameer's treatment of me, since he was equally caustic to Aida and barely acknowledged my grandmother. In fact, I soon realized that the only person who could hold Sameer's respect, if indeed his sullen silence could be called that, was his father.

Birth always brought death. That was what my grandmother said one morning although, at the time, she could not have known whose death she was predicting.

She was reading my mother's coffee cup, the two of them pausing in the morning chore of sweeping and rinsing the courtyard to each drink a small cup of orange blossom flavored coffee. With dresses tied above their knees, they sat on stools in the shade to sip while I secretly watched them from inside the house, jealous, sensing that it was a private moment for them. More and more I had begun to notice both my grandmother and Aida enjoying the renewed comradeship between them which had been lacking over the past years due to my presence and Aida's need to separate herself from me.

They sat among the large tins of oleanders and jasmine bushes, cooling their bare feet in the water they had just sloshed onto the ground, momentarily oblivious to the morning heat. It was as hard for me to believe that my stern, ungainly grandmother had begotten the beautiful younger woman beside her as it was for me to believe that Aida had begotten me—or Sameer, for that matter. Ladies as young and glamorous as Aida were not mothers.

Except for the shared milky complexion—my grandmother's legacy and one which Aida had not outgrown—the two women seemed as different from one another as the sun from the moon, as a pomegranate from honey. While my grandmother scorched and stung in her own loving way, Aida glowed serenely, especially around me. I could tell that she was eager to make up for the lost years when we had lived apart by indulging me with kisses and sweets.

However, it was the shared moment between this other mother and daughter that I was observing the morning that my grandmother saw in Aida's cup that she was pregnant and then immediately followed that with the pronouncement that a death was imminent.

I wandered out into the courtyard.

"What do you think of that? Aida said, smiling up at me, obviously wondering whether I had overheard about her pregnancy.

"Who's going to die?" I said, ignoring her.

"Nobody's going to die. Your mother's going to have a baby," my grandmother said, clearing her throat and spitting onto the ground.

"I heard you say that a birth brings a death."

They both stood up. Aida opened her arms to me but I fled into the arms of my grandmother. Before, she would have explained to me what she meant right then and there, honestly and without reservation. With my mother present, however, the old woman was no longer as open with me. She had someone else now, someone older and more interesting, to confide in.

I nursed a pang of hatred for Aida, wishing that all of her glossy brown curls would fall out and that she would blow up so big with her new baby that she would explode and die. Deep within me, I knew that the only person around me who was old enough to die

177

was my grandmother. I refused this idea, however. It had to be somebody else. Maybe Sameer would die.

Days later, after my grandmother's prophecy of death, I did something wrong, something which involved lying or stealing or both. Perhaps I took some loose change from my new father's trouser pocket and then denied it. Whatever the childish misdeed, my grandmother was going to settle the matter her own way. For although she, for the most part, had surrendered both herself and me up to my parents to feed, clothe, and take care of, she did not believe that anyone but herself was fit to discipline me.

Sameer, at eight, was far too indulged as far as she was concerned, running off into the street with strange boys he barely knew, never around whenever she or Aida needed something from the market or from the pressing shop. She was not about to allow me to be so ruined.

Now, my grandmother had punished me for lying once before—a long time ago in Zahle. Knowing what was in store, I decided not to submit to it again.

When she came looking for me after Aida left the house to visit some neighbor, I hid behind the dining room door. Through the crack, I could see the reddened tip of the meat skewer sensing its way through the air toward me. For my grandmother's remedy for lying was to sear the tops of the knuckles of both of my hands—ten scars to ward away the ten evil jinns who had taught me to lie!

Of course that hurt, although not as much as I had led her to imagine, but I still had ten small scars on my knuckles from the last time, ten dots that blanched whiter than the rest of my skin, and I did not want ten more. I especially did not want to be humiliated before my new family, especially Sameer, who I thought would enjoy seeing me punished.

As Grandmother searched one room, I quickly sneaked into the next one, once her back was turned. Although not the stronger one, I was certainly the lighter, without her girth and faded hearing. By the time she reached the dining room, I was under the bed in Aida's room, safe and dusty against the cool tile.

She screamed my name: "Hala!"

It was such a rasping, horrible cry, that I nearly crawled out from my hiding place to deliver myself rather than hear that strange, growling noise again. But I stayed still, hoping she would give up and go away.

All at once, there was a loud thud and the clinking of metal against stone. I froze in my spot, afraid to move or look out. I knew she had fallen, for I heard the sound of the skewer dropping onto the floor. The whole house seemed to shake and ring, each sound separate, dissected in my mind. Yet, I could not move. Even though I suddenly envisioned her dying, even though I wanted one last look at her while she still lived, I lay still, paralyzed.

I waited for one more sound, a stirring to indicate that she had merely stumbled, but there was only the sound of my own breathing, the distant echo of voices in the streets mingled with the cry of noon prayers from the mosque down the road, and the dust tickling my nose.

Aida returned and found her mother sprawled on the dining room floor, eyes wide, arms rigid as the steel skewer in her hand. She began to scream to the neighbors, to God, to Sameer, for help (she repeated this over and over to us afterwards as though it would rid the image from her memory).

Finally, someone found my father. When he got home to a house full of alarmed neighbors and a draped body on his dining room floor, his only words were: "Where is Hala?"

Still under the bed, terrified by Aida's howling and too stunned to reveal myself, I waited while they searched.

I had killed her! She had crumpled in anger.

I held my breath, hoping to suffocate like my grandmother, to be put out of the confused misery of this new life. However, my grandmother had predicted only one death. Obviously, it was not mine.

It did not take long for someone to look under the bed and to coax me out, but it was my father who lifted me into his arms. Hot, dusty, and crying, I lay my aching head against his shoulder, rubbing my face against his shirt until my nose stopped itching.

"Poor one, poor little one," he kept murmuring, never minding that his white shirt was becoming gray beneath my face, as though he knew exactly what had happened.

Even Sameer tried to comfort me. He lay down on my bed and said that I could hold onto him if I wanted. Aida sent him away and let me touch her belly, instead, reminding me that we were a family, that a new child was coming.

We cried together a while, Aida for the mother she had just come to know again in a new way, I for my very life, for the future of the entire universe. For with Grandmother gone, surely nothing and no one was safe anymore.

Aida pulled me close to her and told me that I was young, that my life was just beginning. I would be starting school soon in Shuaiba and would be too busy to be sad.

I said that I was unhappy and wanted to go back to Lebanon. That is when she told me that we would never go back.

"It's because of Issa. Your father wants to forget Issa," she said. Then she sighed and wiped her hands over her face as though to protect herself from some curse. "Sometimes I think Sameer is a little like Issa. But maybe not."

Lying there, I thought of Issa, my father's older brother. Nobody in our village of Zahle had ever had the heart to come right out and say that he was crazy although they all knew it, just as they had known about his two main pastimes—weddings and funerals.

Both weddings and funerals involved a good deal of eating for those who took part in the processions—even when they were dismal—and Uncle Issa would string along at the end of the impassioned crowd making its way through the village, in eager anticipation of this.

It was not that Issa was ill fed at home. His wife, despite her quick temper, had spent most of her day preparing elaborate meals for her three children and stout husband. However, my uncle's mind had gone limp to the point that he seemed to want immediate gratification of whatever need presented itself to him at the moment. If he was hungry and he happened by a crowd, he would lumber along foolishly, patiently, knowing that the end result was bound to be a feast.

Frequenting the village streets more than his home, Issa would be lost for days before being found in the most unpredictable spots—slumped along a wall in the shade of some balcony, his tongue stretched out to catch the drops of water trickling down from a pot of just-watered geraniums, bent over onto his knees with his face in the dust, whispering to himself as he worshiped the sun. Usually it was my father who found him and took him home to his wife.

His wife would scream at Uncle Issa and tuck him into bed, only to find him risen and gone again later. Toward the end, Uncle Issa claimed that the village square was the only place from which to watch the sun rise. There my father had found his brother one morning, dead of a heart attack at the age of thirty-five.

I never knew Uncle Issa, but my grandmother had talked about him. She told me that he had been responsible for our leaving the pretty mountain village in Lebanon and moving to the desert. Far away from all that he loved, my father must have believed that he could forget his older brother once and for all. Maybe he thought that putting such distance between him and his roots would sever the possibility of his inheriting his brother's illness.

"We are not going back to Lebanon," Aida said the night that grandmother died. "Soon you'll be in school. And think of the friends you have already. Why look back?"

I nodded. I did have new friends in Shuaiba.

"I only wish that Sameer had more friends," Aida said. "He's not exactly like Issa, but he isn't like you. Everyone on this street knows Hala."

181

I smiled, knowing what she said was true. Everyone in our alley knew me. I had made friends. Unlike Sameer.

I never knew whether or not I had killed my grandmother. Perhaps it was the job of raising a child at her age that sent her off. For months afterward I felt her presence around me, as if she were swallowed up by the house and yet still in it.

I knew that her spirit was with us for the forty days following her death—that she walked these rooms, sat with us at mealtime, and lay down to sleep right along with the rest of us. Even though I never spoke about her to anyone, not even to Aida, I knew that she was present. It was almost as if she had burrowed into me.

For instance, I began to crave onions. She had loved onions, herself, and used to add them to almost anything she cooked. She would chop and then fry them, turning them into tiny pearls, teardrops, in the hot oil before adding them to rice or meat. As though her addiction to onions were transferred to me, I specifically asked Aida to put them into anything I ate.

Then, of course, there was her peculiar smell of decomposing fruit that lingered about the house. Once she was gone, the smell grew stronger, as though it were fermenting. Aida aired the house, opened all the windows, and washed the sheets, pillows, and blankets. The smell only increased. Finally, she carried my grandmother's abandoned mattress all the way up to our roof to dry out in the sun.

By then, Aida's pregnant belly had started to show. It was no easy matter for her slender, awkward form to balance the heavy mattress up the spiral stairway to the roof. Looking at Aida that day, carrying the weight of her mother's cotton mattress, I could not help comparing her to my grandmother, the one solid and stubbornly fixed in the ground while my own mother seemed transient and fluid as water. I knew then that I had outgrown Aida as a mother before she had even had a chance.

Not long after, the event that I had been dreading ever since my grandmother announced it months ago to Aida over coffee came to pass—my brother Bilal was born. Contrary to what I had imagined, however, I grew extremely fond of this baby who was the picture of health and ruddy beauty and only wished to be allowed to carry him as much as I would have liked. My father and Aida, though, allotted me only moments now and then whenever they were right beside me. Their attempts to safeguard him, however, led to a secret mishap.

Going into Aida's room one morning, I found Bilal, alone, asleep on her bed. He must have been four months old at the time, with a shock of black hair and red cheeks. I watched him breathe, his mouth open in a tiny O, his round cheek flattened where he lay on it. I knew that he had just nursed because his open mouth was oozing milk onto the sheet. Gazing at him, listening to his short breaths, I was swept away by such a thrill of love as I had never felt before, especially with no one else in the room from whom to censor my feelings.

I tiptoed to where Bilal slept and, careful not to wake him, rolled him into my arms. Almost without realizing it, I lifted up my nightgown and placed his head at my breast, as I had seen Aida do, as I had once tried to nurse my grandmother's kittens back in Lebanon. I wanted to nurse Bilal! I nudged his cheek gently, coaxing him to open his mouth and latch onto my flat nipple. However, nursing a baby who was neither awake nor hungry was quite different from nursing eager kittens who would immediately gnaw at my skin.

Bilal was a disappointment. I was trying to return him to the bed before Aida could come back and discover me with my nightgown over his head when he slipped out of my grasp.

It happened so quickly, as quickly as he must have wriggled out of Aida's belly, that I heard his head hit the tile floor before I realized what had happened. I heard his feeble wail but, too frightened to check him, I scooped him up, dumped him on the bed, and ran out of the room.

The same guilt that infested me after my grandmother's death crept into me once more, sinking deeply into my skin like a tick.

Starting school in Shuaiba diverted me somewhat. On the morning I was to go, Aida examined me carefully to be sure that I was neat, then she combed and braided my dark hair and tied the ends with two large, white ribbons. Sameer watched as I kissed Bilal good-by and I could feel his jealousy of the baby, although he tried to cover it. He, too, was off to school, but he ran out ahead of me since the boys' school started ten minutes before the girls' school.

I hesitated at our door, imagining for a moment that I was back in our white village in Lebanon where the voice of the sweet roll vendor in the road announced each day, and the smell of my grandmother heating *samne* to fry my egg filtered into my bedroom.

I joined the other girls on the way to school, confident of my popularity. With my grandmother gone, I sought out the girls in the Shuaiba alleys more and more out of immense loneliness and also because of another feeling: a sudden freedom that I had never known when she was alive.

The first minutes of that first day at school led me to believe that maintaining my lead among my fifteen classmates would be simple. How was I to know that my position would be challenged only too soon by a girl even more intriguing than myself?

No sooner had we been assigned seats in our new classroom that overlooked the sandy beach than a tall man and an imposing woman with hair the color of the sunrise stopped at the door. The class fell suddenly silent. Even I, who had seen red hair in Lebanon, stared at the woman and at her strange, bleached skin. Holding onto her hand was a girl our own age who had the same hair and pallor as the woman. The two of them were astonishing, their skin like buffed ivory, their hair like crowns. It took us all several minutes to realize that the girl was being placed in our class and was being given a seat next to skinny Aisha Rashid.

184

I knew that I would have to establish myself all over again the moment I saw that flame of orange hair. My heart sank at that instant, not only because this startling creature—Isabelle—was not seated beside me, but because I could see that she would be my nemesis.

Isabelle had only to appear in the doorway of our classroom that morning to prove herself. She was unique. Anyone could see that.

She was odd, too, of course, but somehow that made her even more powerful. She had an aura about her, a circle into which none of us could enter.

Once the teacher forced us to settle down and stop leaning forward to try to touch Isabelle's chalky arms and blazing hair, I was able to study her from where she sat two desks ahead of me. She was as quiet as a mouse, not looking at anyone or seeming to understand anything that was said to her. That was because she was—as the girls called her—*Englisia*, an English girl, although we were to learn later that her mother was American and her father was Arab. Only once, when a girl ran up to the blackboard during break and made faces at us did Isabelle break into laughter along with the rest.

I began to think of a way to win her.

Despite myself, I found myself wanting to be her friend. Also, having learned early on from my grandmother that people admired strength, I decided that the sooner I displayed my own strengths, the better chance I had of keeping this girl in her place.

My chance came at lunch time. We were led out of class, first to a room where we were measured for uniforms and school shoes and given books, notebooks, pencils, erasers, and white ribbons to tie in our hair. Then we went to a large hall with rows of tables and chairs and a smoky smell of cumin and lentils. I went blind from the aroma! Too excited to eat the egg that Aida had fried for me at breakfast, I had deposited it in the flower pot in our courtyard and joined the girls on their way to school on an empty stomach. Now, my insides were growling. I was famished. I could not wait to get a mouthful of food.

At first I was too hungry to care that Isabelle stood behind me or that she sat right down next to me. I had eyes only for the slabs of white bread and cheese that were put on my plate along with a single boiled egg and a tin cup of yellow, lentil soup.

Then, suddenly, I looked about me. Everyone seemed to be eating at once, chewing and slurping greedily. I stared at the white cup with blue and orange flowers on it, watched the steam rise from the thick soup. I glanced at the pale girl beside me who was carefully biting into the bread the color of her slim fingertips. That was when I decided to ignore my pleading body. I ignored my eager taste buds, too, slowly pushing my plate away. Finally, I shoved my steaming cup away and turned my back on the food.

Leaning back against the table, stretching out my legs, watching as the multitude of other girls plunged their faces into their plates, I felt incredibly satisfied, more stuffed than if I had eaten twice as much as any of them. I was the most blessed girl in the world! Next to me, Isabelle had completely stopped chewing and sat staring at me, her cheeks full, as though her very teeth would fall out with surprise.

Isabelle and I did become friends. Despite her red hair and green eyes the color of the sea just outside our school playground, I was able to hold my ground as the only Lebanese in the class. Several of our teachers were Lebanese and took a special interest in me. Also, although the sun turned my skin brown in the long summer afternoons playing in the alleyways of Shuaiba, in winter my face grew white again, glowing with the rosiness that the other darker girls and my teachers found so curious. I was saved from obscurity because I was prettier than Isabelle. Isabelle could not deny this.

Isabelle's name was frequently on my tongue at home and I yearned to show Aida this girl whom I talked about so much. It was not until a few years later, however, that Isabelle, who did not live in Shuaiba but in a compound several miles up the coast with the other foreigners, was allowed to walk home from school with me. I had not realized how bothersome this walk would prove to be until the Shuaiba boys who went to the school next to ours and were not accustomed to Isabelle's hair and eyes began to run after us, hissing at her as though she were a cat. Even Sameer, who usually lurked about in the road after school, joined his friends in the jeering.

Aida had cooked my favorite dish of green beans with tomatoes and rice that day, and I showed Isabelle how to use her fingers and the fresh, round bread to soak up the sauce. Aida sat with us on a stool in the corner of the kitchen, fascinated, nursing two-year-old Bilal who squirmed incessantly in her lap to get a glimpse of the strange girl who dabbed inexpertly at her food.

"Your mother's pretty," Isabelle said to me, later.

"Isn't your mother?"

She considered this a moment. "Not as pretty as yours."

I had just washed our dishes and was boiling coffee for my father and a guest who had come home from work with him. Just then, as though to prove Isabelle's point, Aida walked into the kitchen. She had changed into a silky, new dress and had painted her eyes with fresh, black kohl. Without a word, as though she barely saw us, she took the tray of coffee from me and disappeared, leaving a storm of jasmine perfume in her wake.

Isabelle and I were sent to occupy Bilal in the courtyard and he ran from one to the other of us stumbling and squealing with laughter at Isabelle.

"When can I come to your house?" I said to Isabelle, suddenly. I was tired of playing with Bilal, tired of my house, of my family. I wanted to see the compound where Isabelle lived, to play in her pink room that she had told me about with the toys that she had brought with her from America.

"Come tomorrow," Isabelle said, without hesitation.

"I could ride home in your car," I said, satisfied.

"Let's ask your mother," she said.

I looked about me. My father stood in the shadows of the sitting room, alone, smoking a cigarette. Something in his stance, the way

187

that he seemed to hold the smoke within himself a long while before releasing it into the dark air told me that my mother was not to be disturbed.

Only after Isabelle's driver came to fetch her home, after my strange friend had gone, promising to take me home with her in that same white car the next day, did I see Aida return to the sitting room. A moment later, my father's guest left.

"You idiot," Sameer said when he came home that night. "How could you bring that girl here?"

"Isabelle's my friend. I'm going to her house tomorrow," I said.

"No, you're not," he said.

"She's going to take me in her car," I added, smugly, knowing that this part would make him burn with jealousy.

"You're not going—and she's not coming back here!"

"I am going!" I screamed back. "She said I could!"

Now Sameer's eyes did burn, but not with jealousy. His voice was flat, cold: "She would never invite you if she knew your mother was a whore."

His words thundered down on me. I did not understand what he meant, but I knew he had said something terrible about Aida.

I started to cry, confused and angry that he was threatening to disrupt my plans for the next day. Isabelle had liked Aida. She had said that she was pretty. She had invited me to her house in the compound and I was going to go!

Sameer took a step toward me. I knew that he was sorry he had spoken harshly of Aida. But before he could say another word, before he could explain what he meant, I made a fist and punched his stomach with all my might.

One spring morning, about a year later, my father appeared in the doorway of our classroom. I did not recognize him at first. He wore a dark suit and dark glasses and looked from one girl to another until his gaze fell on me.

A flood of memories came over me as we walked home together

in silence. I dared not ask him why he had come for me, but I assumed that it was for the same reason that he and Aida had come to my grandmother's house that morning in Zahle several years ago—we were going to move yet again to some place where he could finally make enough money for us to live like kings.

When we reached our alley, however, he stopped. A hush settled about us, hovered above the unpaved patch of road leading to our house. The dusty realm outside my blue front door where I played nearly every afternoon with my friends, appeared strangely alien to me now, empty at this time of day when everyone was still at school. Suddenly, yet very gently, as though afraid he might break it, my father took my hand in his. We started down the road.

All at once I realized why the alley looked so changed. The mud walls near our house were streaked with black and at the end, where our blue door used to be, was a dark, smoking hollow. What I mistook for an instant to be the call to prayers in the still air were a woman's screams.

"Aida!" I cried, and started running towards the sound.

My father caught me and tried to hold me still but I wriggled free.

"Aida!"

"She's all right," he called after me, his voice breaking.

I stared at the blackened windows and walls of our house. Gray dust—ashes—blew about the courtyard, coating the white jasmine blossoms and pink oleanders still intact in their tins. The wails stopped suddenly and then started again, filling the dark shell that had been my home.

My father caught up with me. He took off his glasses. His eyes were red and as hard as stone.

"There's been a fire—after you left for school."

I felt dizzy. "Aida?"

"Aida was out."

"Why is she screaming?" I said, suspicious, covering my ears. "Where's Sameer?"

"Sameer is with her, inside."

189

I found this strange. Sameer was rarely with Aida these days. Then my stomach tightened. "Bilal?"

Bilal was dead. He had been taking a nap. By the time Aida had returned from the neighbor's house next door where she often drank coffee, and had run through the flames into his bedroom, it had been too late. Bilal had already suffocated.

Bilal!

At first, I screamed like Aida, howls that broke the thin air of the spring day. I screamed until I was weak, until all of Shuaiba seemed to be burning along with my house, with my brother. Bilal—the one sparkle of joy in my life. Without him I could not go on!

I do not remember what else happened that day but later that evening Isabelle and her parents came to see us bringing toys, blankets, and a big, chocolate cake. As Isabelle watched, I swallowed mouthfuls of the cake, trying to taste the sweetness, to drown in the chocolate that would take away the bitter emptiness of the terrible and inconceivable loss.

Still later, after Isabelle and her family left, after the neighbors had taken us to their house and spread mattresses for us to sleep on their sitting room floor, after my father had calmed Aida somewhat, Sameer came up to me.

In the dark, I felt him shudder beside me, felt his tears on my shoulder as he touched my hair every now and then to ease his own pain.

I did not move away from him as I usually did. Instead, I allowed him to soothe me, allowed his muffled croons to ease the shock of what had happened and his fingertips to stroke away Aida's sharp, fitful moans that pierced my dreams throughout that long night.

PETRA

Petra at five in the afternoon. The desert breeze begins to sift through the hills. The sun turns a pale watermelon.

Joanna and Bob have driven along the Amman-Aqaba road in Jordan past crusader fortresses on craggy mountaintops, past villages with terraced fields of olive and cyprus trees, village women winnowing grain. The houses of the village of Wadi Musa adjoining Petra jut out sharply from the rounded hills on either side of a ravine—an oasis—like some centuries-old California gold mining town to nugget-crazed prospectors. Through the ravine and up a hill is the new hotel, a low building of the same pink rock as the legendary city itself.

Bob signs the register at the front desk while Joanna drops her camera-laden duffel bag to gaze out at the pink patio and wind-clipped surface of the azure swimming pool. The drafty, marble lobby echoes the silence of the surrounding canyon. *Petra.* She can already sense the Nabatean city just beyond the glass doors.

Rose-red. Salmon. Russet. Coral. Joanna and Bob—she, a high school history teacher, he a petroleum engineer with extensive experience in the Middle East—have come to Jordan to witness this wonder of the ancient world. Joanna is pleased, at least, that the rock is as pink as in the photographs, although she has yet to see evidence of the ruins of this ancient caravan sanctuary beyond

191

the cliffs some distance down the road. They have saved Petra for last so as not to dwarf the other sights by comparison.

In Amman, the capital, they had only to drive several minutes from their hotel to reach the Roman amphitheatre of ancient *Philadelphia* set smack in the middle of the busy downtown. At *Jerash*, Roman archways and columns had announced the city even before the blazing white sign. Even the Dead Sea had been visible almost from the start of their descent through the barren mountains to where it lay eight-hundred feet below sea level winking up at them like a pearl. Here, however, they have driven through the town and marketplace and still have had no glimpse of the gargantuan monuments that they have come to know by heart. Joanna is beginning to worry that Petra might prove as deceptive as the Georgia O'Keeffe paintings she had seen for the first time in the museum, oils that in art books had seemed massive but which had in reality proven to be smallish squares that could barely fill a narrow wall.

The hotel is empty mid-week in August, so they have their pick of the bungalows overlooking a canyon of limestone hills. Pink and white oleanders flutter outside the glass doors of their room. There are the usual narrow beds separated by a night table and lamp. Bob flings open his suitcase on one, retrieves his shaving kit, and heads for the shower while Joanna pays the porter. A falcon-eyed boy of about fourteen, the porter seems to have been plucked from his flock of goats for the afternoon. He pauses at the door as he slips the heavy coins into his pocket, startling Joanna with a gaze that penetrates like a prophet's and yet seems to her altogether too lascivious for a fourteen-year-old.

Joanna has been unnerved by these stares from the Arab men since the day they arrived in Jordan from Minneapolis, although she is still not sure whether they are actually the lustful looks she perceives them to be or whether it is some latent yearning on her part for such glances that leads her to suspect this.

Staring through the oleanders to the sand and limestone hills,

Joanna remembers Eve's words last night. Eve Calahan, a child-hood friend of Joanna's and currently the cultural attachee at the American Embassy in Amman, had joined her for drinks at her hotel last night. As she and Joanna sipped gin-and-tonics on the terrace and watched Amman's windows turn gold and tarnished silver in the sinking sun, Eve had confided that she had requested an extension of another year because she found the Arab men so agreeable.

"Agreeable? Arab men?" Joanna had been surprised. Eve had always been reticent with men. Throughout their dating years Joanna had been the more gregarious and sultry of the two, managing almost effortlessly to attract the men she fancied. Moreover, although Eve had never married, she had grown plump and matronly as a contented partridge. Joanna had assumed that now, on the brink of middle-age, men—any men—had become a low priority in Eve's life.

Joanna, appraising her friend against the Arab landscape of rough-hewned white stone houses, of minarets and pungent, ancient smells, had suddenly noted the luster in Eve's cheeks. "Just how well do you know Arab men?"

Eve had chuckled. "I've been here two years. I haven't exactly been in a convent. I meet people all the time, besides," she had looked at Joanna slyly, "they like full-bodied women. I'm just right over here."

Joanna had sipped the gin, drowning an unexpected spasm of jealousy. "Tell me about it."

Eve, smiling, had lowered her voice. "I'm not sure what it is. They're not afraid, if you know what I mean."

"Not afraid of what?"

"Well, they flirt, but with intention. At first I flirted back. Then, I realized they were serious. It was a sort of foreplay."

"Foreplay?"

"If you respond to their signals, they expect you to give them what they want."

"How awful," Joanna had snickered. She had tried to imagine

193

Eve in the arms of one of the dusky, bearded men in the streets. Although she did not care for beards, the short ones on many of the men here were different—youthful, somehow. Potent.

"Not so awful, really," Eve had said, suddenly serious. Her eyes had succumbed to the smoldering glow they used to take on when they were children and she had discovered where her mother had hidden the Christmas gifts. "It's easier. If you respond, they go further—no wishy-washy ambivalence, no mother-haters. *And* guaranteed to please."

Joanna had stared at her friend. "Eve—I never thought—"

"Never thought what?"

Joanna had felt her hand shake slightly, the years of discontentment in her marriage strewn before her like children's blocks. Although she had always felt lucky to be married, to have had children, often regarding Eve's life as sad and empty, now, she realized that was not so.

Eve had simply grinned. "Just remember what I said. Don't flirt."

"I'm with Bob, for heaven's sake."

"They don't care. If you're a foreign woman you're fair game. Just be careful."

Joanna had shivered, piqued yet intrigued by Eve's enthusiasm. "I don't find them all that attractive. Most of them could use a haircut and a shave."

Eve had laughed. "My initial feelings, exactly! I'm telling you, watch out!"

Joanna finds her friend's words singularly poignant now that sensuality is so absent from her own life.

She and Bob have recently abandoned sex. They have not made love in the past six months, have not been in love, it seems, for more years than she wants to remember. Dropping the carnal aspect of their marriage had been Joanna's idea. Although Bob had fought it in the beginning, insisting that there was no reason to give up the one thing they still managed well together—not now that the children were almost grown and they would be left alone together more and more—he now seems secretly relieved not to have to cajole her into the erratic encounters which she later claims depress her.

But it is not simply physical intimacy that distresses her. Bob is right about one thing—they *did* still manage it well. But that, in itself, is not enough. Rather, it is the increasingly passionless nature of it that seems to cheapen it and makes her feel used in the act of love. She is not sure when it started, but she and Bob both know it has been spiralling over the years—first with her resentments for seemingly trivial things such as his frequent business travel, his neglect of his once-athletic body. Then with her growing, almost visceral rejection of his very being. Finally, it seems, they have reached rock bottom. The bitterness between them has ground what they once knew as love into a subtle, gritty anger.

Traveling seems to be the one thing left for them to share, the thrill of experiencing new landscapes and peoples reminiscent of the early, tantalizing terrain of their marriage. Mapping out unexplored routes, delving into alien customs and history, comes closer than anything else to salvaging some of the headiness of their youth. They have dreamed of coming to Petra for twenty years and have prepared for this moment as though for some sacred ritual, learning all they can of the ancient Edomites and Nabateans who thrived here two thousand years ago.

Bob's splashing in the shower is a rainstorm behind her. He has been waiting to shower ever since they left Amman, the dust of the three-hour drive brutal to his allergy-prone nostrils. He had repeated it so often during their relentless trek along the historic King's highway behind rock-hauling trucks and diesel fumes that Joanna had finally stopped listening.

Outside the glass doors, opalescent oleanders rise up from a carpet of sand. Joanna walks the few yards to the edge of the hill. There is an abrupt drop into a canyon with more hills like sculpted mushrooms glowing pink, grey, and blue in the fading light: A coral sea bed without the water. The wind whispers across the globes of the giant limestone boulders. They seem to glare at her like the faces of grotesque, other-world life forms. She swallows, tears welling in her dust-weary eyes. Never has she come across nature in such harrowing, human shapes before.

"Where is Petra?" she asks, irritably.

They are sitting on the veranda across from the swimming pool. The weathered, golden hills of the surrounding desert peek at them from behind the pool and the hotel bungalows. Beyond is the desert of *Wadi Araba* and then *Aqaba*—battlefield of T. E. Lawrence.

Bob has put on a her favorite lavender Izod shirt. He has parted his sandy hair with his brush, the part crooked as a schoolboy's.

"It's somewhere in those hills," he says, glancing toward the canyon.

"Do we have to go with the guide?"

"He's planning on us. It would be rude to Eve not to."

Eve, over Joanna's protests, had made arrangements for someone from the Department of Antiquities in Petra to personally escort them to the ruins. At the desk, when they checked in, there had been a note saying that they would be picked up at the hotel at six o'clock. It is already five minutes to six.

At seven o'clock, they are still waiting. They eat supper in the empty restaurant, dipping pieces of floppy pita bread into earthenware bowls of *hommos* and eggplant puree, wrapping strips of bread around the bitter green and black olives. They sip small glasses of cloudy, mentholated *arak.*

Almost as much as the historic sights, the food in Jordan has become an obsession to Joanna. As a rule, anything she eats with her hands tastes richer and more flavorful to her. So, she has adopted Arab table manners, her usual guilt at discarding her fork and knife in public giving way to an uninhibited mealtime revelry. She scoops up yogurt-dip floating in olive oil. Mouthfuls of chickpeas disintegrate on her tongue, cleansed by the ice-cooled *arak.*

"Where do you suppose he is?" she says, tearing the bread with her fingertips.

Suddenly, Bob stands up.

Joanna puts down her bread and turns around. A man is approaching them.

He is of medium height, compact, and dressed in a khaki safari suit like a soldier. His skin is the brown, desert color of mud-brick and his black hair, although neatly cut, is stiff, as though it has been ironed flat. To Joanna, he looks about thirty.

"Wahbi Matar," he says, introducing himself as the assistant Director of antiquities. He extends a dark hand first to Bob and then to Joanna. He quickly looks away from her, an almost shy, butterfly's flutter of his lashes that takes her in and abandons her in the same instant.

"It's nice of you to come," Bob says, pulling out a chair.

Wahbi Matar sits down. "Anything I can do for Miss Calahan..." He smiles broadly at Bob, and Joanna wonders whether this is one of the men Eve has known, one of the specimens 'guarantied to please.'

He makes no apology for being over an hour late and addresses his questions about their journey to Petra and their impressions of Jordan directly to Bob as though Joanna were invisible. Joanna is struck by a certain serenity in his face, a complaisant affinity with life that she has marked in the faces of so many of the people here.

The waiter brings cups of Turkish coffee. The man slurps his quickly and noisily—another local habit she has noted—apparently without scalding his mouth. He and the waiter chat with a familiarity that seems to come from his being a frequent guest at the hotel. Joanna realizes that she and Bob are probably the latest in a stream of tourists that he is obliged to make time for by important people such as Eve.

He suddenly rises. "Shall we go?"

Bob looks up. "Where?"

"To Petra."

197

Bob and Joanna look at each other. The sun has already set. A shimmering echo of its rays hovers along the horizon. .

Bob seems skeptical. "Shouldn't we wait until morning?"

"This is the best time," the man says.

"It's almost dark," Joanna says.

Bob and Joanna look at each other, again.

Wahbi Matar glances at Joanna, his eyes brushing her breasts, the small St. Christopher at her neck, and finally resting on her eyes. His own dark eyes seemed to say, "trust me."

They climb into the sleek white jeep with PETRA DEPART-MENT OF ANTIQUITIES plastered in black on both sides. Joanna sits on the meager cushion in back while Bob takes the front seat next to the guide—Joanna is embarrassed to have already forgotten his name.

The sky is a luminous copper over the molded hills as they drive away from the hotel. A camel and some horses are being led away through an adjacent ravine by young boys and a bent, bowl-legged man in a striped robe and white headdress. The jeep winds through the empty town and surges up an adjoining hill, deftly circling the edge like a knife peeling an apple. When they reach the summit, the guide gets out.

"First, we see the sunset," he says.

Bob helps Joanna out of his door.

It has grown darker, still, the horizon now a graying, faded peach. The Nabatean plain below has taken on a subdued fuzziness, as though it were being photographed through a lense smeared with vasseline. Patches of tilled earth, soft squares of velvet jade and brown, are sprawled out like a damp quilt. Cones of limestone hills, some sharp as funnels, others round as a woman's breast, dissolve up into the dusk. The entire plain is the pale pink of an unripe rose.

Still, there is no sign of the famous sandstone city, no mono-lithic red boulders, no giant temples.

"Where is Petra?" Joanna asks.

"Petra?" The guide seems to shake himself from his reverie.

"The city," she says.

The guide points to the cliffs forming huge barrier walls in the distance. He jerks his head toward the jeep. "Now, we'll go."

"Shouldn't we wait until morning?" Bob says, again.

The guide smiles.

"We're going on horses?" Bob says. They have seen countless photographs of visitors entering the hidden city single file on horseback.

"Yes," the man says. He pats the jeep. "This horse."

Bob looks at Joanna.

"Let's do it his way," she whispers, shrugging, as Bob helps her into the back. "We'll go back tomorrow on our own."

Bob's eyebrows lift in surprise. He has obviously protested for her sake, knowing how meticulously she likes to study things.

The jeep jolts back down the valley, through the town, past the hotel, until they reach a solitary guard house. An old man with a flashlight peers at them.

"*Massa-al-khair*," the guide calls out. Realizing who it is, the guard salutes and lifts the metal bar that blocks the road.

The jeep bounces over the rocks and holes in the desert. Joanna grabs onto the bare metal frame of a canopy which has been removed. The headlights shoot a blade of silver onto the road, cutting into the black before them.

"Petra by night," the guide announces, chuckling.

"Petra by night!" Bob echoes into the dark.

"Bob," Joanna protests, her half-hearted laugh drifting feebly into the night. She is annoyed by Bob's snicker, visualizing a batallion of feathered Las Vegas show girls darting in and out of the bleak shadows. The *arak* they drank with dinner has fogged her head, slightly. It has evidently emboldened Bob. A budding, male camaraderie seems to link the two men in the front. Joanna feels excluded, cast into the Arab night like a frivolous veil.

They round a corner and pull to an abrupt stop. "Petra!" the guide says, solemly, as though they are in the presence of a hallowed sanctuary.

Joanna sits up. Ahead of them are the shadows of the cliffs that she saw earlier. The jeep's headlights ricochet off the high and menacing shadows. They press slowly forward, the jeep's lights transmitting a ghostly code as if to signal the arrival of aliens.

"The Obelisk Tomb," the man says, pointing off to the right. "Egyptian inspired."

Joanna can discern nothing until the jeep's lights hit the four obelisks set in the cliff, pointing toward heaven.

The jeep halts, again.

The guide turns to the back. The motor rumbles. His hand vibrates with the steering wheel. "O.K.?"

Joanna looks at him. "O.K.?"

"Petra by night," he says.

"This is it?" she says.

The guide shrugs. "There is no more road." Then, he smiles. His strong white teeth run in a straight ridge across his lower lip as though he spent his life gnawing on bones. She likes him better when he laughs, although she suspects that he is laughing at her.

He turns back to the steering wheel and shifts into first geer as they inch toward the tall shadows. Joanna grips the canopy frame.

She watches the back of Bob's head. She cannot tell whether he is annoyed or as confused as she is. Perhaps he is secretly satisfied that he has been right not to want to come out here at night. She has been wrong, wrong to have let Eve and this stranger take control of their journey.

"Can you see anything?" she asks.

"No," Bob says.

Suddenly, a shaft of light like trapped moonbeams erupts before them.

"The entrance to Petra," the guide says. "The *Siq.*"

Joanna knows it from photographs—the high, narrow fault in the massive rock that forms the natural entrance to Petra, widening slightly at the bottom to accomodate horses or pedestrians. She tries to imagine the pink color.

She wants to ask the guide how he expects them to see anything in this dark. Yet she does not want to offend him or to betray her ignorance of Petra being best seen, as he claims, this way. She certainly does not want him to feel that she is afraid.

They are face to face with the *Siq.* The crack in the rock gapes at them. She waits for the guide to order them to disembark, for from here on they must surely go by foot. Instead, the jeep eases forward, stopping and starting in spurts, entering the narrow *Siq* like a skittish horse.

Joanna leans forward. "Can we go in this way?"

"He knows what he's doing," Bob says.

"Don't be afraid," the guide says, calmly.

Joanna's shoulders stiffen. Her neck grows small. Though she knows it is absurd, she feels it is crazy for them to be out here in the night on a deserted plain with a stranger—even one recommended by Eve. Blinded, love-sick Eve. Eve who has acquired a taste for Arab men. This man could kill them, knife them, rape her, and nobody would ever know.

The steering wheel twists in the guide's hands as the jeep rocks forward. The moonlight beckons from within the shaft of the gorge.

Inside the *Siq,* the dark enshrouds them even more. Now Joanna smells rather than sees the rock walls that hover on either side of the jeep. Joanna stretches out her right arm. Her hand scrapes against the dry stone. There is a faint trickle of water above them, a reminder of the natural spring that nourished this ancient civilization, of the famous clay pipes that the Nabateans had ingeniously engineered to channel water from cisterns and underground springs into their city thousands of years ago.

"This is the path of the stream of *Ain Moussa,* Moses' spring," the guide says. "In rain it is dangerous."

Joanna remembers reading of a group of Italian tourists who were swept to their deaths by a flash flood in this very passageway. "Is this where the people died?"

"We now have a dam," the guide says.

"A brutal culmination to a holiday," Bob says.

"Look, up," the guide commands. Bob and Joanna tilt back their heads. The gorge opens to a narrow flood of sky. An indigo river swims above them floating tiny blinking stars.

"God," Bob says, his voice reverberating up the gorge.

"It's part of the Milky Way," Joanna says.

There is no other light save this starlight. Joanna tilts back her head even further until her face is a flat page open to the sky. The faint light ignites the tips of the cliffs above them, revealing the niches carved into the walls. Occasionally an entire zigurat-like cornice can be glimpsed. On either side of the jeep, tufts of bushes undulate from rocky nooks.

"Glorious," Bob says. She leans back and lets the jeep jostle her through the dark labyrinth. She puts out her right palm. Occasionally she can touch the rock wall. Her neck is now exposed to the jagged blue sky, raw, defenseless. Suddenly, she imagines a dagger slitting her throat. Blood throbs at her temples. She drops her head forward.

The guide is silent, as if as overcome as she and Bob by this ghostly sliver of sky. *Forget all you have heard of the pink colors, the grain of the sandstone, the shape of the monuments,* he seems to say. *Just imagine it from these shadows. Feel it.*

Joanna allows the dark to absorb her. Slowly, a faint memory of love-making ripens in her. She used to try to explain to Bob her preference for making love in the dark. Not, as he thought, because she was ashamed to have him see her in the light, but because it was less distracting, like being drawn into outer space with nothing to bind her—limitless. A sadness seeps into her spine. Something is being unearthed against her will.

The tunnel seems to grow narrower and deeper, as though at

any moment the rocks will scrape the paint off the sides of the jeep.

"Lawrence—you know Lawrence?" the guide says.

"Lawrence of Arabia?" Bob says.

"Lawrence," the guide repeats with a sweep of his arm, "killed many Turks when they tried to enter Petra. He had only two guns—two guns and two Bedouins. They hid up there."

"So, Lawrence was here?" Bob says.

Joanna looks back up at the high ridges. The Turks had been trapped down here like the Italian tourists.

"My grandfather fought beside Lawrence," the guide says. "He was the *Sheikh* of the Petra Bedouins."

The gorge suddenly opens up. Above them, the sky grows into a vast ocean. The jeep stops.

"*Al-Khazna*," the guide says. "The treasury."

The massive portals of the Nabatean treasury—the most famous and familiar building in Petra—erupts before them. Joanna notes the urn at the very top, said to have held the Pharoah of Egypt's secret treasure. This is the building that dwarfs the astonished traveler coming upon it after the narrow *Siq*, the scene that stunned John Lewis Bruckhard in 1812 when he rediscovered the hidden city for the Western world. Joanna knows the rose-pink hue of this Greek-inspired wonder despite its yellow tint from the jeep's lights. But, Just as her eyes gather in the Corinthian columns and begin to taste the fluid Alexandrian classicism, the headlights are extinguished.

"Ancient city—we don't like to disturb it with light," the guide says, softly.

A purple shadow hovers where the treasury stood. The moon is a feeble arc above them.

Joanna leans forward. "Can't you keep the light on it a little longer?"

"Don't worry," the guide says, "you will see everything."

"Are you afraid Joanna?" Bob asks. His voice seems strangely vindictive.

"I want to know what I'm seeing," Joanna says. She *is* afraid, not only of this unknown place and unknown driver who has brought her into this deserted city practically against her will, but also, of her own husband, Bob. The subtle alliance that has sprung up during the past half-hour between the two men seems to have deepened. They seem to find her a nuisance. Bob, apparently no longer ambivalent about placing his fate in the hands of this stranger, now seems almost too eager to risk the unknown.

For a moment, Joanna wonders whether he is avenging himself for her coolness toward him these past months. She imagines, oddly, that he will unite with this stranger and, for the satisfaction of seeing her submit to sex—any sex—will allow him to rape her. She imagines that he and the guide have already made some secret pact to this effect. In this tight moment of delirium, the red rock walls seem to close in on her.

Once again they wind through a narrow tunnel, dust rising about them, only this time the guide has not bothered to turn on his headlights. The smell of the rock walls guides them through the dark gorge until they emerge into another open plain. The air around them clears. The sky blossoms above them again.

"Did you hear, Joanna? The facades? Remember?" Bob's voice is impatient, a missile seeking her through the dark.

"What facades?" She does not know whether or not he has said this before.

The guide rescues her. "Assyrian facades. Homes. Perhaps tombs. We do not know."

Joanna stares at the distant cliffs which glow like mirrors in the moonlight. She discerns the dark rectangles. She remembers reading about them.

"Below us," the guide says, somewhat mechanically, "is the amphitheatre. Carved by the Romans in the first century A.D. It seated 3,000 spectators."

They observe the full crescent of the Roman steps cut into the mountain in the valley below. Joanna can picture the bustling Nabatean marketplace on a cool summer evening. She imagines the travelers before her who had discovered this hidden city for the first time, from this height, though probably never in quite this way, in the dark, and with such hollow trepidation.

The jeep comes to a stop. This time the guide turns around to include Joanna, as though about to embark on a well-practiced sermon. "Welcome to the city of Petra."

He flings open his door and gets out of the jeep. Bob does the same, with such reckless speed that Joanna gasps when she sees that their side of the jeep opens onto the steep hillside.

Something flashes in one of the "facades" in the mountain wall across the valley. On and off. On and off.

The guide points to it. "Abu Yousef sees us."

Joanna stares at the dim outline of a cave. "There's someone up there?"

"Abu Yousef guards Petra."

"Alone?"

"Every night—for fifty years. He used to have the Bedouins for company, but two years ago we sent them away." The guide waves his hand as though disbanding a horde of gnats. "They used the caves as homes."

"They lived in them ?" Joanna says.

"They were destroying them," the guide says. Then, as though to justify his insensitivity to rendering the nomads homeless, he reminds her, "I am originally Bedouin, myself. I grew up in those caves."

Joanna stares at the dark patches in the cliffs to which he is pointing. Then she looks back up at the blinking light. "How do you get up there? Are there steps?"

The guide climbs back into the jeep and flashes his own lights off and on in response to the signals. "We climb there—we are Bedouin."

Bob, meanwhile, has moved through a thicket of oleanders

toward the ledge of the hill overlooking the amphitheatre. His back is to them as he stands teetering, it seems to Joanna, on mere air.

"Bob," Joanna says, over the jeep's rumble. "Bob!"

He looks back, slowly, as though forcing his eyes away from some hypnotic vision. Suddenly, he stumbles.

She catches her breath. "Bob, be careful!"

Bob stands taut as an arrow, as if he were sleepwalking, unable to pull himself back to the jeep.

Joanna looks to the guide for help. He, too, is alert, shifting his eyes intently from Bob to her as though asking whether her husband has been known to do bizarre things. She reaches forward to grab the door handle but the guide's hand shoots over hers to stop her. He silently opens the door.

But Bob is starting back towards them. "Marvelous, isn't it?" he breathes, looking somewhat stunned. In the dark, his hazel eyes burn a cat-like yellow. He appears oblivious to the guide's tense grip on the door handle, to the thud of Joanna's heart.

Some minutes later they are drinking strong mint tea brewed by the robed watchman. Joanna clutches the dusty, gold-rimmed glass, still marveling at the stamina of the old man who scampered down to them from his lanterned post carved into the face of the mountain. Abu Yousef apparently has no reservations to using light in Petra. His battery-operated lantern glows brazenly from the center of the wooden table between them.

As the guide chats with the watchman in Arabic—this tea-break is obviously an integral part of a night visit to Petra—Joanna studies her husband's face. Gone is Bob's dreamy expression. Now he simply looks confused, lost, as though wondering what he is doing here, why they are drinking tea in the moonlight in a dead city. Yet rather than be annoyed by this return to his true nature, Joanna is comforted by the familiar, cautious Bob, the husband she normally feels so stifled by.

The old watchman's toothless gums shine like glass as he speaks in a thin voice to the guide. At one point, Joanna notices both the guide and the watchman looking at her. When she glances back at them, they look away, as though they have been talking about her.

She turns to the guide. "Doesn't he feel lonely all by himself, every night?"

The guide translates. The watchman wheezes into the lantern's frail, dancing light without looking at her.

"He says *Al-'Uzza* keeps him company," the guide says.

"Who?" Joanna says.

"*Al-'Uzza*. The lion. The Nabatean goddess of Petra. He says she roams the caves and the theatre after dark."

The old watchman is smiling. Even Bob is smiling.

"Does the lion ever get hungry?" Joanna says, undaunted.

The guide looks at her a moment longer than he needs to before translating. The watchman mumbles something and laughs.

"Never hungry enough for an old man," the guide says. "He says that you can see her shadow from his cave."

Joanna looks at the watchman. "The lioness's shadow?"

"Down in the theatre," the guide says.

Joanna stares at the circular steps. Not so much as a wisp of air stirs. "Would you like to go up and see?" the guide says.

Joanna gazes up at the mountainside. She turns to Bob. "Would you?"

"Climb up there?" Bob stares at the shadow of the cave high in the rock.

"It is not difficult," the guide says with a sweep of his hand toward the hill. "Abu Yousef does it all the time and he is half blind."

Joanna looks from her husband to the guide and back to her husband.

"My ankle's a little shaky," Bob says. Since his stumble on the edge of the canyon, he has rubbed his ankle frequently.

The guide looks at the watchman. The watchman blinks and waves toward his cave—a dark, hungry mouth.

"Go on," Bob says. "See the lion, the lioness—whatever. You'll wish you did it."

"I can go tomorrow."

"Tomorrow it'll be daylight. Lions don't prowl in daylight."

Bob's grin seems to stretch beyond infinity. Joanna looks away to avoid the grotesque spread of her husband's teeth in the torch light.

"I'm afraid of heights. I'm clumsy in the dark," she says.

The guide says nothing. He merely looks at her. His eyes, like deep wounds, draw her to him. Although they merely graze her face, they seem to understand that she will go with him. The warmth of his hand which had covered hers minutes ago in the jeep rushes through her. She thinks of Eve. Eve would thrill at the thought of being alone with this rugged man.

Joanna looks a last time at Bob. It seems settled. She is to follow this stranger as if it were part of the travel itinerary.

His fingers curl tightly about hers as he helps her up off the last boulder to the ledge of the watchman's cave. She gasps, astonished by her own ability to ascend what must surely be two hundred feet with such speed.

The guide smiles, looking no more exhausted than if he had skipped up a single flight of steps. He releases her hand.

As she stands beside him at this new height, she realizes why she has come all the way to Petra. If in a lifetime there are certain rare glimpses at life's glory, this extinct city showered in blue starlight is, surely, one of them. The plain throbs with life, past and future, as though the millenia separating it from the present have suddenly disintegrated in this one leap up from the ground. The night, itself, has come to life. Joanna's eyes filter out the black and draw in the luminous lavender rays. The market promenade, the columns, the empty theatre, are remarkably lucid. The majesty of the cliffs, the monumental carved doorways—entrances to homes, tombs, shrines—the sheer spread of the city and its necropolis cascading down the cliffs is heartbreaking.

The guide steps toward the edge of the ledge. Joanna follows him, amazed by her lack of fear, by her trust in him that her feet will touch hard ground. She looks to where he is pointing—the street of Assyrian facades carved into the rock, the Carmine tomb, the High Place of Sacrifice with its efficient blood-draining system. She hears familiar names from his lips: the Temenos Gate, *Kasr el Bint*, the impregnable plateau of *Umm el Biyara* on which nested the early Edomite settlement.

"Tomorrow I will take you to Aaron's tomb, *Nabi Haroon*," he says. "That is a difficult climb." His voice seems to be infused by a new respect for her.

She takes in the view in a single gulp, pleased with herself. Then her eyes drift across his back, at the dip between his shoulder blades, the rounded muscles beneath the jacket.

He points down to the waiting men below so that she can see how high they are. Joanna can see a sliver of Bob's blond hair beside the watchman's *kafiya*-draped head. Then, she remembers why they are here.

"Is the lioness out tonight?" She tries to sound serious as her eyes drift across the theatre, searching for the goddess who supposedly keeps nightly vigil with the watchman.

The guide puts his hands on his hips and scans the theatre. "She will come."

The Roman columns grow up from the earth like inverted stalactites. The echo of the watchman clearing the tea glasses from the table below resonates across the canyon.

"Do you believe in the goddess?" she says.

"*Al-'Uzza*," he says.

"*Al-Uzza*," she repeats, crisply, striving to get the gutteral pronunciation. "Does she really lurk here? Or does the watchman enjoy frightening tourists?"

The guide does not look at her. "A lonely man needs a companion—even if she is only a ghost."

Joanna is silent. She can hear the air about her.

The guide goes on, his voice low. "A woman died here last month. An American woman."

Joanna glances at his profile, partially invisible in the dark.

"She went on her own, up to *Um al Biyara.* Then she got lost. At night, the Bedouins heard calling. They thought it was *Al-'Uzza.*"

Joanna shivers.

"How did she die?"

"She fell."

Joanna feels as though she is drowning in a halo of ice.

Suddenly, he turns to her. Despite the dark, her eyes trace the wide curve of his jaw, the clean-shaven skin. A stab of recognition grips her. Is it Bob's jaw, when she first knew him? Is it the face of each of the men she has ever been aroused by when she first knew them? She finds herself counting the number of men who over the years have pierced the fragile serenity of her marriage. Five? Seven? Starting with the young theologian in college who, upon hearing that she had been married three months promptly asked, "Had any extra-maritals yet?"

All of the sweet, unrequited desire of these years comes back, desire for those men she had allowed to divert her from the void of her life with Bob. She tries, but cannot remember when Bob stopped being enough for her—perhaps she for him. She could not be sure for him, but only once had she actually strayed—a miscalculated episode which she thought had left her cured forever of these sporadic temptations. All of these men merge together now, like a strand of beads, as she listens to this stranger's breath.

Their eyes meet. Could this man be seeing her for the first time tonight—her blond hair, her green eyes? She wants to embrace the dark for hiding the papery lines about her eyes that she has grown so concious of lately. He is, perhaps, ten years younger than she, yet from the way he looks at her he seems to find her beautiful. She feels so vulnerable suddenly! Already, he makes her feel old.

She smells the earth in his skin, the same aromatic smell she had found so intriguing on the Bedouin women in downtown Amman. It is a smell not of sweat but a dry, clean aroma of grass and soil, as though the pores in the skin have been permanently sealed by life in the desert heat.

Then he comes to her.

He puts out his hands and takes her arms above the elbows. He pushes them back gently. She shuts her eyes, tilting back her head, baring her neck to him the way she bared it to the sky in the *Siq* earlier. She waits, a shard of fear slashing her throat.

But he does not touch her further. She opens her eyes as he loosens his grip on her arms.

He seems to know everything—how much she wants him just now, how long it has been since she has had a man, how she has yearned to give herself to other men but has not.

A tremor of sound floats up from below—a transister radio, the scratchy sound of a flute spiraling up to them along with the muffled humming of the watchman.

She takes a step backwards, wading into the shadows of the cave, slumping against the cool rock.

Tentative, he steps toward her into the cave. Then, as though responding to some mysterious signal, he reaches around her and draws her to him. She gives herself, feels her body yielding like soft clay in a potter's hands.

He is smaller than she imagined, his shoulders hard and tight beneath the safari suit. Her fingers came up to his face, to his smooth cheek.

She keeps her eyes closed. She will see him through touch and smell as he has forced her to see Petra.

He presses her gently against the hard stone of the cave, the dampness like a sea breeze on her skin. She is suddenly frightened by the lengths that she is willing to go...

Overcome by an exquisite recklessness, she waits for his hand to seek her breast beneath her shirt, waits for his lips, for their softness, remembering what Eve had said about Arab men pleasing women.

Then, all at once she cries out. Her chest rises and falls fast. Everywhere, her skin burns.

He is backing away from her, looking confused, his still form silhouted sharply by the blue of the open sky outside the cave.

She hears the static from the radio again and thinks of Bob.

She smoothes her clothes. Why did the man stop? Has Bob bribed this guide to seduce her? Is her husband punishing her through this man?

The night is broken into tiny, crumbling bits. Her dreams fly at her like sherds of the sandstone monuments of Petra. She walks again along the colonnaded street, sees the temples, the silk tomb with its blue, orange, black, and coral waves. All that was pointed out to her tonight—the treasury, the urn tomb with its great height and courtyard, the cornices of the facades—become clear in the dream because she has already breathed it in the dark.

Suddenly, the guide is coming toward her, passing by her. In his hand is a sharp cane or a metal pipe. Even in sleep she recognizes the erotic symbol.

Rousing briefly, she is startled to find Bob's long body beside hers in the narrow, single bed. It is hard to move between the stiff hotel sheets but when his hand drifts up her thigh, she turns to him. They make love quickly. Her body is unresponsive and heavy with sleep.

She dreams again, sees herself lying on the high place of sacrifice, lifting her hips to someone—To Bob? To the guide? On the face of a cliff is the watchman's cave. Its facade has a watered look as though it has been buffed over the centuries, its sharp angles worn away. Bob is gazing down at her from the oleanders. From the street below she suddenly panics, realizes that she is losing him. She reaches up to him, tries to call him, but he has dissolved into the threadbare rock.

212

A ray of white light simmers below the curtains. Joanna lies awake in the dark several minutes before realizing that it is morning. She sits up. Bob is no longer beside her. His bed is empty.

She slips on the jeans of last night. The back of her white shirt is smeared red where it had rubbed against the rock of the cave. She quickly looks down at the white of her breasts and arms, almost surprised that there are no marks from the man's lips or teeth.

She leaves the room, leaping up the steps from their bungalow to the main terrace with the sinking knowledge that Bob has left her.

But he is sitting on the pink terrace near the swimming pool reading the *Jordan Times*. Both cameras—his Nikon and her small Canon—lie on the table. Behind him, the sun is lifting off the swirling pink-gray hills like a weightless basketball.

"Bob?" she calls, lightly.

They are silent over coffee—instant nescafe that Joanna mellows with tinned milk. She sips it, wanting to ask him about last night. Had he purposely allowed her to go up to the cave alone with a stranger? But he is totally absorbed in his reading.

When she finishes, they go through the lobby to the hotel entrance where they have agreed to meet the guide. Joanna's heart sails when she sees him waiting at the entrance.

The guide greets them cheerfully. In the morning light, his face seems fuller, his cheeks sag slightly. Today, he is wearing a light blue safari suit that makes him appear even more youthful than yesterday.

Her eyes take in his strong chest, his shoulders that she had clung to last night, the rough, archaeologist's hands that had held her. Her chest and head throb in anticipation of climbing up to Aaron's tomb with him this morning. The recklessness surges through her, once again. Then, her eyes are drawn to the white jeep behind him. Her mouth parts, slightly.

In the front seat sits a young woman, her head completely covered by a drab, yellow scarf. In the back where Joanna had sat last night, are three small boys.

The guide nods toward the jeep. "My son is sick. I must take him to the Doctor."

The woman in the jeep reaches behind her to rebuke one of the boys. She looks toward Joanna, shyly, as though to apologize for her son's behavior. Her eyes are wide and liquid, set like jewels in her plain face.

"You will be alright?" the guide says.

"We'll be fine," Bob says, waving vaguely in the air, assuring him that they can rely on themselves.

"You know Petra, now?" The guide glances at Joanna. She looks away.

"We do," Bob says. He turns to Joanna. "Think we can make it alone?"

Joanna glances at the guide for some glimmer of recognition of what had happened between them last night. Last night he had promised to take her to Aaron's tomb. He seems to have forgotten all about it, about last night, about her.

"Of course we can," she says. An absurd rage grips her as the guide walks back to the jeep and gets into the driver's seat. He leans close to the young woman to tell her something. Joanna remembers his breath on her own face and neck last night. There is a dry twist in her stomach.

Then he is driving away. The three boys wave madly at Joanna and Bob as they bounce recklessly in the back seat.

"Shall we ride in?" Bob says, suddenly.

"What?" She feels weak, hot. The sun burns down on the hotel, the sand, the cliffs.

"Let's do it on horseback," Bob says, "the old-fashioned way."

She does not understand. She watches her husband go up the road a bit to where some old Bedouin men, their legs bowed by rickets, saddle horses for some tourists.

She looks back to where the jeep had stood a moment ago. The dust from the tires has cleared. Last night is gone. In its place is a young wife and three small boys.

Joanna wonders whether the guide bites his wife's neck as she had wanted him to bite hers last night. She shakes her head, as though to dislodge the thought.

Bob is haggling with one of the old men. Young boys on horse-back, bedouins, canter recklessly toward the *Siq*. More boys gallop out of the rose-red crack, showing off their skill, calling out glee-fully, as their horses hooves fly, their tails lifted in a salute. A Bedouin in majestic black robes and bandoleers follows on a white horse.

They could be back at the dawn of time. Joanna is spellbound. They have waited so long for this!

Bob is riding toward her on a smoke-colored horse.

"We'll have to share this one," he says, looking like a happy boy scout on a wilderness outing.

She waits for him to draw near, waits for him to pull her up in front of him so that they can ride into the gorge together and see Petra for themselves in bright light, quench their thirst for the pink rocks.

She imagines the ride through the narrow *Siq*, then envisions the giant treasury that had been obliterated last night. She won-ders whether the amphitheatre and the tombs will be as she imag-ined or whether they will prove to be lesser in the daylight. The dark had made them limitless, their shapes and colors taking on whatever her imagination demanded.

Bob reins in the horse. She struggles onto the blanket strapped in front of the saddle, still thinking of her arms outstretched to him in her dream, how he had faded into the worn rock of Petra. She thinks of the guide's lips that had not once touched hers, that would never touch any part of her.

She drops her head back onto Bob's shoulder, settling begrudg-ingly, deeply, into the warmth of his shirt as the horse gently rocks them forward.

She knows that there is no turning back, the marriage is over. The last twenty years of her life are gone. This thought suddenly makes her weak.

Then, the *Siq* is before her once again—a jagged shadow against a burst of apricot. Somehow, she is no longer frightened as she had been last night.

This last thing they will do together. They will seal their twenty years, cross over the frontier of youth.

Petra. It is waiting for them.

Kathryn K. Abdul-Baki was born in Washington, D.C. She grew up in Iran, Kuwait, Beirut, and Jerusalem where she attended Arabic, British, and American schools. She attended the American University of Beirut, Lebanon, and earned a B.A. in journalism from George Washington University in Washington D.C. She has an M.A. in creative writing from George Mason University, Virginia.

Ms. Abdul-Baki worked as a journalist and features-writer for an English weekly newspaper in Bahrain before devoting her time to writing fiction. Her two novels include *The Tower of Dreams*, a coming-of-age novel set in Kuwait, and *Ghost Songs*, a family saga set in modern Jerusalem. She received the Mary Roberts Rinehart award for short fiction in 1984, for the stories "Nariman" and "Skiathos."

She currently resides in McLean, Virginia with her husband and three children.